PUBLIC LIBRARIES

3 3288 50102115 0

D0778195

The Fantastic Book of
Everybody's Secrets

Also by Sophie Hannah

The Fantastic Book of Everybody's Secrets

SHORT STORIES

SOPHIE HANNAH

WITNESS
IMPULSE

An Imprint of HarperCollinsPublishers

This is a work of fiction. Names, characters, places, and incidents are products of the author's imagination or are used fictitiously and are not to be construed as real. Any resemblance to actual events, locales, organizations, or persons, living or dead, is entirely coincidental.

THE FANTASTIC BOOK OF EVERYBODY'S SECRETS. Copyright © 2008 by Sophie Hannah. All rights reserved under International and Pan-American Copyright Conventions. By payment of the required fees, you have been granted the nonexclusive, nontransferable right to access and read the text of this e-book on-screen. No part of this text may be reproduced, transmitted, downloaded, decompiled, reverse-engineered, or stored in or introduced into any information storage and retrieval system, in any form or by any means, whether electronic or mechanical, now known or hereafter invented, without the express written permission of HarperCollins Publishers.

The Octopus Nest won first prize in the 2003 Daphne du Maurier Festival Short Story Competition.

Originally published in 2008 (and as an eBook in 2011) by Sort Of Books, PO Box 18678, London, NW3 2FL.

EPub Edition OCTOBER 2016 ISBN: 9780062562098

Print ISBN: 9780062562111

AM 10 9 8 7 6 5 4 3 2 1

The Octopus Nest

IT WAS THE sight I had hoped never to see: the front door wide open, Becky, our sitter, leaning out into the darkness as if straining to break free of the doorway's bright rectangle, her eyes wide with urgency. When she saw our car, she ran out into the drive, then stopped suddenly, arms at her sides, looking at the pavement. Wondering what she would say to us, how she would say it.

I assured myself that it couldn't be a real emergency; she'd have rung me on my mobile phone if it were. Then I realised I'd forgotten to switch it on as we left the cinema. Timothy and I had been too busy having a silly argument about the movie. He had claimed that the FBI must have known about the people in the woods, that it must have been a government relocation programme for victims of crime. I'd said there was nothing in the film to suggest that, that he'd plucked the hypothesis out of nowhere. He insisted he was right. Sometimes Timothy latches on to an idea and won't let go.

'Oh, no,' he said now. I tasted a dry sourness in my mouth. Becky shivered beside the garage, her arms folded, her face so twisted with concern that I couldn't look at her. Instead, as we slowed to a halt, I focused on the huddle of bins on the corner of the pavement. They looked like a gang of squat conspirators.

Before Timothy had pulled up the handbrake, I was out of the car. 'What is it?' I demanded. 'Is it Alex?'

'No, he's asleep. He's absolutely fine.' Becky put her hands on my arms, steadying me.

I slumped. 'Thank God. Then…has something else happened?'

'I don't know. I think so. There's something you need to have a look at.' I was thinking, as Timothy and I followed her into the house, that nothing else mattered if Alex was safe. I wanted to run upstairs and kiss his sleeping face, watch the rhythmic rise and fall of his Thomas the Tank Engine duvet, but I sensed that whatever Becky wanted us to see couldn't wait. She had not said, 'Don't worry, it's nothing serious.' She did not think it was nothing.

All our photograph albums were on the floor in the lounge, some open, most closed. I frowned, puzzled. Becky was tidier than we were. In all the years she had babysat for us, we had not once returned to find anything out of place. Tonight, we had left one photo album, the current one, on the coffee table so that she could look at our holiday pictures. Why had she thrown it and all the others on the carpet?

She sank to the floor, crossing her legs. 'Look at this.' Timothy and I crouched down beside her. She pointed to a picture of Alex and me, having breakfast on our hotel terrace in Cyprus. Crumbs from our bread rolls speckled the blue tablecloth. We were both smiling, on the verge of laughing, as Timothy took the photograph.

'What about it?' I said.

'Look at the table behind you. Where the blonde woman's sitting.'

I looked. She was in profile, her hair up in a pony-tail. She wore a sea-green shirt with the collar turned up. Her forehead was pink, as if she'd caught the sun the day before. Her hand, holding a small, white cup, was raised, halfway between the table and her mouth. 'Do you know her?' asked Becky, looking at Timothy, then at me.

'No.'

'No.'

She turned a page in the album and pointed to another photograph, of Timothy reading *Ulysses* on a sun-lounger beside the pool. 'Can't you read John Grisham like everybody else?' I'd said to him. 'We're supposed to be on holiday.' In the pool, the same blonde woman from the previous photograph stood in the shallow end, her hands behind her head. I guessed that she was adjusting her pony-tail before beginning her swim. She wore a one-piece swimsuit the colour of cantaloupe melon.

'There she is again,' said Becky. 'You didn't talk to her at all, in the hotel?'

'No.'

'Didn't even notice her,' said Timothy. 'What's this about, Becky? She's just another guest. What's the big deal?'

Becky sighed heavily, as if, by answering as we had, we'd confirmed her worst fears. I began to feel frightened, as if something unimaginably dreadful was on its way. 'She doesn't look familiar?'

'No,' said Timothy impatiently. 'Should she?'

Becky closed the album, reached for another one. This was one of our earliest, from before Alex was born. She flipped a few pages. Cambridge. Me, Timothy and my brother Richard outside King's College, sitting on a wall. I was eating an ice-cream. The day had been oven-hot. 'Sitting next to you, Claire,' said Becky. 'It's the same person.'

I looked at the blonde head. This woman – I was sure Becky was wrong, she couldn't be the same one – was turned away from the camera towards her bespectacled friend, whose face was animated. They looked as if they were having a lively conversation, utterly unaware of our presence. 'You don't know that,' I said. 'All you can see is her hair.'

'Look at the freckles on her shoulder and arm. And her earring. She's wearing the same ones in Cyprus – gold rings that are sort of square. Not very common.'

I was beginning to feel a creeping unease; otherwise I might have pointed out that rings could not be square. 'It's a coincidence,' I said. 'There must be more than one blonde woman with freckly arms who has earrings like that.'

'Or it's the same woman, and she happened to be in Cambridge and then Cyprus at the same time as us,' said Timothy. 'Though I'm inclined to agree with Claire. It must be a different woman.'

Becky was shaking her head as he spoke. 'It isn't,' she said. 'When I looked at the Cyprus photos, I noticed her. I thought I'd seen her somewhere before, but I couldn't place her. I puzzled over it for ages. Then later, when I was standing by the shelves choosing a DVD, I noticed the picture in the frame.'

All our eyes slid towards it. It had been taken by a stranger, so that all three of us could be in it: Timothy, Alex and me. We were in the grounds of a country house hotel just outside Edinburgh. It was the week of the book festival. Many of our trips, over the years, had revolved around Timothy buying books. Behind us were two large sash windows that belonged to the hotel's dining room. Clearly visible at one of them was the blonde woman from the Cyprus photographs. She was wearing a blue shirt this time, again with the collar turned up. Her face was small, but it was unmistakably her. And the earrings were the same – the square hoops. I felt dizzy. This had to mean something. My brain wouldn't work quickly enough.

'That's why she looked familiar,' said Becky. 'I've seen that photo millions of times. I see it every time I come here. Alex is just a baby in it and...I thought it was an amazing coincidence, that the same woman was wherever you were in this picture four years ago and also in Cyprus this summer. It seemed too strange. So I got the other albums out and had a look. I couldn't believe it. In each one, she's in at least nine or ten of the photos. See for yourselves.'

'Jesus.' Timothy rubbed the sides of his face. When he removed his hands there were white spots on his skin. I began to turn the pages of another album. I saw the woman, once, twice. In Siena, at a taverna. Walking behind me in a street market in Morocco. Three times. She stood beside Timothy outside the Tate Modern, again with her short-sighted, frizzy-haired friend.

'But...this *can't* be a coincidence!' I said, expecting to have to convince Becky, or Timothy. Nobody disagreed with me. I felt sharp, piercing fear.

'What does it mean?' Timothy asked Becky. He rarely asked anybody for advice or an opinion, let alone a nineteen-year-old babysitter. His lips were thin and pale. 'She must be following us. She's some sort of stalker. But...for nearly ten years! I don't like this at all. I'm ringing the police.'

'They'll think you're crazy,' I said, desperate to behave as if there was no need to take the matter seriously. 'She's never done us any harm, never even drawn herself to our attention. She's not looking at us in any of the photos. She doesn't seem aware of our presence at all.'

'Of course not!' Timothy snorted dismissively. 'She'd try to look as innocent as possible as soon as she saw a camera coming out, wouldn't she? That's why we've not spotted her until now.'

I turned to Becky. 'Is every album the same?' I didn't have the courage to look.

She nodded. 'Some, she's on nearly every page.'

'Oh, God! What should we do? Why would someone we don't know want to follow us?'

'Timothy's right, you've got to tell the police,' said Becky. 'If something happens...'

'Christ!' Timothy marched up and down the lounge, shaking his head. 'I don't need this,' he said. 'I really don't.'

'Tim, are you *sure* you don't know her?' An affair, I was thinking. A jealous ex-girlfriend. I would almost have preferred that; at least there would have been a rational explanation, a clarifying link.

'Of course I'm sure!'

'Do you want me to stay?' asked Becky. What she meant was that she was keen to leave.

'She's not some woman I've slept with and discarded, if that's what you're thinking,' Timothy snapped.

'You have to tell me if she is,' I said. Neither of us cared that Becky was listening.

'Have I ever done anything like that?'

'Not that I know of.'

'Claire, I swear on Alex's life: not only have I never slept with this woman, I've never even *spoken* to her.' I believed him. Alex was sacred.

'I should go,' said Becky. Our eyes begged her not to. She was a symbol of safety, the only one of the three of us who was not dogged by a stalker. We needed her normality to sustain us. I had never been so frightened in my life.

'I'll drive you,' said Timothy.

'No!' I didn't want to be left alone with the photo albums. 'Would you mind if we phoned you a cab?'

'Of course not.'

'I said I'll drive her!'

'But I don't want you to go out!'

'Well, I want to get out. I need some air.'

'What about me?'

'I'll be back in half an hour, Claire. Why don't you ring the police while I'm gone? Then we can talk to them when I get back.'

'I can't.' I began to cry. 'You'll have to do it. I'm in no fit state.'

He frowned. 'All right. Look, don't worry. I won't be long.'

Once he and Becky had left, I went upstairs and looked in on Alex. He was sleeping soundly, his hair covering his face. Despite my pleas, I found that I felt less afraid once Timothy had gone. I thought of one of our honeymoon photographs, one that could not possibly contain the blonde woman: Timothy in our en-suite bathroom at the Grand Hotel Tremezzo. He insisted on lavish holidays. Perhaps that was why we were always short of money. That and his book-collecting. In the picture, there is a mirror in front of him and one behind, reflecting an endless row of Timothies, each smaller than the last, each holding the camera to his eye, pressing the button. They dotted an invisible line that led from the foreground to the background. I knew why the picture had sprung to mind. It was the principle of magnification: seeing my own panic reflected in Timothy's eyes had added to my paranoia.

I went downstairs and began to look through all our photographs. This time I was methodical, unsuperstitious.

I found the blonde woman with the upturned collars and the square hoop earrings again and again: on a boat, in a park, walking along a canal tow-path. Sometimes she was right behind us, sometimes nearby. Who was she? Why was she following us? I had no way of knowing. Neither would the police, not with only our photo albums to work from. Of course, they could track her down if they wanted to – they could appeal on television and somebody who knew her would be bound to come forward – but the idea of them doing such a thing was laughable. She had committed no crime. Stalking was against the law, I was fairly certain of that, but the direct accosting of one's prey was surely a pre-requisite. What, I wondered, would the police have to say about a stalker so unobtrusive that, were it not for Becky's meticulous eye, we might never have become aware of her? Her presence in our lives, unnoticed for all these years, felt more ghostly than criminal. I was suddenly very aware of myself, my thoughts and my actions, and looked around the room, up at the ceiling, half expecting to find someone watching me.

I concentrated on the woman's face, trying to see a character or a motive behind it. She was either beautiful in a classical, well-proportioned way, or very bland-looking – I couldn't decide. I found it unsettling that, however hard I stared, I couldn't commit her face to memory; it was almost impossible to take in as a coherent whole. I looked at her features one by one and judged each of them regular, flawless, but together they made no lasting impression. I'd had this feeling before, usually about famous people. Sharon Stone, the late Jill Dando. They too had faces one could study in detail and still not know what they looked like.

In one photograph our blonde ghost was touching me. Her shoulder was pressed against mine in a crowded wine bar. Hay-on-Wye? No, Cheltenham. Another of Timothy's literary holidays. I was holding a tall cocktail, dark red and fizzy, like carbonated blood. I pointed to it, an apprehensive expression on my face. Timothy had labelled the photo 'Am I really expected to drink this?' He assigned titles to all our pictures; his parents did it too. It was a Treharne family tradition.

The blonde woman had a book in her hand. It was on the edge of the picture, some of it missing. I screwed up my eyes to read the title. *The Octopus* – that was all that was visible. My heart jolted. *The Octopus Nest*, I whispered. It was a novel I hadn't thought about for years. Timothy used to own it, probably still did. He'd tried to persuade me to read it, but I gave up. Sometimes it is apparent from the first page of a book that nothing is going to happen. A Timothy book.

I slammed the photo album shut and rang his mobile phone. It was switched off. I paced up and down the lounge, desperate to talk to somebody. I nearly rang Becky's mobile, but I didn't want her to make excuses when I asked her to babysit in the future. If I started to talk to her about obscure novels with strange titles, she'd think I was insane. Timothy had said he'd be back within half an hour. This could wait half an hour.

I forced myself to calm down, sit down, and think about how I was feeling. Was this surge of adrenaline justified? Seven years ago, the blonde woman had been in a wine bar, holding a novel that Timothy once raved about. It was a link, but then, I reminded myself, I did not need to look for a link. A woman we didn't know was in the backgrounds of dozens of our photographs. Wasn't that connection enough?

Still, I was too agitated to do nothing. I searched all the bookshelves in our house. There was no copy of *The Octopus Nest*. I tried Timothy's phone again, swearing under my breath, furious with impatience. How could he not have remembered to switch it on? He knew what a state I was in. Irrationally, I took my not being able to speak to him while he was out as an omen that it would take him much longer to return, that he might never come back. I needed to occupy myself, to drive away these groundless fears. That was when I thought of the internet.

I rushed to Timothy's study and switched on the computer, certain that Amazon, the online bookshop, would have *The Octopus Nest* listed. I wanted to know who it was by, what it was about. It might lead nowhere, but it was the only thing I had to go on. In none of the other photographs did our ghost have any identifiable accessories.

The Octopus Nest was available from Amazon, but not easily. Delivery might take up to six weeks, I read. This didn't matter to me. I didn't necessarily want a copy of the book. I just wanted to know more about it. The author was a K V Hammond. I clicked on the small picture of the novel's cover, a white background with one black tentacle running diagonally across it.

The book was number 756,234 in the Amazon chart. If Timothy and the blonde woman hadn't bought it all those years ago it would probably have been number 987,659, I thought, half-smiling. I was surprised I was able to joke, even inside my head. Somehow our ghost didn't seem quite so threatening, now that I had seen her holding a book that Timothy had once thought highly of, though I didn't understand why this should be the case. The optimist in me reasoned that she hadn't done us any harm in nearly a decade. Maybe she never would.

No description of the novel was offered. I had bought books from Amazon before, and there was usually a short synopsis. I clicked on the 'Google' button and typed 'K V Hammond' into the search box. The first result was the author's own website. Perhaps here I would discover more about *The Octopus Nest*. I drummed my fingers on the desk, impatient for the home page to load.

A photograph began to appear on the screen, from the top down. A blue sky, a tree, a straw hat. Blonde hair. Gold, square hoop earrings. I gasped, pushing my chair away from the computer. It was her. A letter welcomed me to her site, was signed 'Kathryn'. Only minutes ago it had seemed out of the question that we would ever know her identity. Now I knew it beyond the slightest doubt.

I tried Timothy's mobile again, with no luck. 'Please, please,' I muttered, even though noone could hear me, even though a mechanical voice was already telling me to try again later. I felt as if Timothy had let me down badly, deserted me, though I knew he was probably too preoccupied to think about a detail such as whether his phone was on or off. He would be back soon, in any case.

Fear and excitement rioted in my mind, my whole body. I had to do something. Now that I was in possession of certain knowledge, calling the police did not seem such an absurd proposition. I didn't want to go into the whole story on the phone, so I said only that I wanted to report a stalker, that I knew who it was, that I had evidence. The woman I spoke to said she would send an officer to interview me as soon as possible.

Willing the computer to work faster, I moved from one section of Kathryn Hammond's website to another. She had published no books since 'The Octopus Nest', but her newsletter said she was working on her next novel, the story of fifty years in the life of a ventriloquist's dummy, passed from one owner to another. Another Timothy book, I thought. The newsletter also informed fans (it seemed to take for granted that everyone who visited the site would be a fan) that Kathryn and her sister – the frizzy-haired woman, I assumed – were going on holiday to Sicily early next year.

For a second, I felt as if my blood had stopped moving around my body. We were going to Sicily too. In February. Kathryn Hammond and her sister were staying at the Hotel Bernabei. I had a horrible suspicion we were too. My terror returned, twice as strong as before. This was as real, as inexplicable, as ever.

I rummaged through the drawers of the desk, thinking I might find a letter from Timothy's travel agent or a booking confirmation. There was nothing. I flew round the house like a trapped fly, opening drawers and pulling books off shelves. I couldn't understand it; there had to be some paperwork somewhere relating to our holiday.

I was crying, about to give up, when it occurred to me that Timothy kept a filing cabinet in the garage. 'Why not?' he'd said. 'The thing's hideous and the house is too cluttered.' I rarely went into the garage. It was dusty and messy, and smelled of damp, turpentine and cigarettes; since Alex was born, Timothy hadn't smoked in the house.

I had no choice but to go in there now. If the police arrived before Timothy got back, I wanted to be able to show them our holiday details and Kathryn Hammond's website. What more proof could they ask for? Even as I thought this, I was aware that it was not illegal for a novelist to go on holiday to Sicily. Terror gripped me as it occurred to me for the first time that perhaps we would never be able to stop her following us, never force her to admit to her behaviour or explain it. I didn't think I'd be able to stand that.

The cabinet wasn't locked. I pulled open the first drawer. A strangled moan escaped from my mouth as I stared, stunned, at what was inside. Books. Dozens of them. I saw the title *The Octopus Nest*. Then, underneath it, *Le Nid du poulpe*. The same title, but in French. Numb with dread, I pulled the books out one by one, dropping them on the floor. I saw Hebrew letters, Japanese characters, a picture of a purple octopus, a green one, a raised black one that looked as if it might spin off the cover and hit me in the chest.

Kathryn Hammond's novel had been translated into many languages. I pulled open the next drawer down.

More copies of *The Octopus Nest* – hardbacks, paperbacks, hardback-sized paperbacks, book club editions.

'Fifty-two in total.'

I screamed, nearly lost my balance. Timothy stood in the doorway of the garage. 'Timothy, what…?'

He stared blankly at me for several seconds, saying nothing. I backed away from him until I was against the wall. I felt its rough texture through my blouse, scratching my skin.

'I was telling the truth,' he said. 'I've never spoken to her. I don't know her at all. She doesn't even know I exist.'

The doorbell rang. The police. I'd said only that I wanted to report a stalker, that I knew who it was, that I had evidence.

Friendly Amid the Haters

'I KNOW IT's a mistake. I told you it was a mistake.'

She is entitled to be angry. All morning she has been considering other people's feelings, looking at things from points of view that oppose her own, breathing deeply, counting to ten, counting her blessings, thinking about the grand scheme of things rather than the tiny speck of time dust that is insignificant today. She has guarded her irritation to make sure no part of it escapes, like a parent minding a defiant, grounded teenager.

She said nothing when the men from Bonners brought the wrong colour carpet. She agreed that marble was 'as near as dammit' to shell. She nodded when the fitter, Keith Halliday, told her that the bottoms of her doors were too low for the thick new carpet, that it was not his job to take off the doors, plane them down and reattach them. She smoked a cigarette to calm herself, then phoned Sol Barber, a joiner she had used before, who agreed to come straight away.

She knows nothing about the process of removing a door, but oil must be involved, because Sol Barber managed to spill some on her new marble-coloured carpet. There were two smears of black in the hall, outside the downstairs bathroom. Sol summoned her from her study to inspect them. 'Sorry,' he said sheepishly. 'Don't know how it happened. But all you need to do is tell the company that sold you the carpet that it was like that when it arrived. Then they'll have to replace it free of charge.' He grinned, and she noticed again his chipped front tooth.

The plan had a certain appeal. She could insist on shell instead of marble. She should have insisted first time round, but the men from Bonners knew more about carpets than she did; who was she to argue if they told her, sternly, that it didn't matter? But now there was a way for her to get the carpet she wanted, had ordered and was entitled to. On the other hand, she could see that it wouldn't be fair to do to Bonners what Sol was proposing.

'I can't afford to replace your carpet, so it's your only option,' he said cheerfully. 'Or, if you don't want to do that, I'll have a scrub at the stains, see if I can get them out for you.'

This is why she has come to the library: not only because she needs a book for her work, but to get away from Sol and give herself time to think about what to do. She sat on the bus with her arms folded and her legs crossed, her whole body a tight knot of resentment. *I've got a stained carpet that's the wrong colour,* she said to herself, *and now I either have to defraud the company I bought it from, fall out with my joiner by turning down his kind offer of a criminal conspiracy and insisting he pay for the damage himself, or just lump it.*

She has always liked Sol. Not that she knows him very well. His name isn't really Sol, but that has been his nickname for years. It is what everybody calls him. Sol is his favourite beer. The main thing she likes about him is that he is always instantly available for work, whenever she needs him. She doesn't know if this is because he is efficient or unsuccessful. His hair is fine and black, and his skin pale, alabaster. He often smells of vinegar. She knows very little about him, only that he is married to a woman named Tina and has two children, Wilfred and Agnes. Also, she remembered on the bus on the way to the library, she knows that his star sign is Capricorn. He fitted a new kitchen for her last year. The manufacturers kept sending units that were the wrong size, which made his job almost impossible and wasted a lot of his time, but Sol never seemed to mind. He remained tolerant and amused throughout. When she said she didn't know how he managed it, he said, 'It's my Capricorn temperament,' and winked at her.

She has left Sol in her house. He is there now, planing and rehanging the doors while she is out. She is nervous about telling him that she cannot lie to Bonners. This trip to the library is supposed to be a calm interlude in an otherwise fraught day. Which is why, when the young bearded man behind the inter-library loans desk tells her that the wrong book has arrived, she reacts as she does. Because she is entitled to be angry.

'You ordered *Leviathan* by Thomas Hobbes,' says the man, waving a small blue slip of paper in the air as if it is proof that he has never in his life done anything wrong. 'And that's what's arrived. Does it really matter who wrote the introduction?'

'Yes. If it didn't matter, I wouldn't have said anything about the introduction when I ordered the book, would I? I'd just have ordered a copy of *Leviathan*. What else does it say on that bit of paper? What have I written under "*Leviathan* by Thomas Hobbes"?' She is beginning to enjoy her anger. Giving vent to it is satisfying, like picking a scab at the perfect moment, when it has hardened enough but not too much, and the degree of resistance is exactly right. 'I've written "must be the edition with Michael Oakeshott's introduction". I believe I've even underlined the word "must".'

'Isn't this better than nothing? How different can this introduction be from the other one? Both are introducing the same book.' He is saying all the wrong things.

She loses her temper. Or, rather, she decides to allow herself to behave as if she has lost it. After the morning she has had, she has earned the right. And she will enjoy putting this nerd in his place. And perhaps if she asserts herself more often, people will treat her better. 'What the hell do you know about it? I've got a copy of Hobbes' *Leviathan* on my shelf at home. This edition.' She shoves the book back across the counter at the bearded man. 'It's specifically Michael Oakeshott's introduction that I need for my work, as I keep explaining to you, and as I clearly wrote on that slip of paper.' People nearby are turning to watch; many are giggling. She doesn't care. She continues to shout. It is the first time she has shouted in her adult life, and she doesn't want it to be over too quickly. 'Do you know what my work is? Do you know the title of the paper I'm writing at the moment?'

'Of course not…'

'No! Then don't *dare* to tell me that I don't need Oakeshott's introduction when I keep telling you that I *do* need it!'

'All right, I'm sorry. My mistake. I'll order you the edition with the introduction by Michael Oakeshott…'

'That's not good enough! I need it now! I need it today! Forget it, just forget it. You're useless. I don't know how you manage to hold down a job of any sort, let alone in a library!' She plunges towards the exit, which is also the entrance: a revolving door. She is so flustered by what has taken place that she walks round twice, two complete circles inside her glass compartment, before tumbling out on to the street.

She feels worse but pretends to herself that she feels better. What she told the bearded man is true: she cannot proceed with her work without the book she ordered, the correct edition. She will have to see if she can buy a copy online. She catches the bus home, rehearsing what she will say to Sol Barber. There is no need to imply that his suggestion was out of order. A simple refusal will be sufficient: 'No, I can't pretend it was the carpet company's fault when it wasn't.'

Option number three, then: lumping it. But maybe not, not if she also says, solemnly, 'I'd really appreciate it if you could try to get rid of the marks with stain remover.' No. Why should she appreciate it? Sol Barber owes her a new hall carpet. 'I've decided I'd like you to tackle it with stain remover.' That's better, more authoritative.

She arrives home to find Sol sitting on her couch, drinking a cup of tea. He has unplugged her television and plugged in his paint-spattered ghetto blaster instead. He is listening to what she would call a folk song. She pauses in the doorway. A deep, male, American voice is singing about finding happiness in quiet things: a pair of geese in flight, the sunset's quiet light.

'Hiya,' says Sol cheerfully when he sees her.

'Hi. That was quick.'

'What was?'

'The doors.'

'I haven't finished them. Haven't even started. I need a mole grip. Have you got one?'

'No. You…So what…?'

'Been anywhere nice?'

'Er, just to the library. So…'

'I wish I had your job! Still in your pyjamas at nine o'clock, shuffle a few papers around, then swan off to the library at midday for a nice leisurely browse through today's papers. At five this morning I was up the top of a ladder pushing a flat-pack bed through a window.'

Well, that's an absurd position to be in and it's entirely your own fault if you were in it, she feels like saying. She is used to the pyjamas joke (Sol once arrived to start work before she was dressed) and the paper-shuffling joke. Both are regulars, and normally she takes them in good humour. She knows that she cannot expect a person like Sol to think that the sort of work she does is anything other than an indulgence. People need kitchens and doors that open and close more than they need articles about Thomas Hobbes' political philosophy; she accepts this.

But Sol is not working now. He is sitting on her sofa, listening to a song about escaping from the rat race in order to lead a tranquil life. This is what he has been doing since she left. 'What about the oil stains?' she asks. 'Have you had a go at them with stain remover?'

'Oh.' He looks surprised. 'No. I thought I'd wait and see what you wanted to do. I thought if you wanted Bonners to replace the carpet, it'd be better to leave it as it is, so they can see the damage.'

'Right,' she says tightly. *Tell him.* 'I've decided I'm not going to do that,' she says. She is pleased. For a moment she thought she might not be able to bring herself to say it.

'What?' Sol wrinkles his face. 'You're crazy! You've got to.'

'I can't lie.'

He shrugs. 'Fine. Well, I'll see what I can do to get rid of them, but I still think you're crazy.'

She is livid. Has he forgotten that he made the marks, that it is his fault?

'Are you sure you haven't got a mole grip?' he says. 'Everyone's got one.'

'A mould grip?' She pretends to give it some thought. 'No, mole. M-O-L-E.'

'I definitely haven't got one. Can you get one from somewhere else?'

He smiles. 'Look, point me in the direction of your toolbox. You're bound to have one. I'll find it.'

She doesn't have a tool box, but she is too embarrassed to admit it. 'I haven't.'

He is about to say something, but bites his lip. She stares at the pink flesh crushed by the chipped white tooth. He shakes his head slightly and stretches, elbows up. She can see that he is impatient. It upsets her. 'I'll…why don't you start on the oil spots? I'll see if one of my neighbours can lend me…a mole grip.'

'Good idea,' he says, smiling again. He stands up, slurps the remains of his tea, then takes his empty mug through to the kitchen.

She stares after him. Now that he is jolly again, indignation begins to swell inside her. Why should she have a mole grip? More to the point, why doesn't he have one? As a joiner, he ought to have a toolbox containing all the necessary tools. *It's his job, not mine, to have a mole grip,* she thinks.

She is still standing where he left her, outside the lounge, when he returns from the kitchen empty-handed. 'Chop chop,' he says, and winks.

'I'll go now. I was just…'

'What?'

'I was wondering: you don't by any chance have a copy of Michael Oakeshott's introduction to Hobbes' *Leviathan*, do you?'

Sol stares at her in silence for a few seconds. She is surprised. She expected him to say 'You what?' or something similar. Well, he asked for it, she thinks to herself. *Chop chop.* Who does he think he is?

'No,' he says eventually.

'Are you sure?'

'Positive.' He stares at her. His face is unreadable.

His reaction strikes her as strange, but she carries on. Maybe she has succeeded in making him think. 'Damn!' She feigns disappointed irritation. 'You're quite sure? I really need one, you see. I can't get on with the article I'm writing until I've read Oakeshott's introduction. You couldn't just…check your toolbox, could you, in case you've got a copy in there that you've forgotten about?'

'I haven't,' he says. He appears to be frozen in place. She stares at his thick arms, which are like perfectly still parentheses around his stocky body. Something is not quite right. She must get out of this situation somehow.

'Oh well,' she says breezily. 'Never mind.' She decides against adding, 'Perhaps you could ask your neighbours if they've got one, when you get home later.'

She does not wait for his reaction. Instead, she runs upstairs. Her heart beats as if it is trying to batter down the walls of her chest. She stands on the landing outside her bedroom, listening for his movements. There is silence for a long time, five minutes. In this context, five minutes is a very long time. Then she hears an abrasive rubbing noise. She decides that this can only be the sound of Sol fixing the carpet, treating the oil stains with a magic substance, the name of which she wouldn't recognise.

She exhales and her body sags. She got away with it. And quite right too. He was out of order. Now she has shown him that she doesn't plan to take any more of his cheek, his unfair demands or his unjustified impatience. *Things have changed between us*, she thinks, *and he knows it.*

She hears the beginning of another folk song downstairs, this time about Billy the Kid not having been shot, but, instead, having got away and spent the rest of his life engaging in various activities of a peace-promoting nature. Shooting Hitler is one of these. She wonders about the chronological accuracy.

She smiles. What next? To the neighbours for a mole grip, as promised. She will be magnanimous in her victory. But she is still too triumphant about her successful burst of assertiveness to risk letting him see her face, so she potters around the bedroom for a while. She takes off her black V-necked sweater and pulls on a green cashmere polo-neck. She straightens the duvet. She takes her new lipstick, 'Marmalade-on-Toast', out of its shiny navy-blue box, and removes the lid. It is only the afternoon, but why shouldn't she look nice? Some women wear make-up all the time, every day, even if they're just staying in.

She stands in front of the full-length mirror in her bedroom and twists the lipstick so that it sticks out as far as it will go. It looks like a small sword with an orange blade. Instantly afraid she will be clumsy and snap it, she winds it back in again so that only the tip protrudes. She starts to put it on, covering her upper lip with colour first, as she always does.

'Very fetching.' Sol's voice comes from right behind her. She jumps, makes a high-pitched, startled noise. He steps sideways, and now she sees him in the mirror. How long has he been there? His face is contorted, fluid, as if there is something horrible wriggling underneath the skin and the features. He puts his right arm round her neck and squeezes. She can still breathe, but only just. She cannot speak at all. Sol's other arm wraps around her waist. He lifts her up. She smells vinegar. In the mirror, she watches her legs kick in the air as her face turns red, almost purple. Then he lowers her so that her feet are on the ground again, but he doesn't release his grip on her throat. 'Think I'm some kind of scum, do you?' he says.

She does her best to shake her head.

'Yes, you do. Or else you wouldn't have tried to mock me with your great fucking knowledge. You think I've never heard of Hobbes and *Leviathan*?'

He releases her, spins her round in his hands, seizes her by both shoulders and slams her against the mirror. 'I'm sorry,' she sobs. 'I'm sorry, I don't think that, I was just joking, please, let me go....'

'I've read...' He pulls her towards him. She recoils from the snarl of bared teeth. '...*Hobbes*. And *Locke*. And *Marx*. And *Rousseau*.' With each political philosopher's name, he slams her against the mirror, harder every time. She is terrified that it will smash, that he will pick up a pointed wedge of glass from the carpet and cut her throat with it.

'I'm sorry, I'm sorry,' she whimpers. 'Please, just let me go and I'll never...I promise I'll...'

He looks down, notices that she has one fist clenched. It is only when she sees him looking that she remembers the lipstick. Her fingers have fossilized around it. 'Open your hand,' he says.

She does as he tells her. The lipstick is broken. Her arm shakes, and the small orange tube, detached from its base, rocks in her palm.

Sol grabs it, holds it above her head. She stares up at it as if it is an executioner's axe, having run out of words that she might say in her defence. Sol moves his left hand from her shoulder to her throat. This time he does not squeeze, but simply holds her neck firmly, in a way that makes it clear that any movement would be dangerous. With his right hand, he brings the lipstick down slowly, until it is level with her nose. It hovers, a small, orange finger, pointing at her. He is smiling, eyes bulging with enthusiasm for whatever he intends to do.

'Please don't,' she murmurs.

Very slowly, he begins to write something on her forehead. A word. An orange word. Or maybe more than one. How many words can one forehead accommodate? As soon as she realises this is what he is doing, she starts to roll her eyes and wag her tongue inside her mouth and strain to get away, even though, with his hand still in place like a choker necklace, it is agony for her already bruised throat. But she would rather feel the pain, even risk unconsciousness, than stand still and allow herself to work out what he is writing.

He is soon finished. He releases her neck and grips her by the shoulders again. 'I'm going to go downstairs now and try to get the oil out of your carpet,' he says, deliberately and obtrusively patient. 'You are going to stay up here in this room and think about what a patronising bitch you've been, and you are not – repeat, not – going to wash this…' – he jabs her brow with his finger – '…off until I come back up here and say you can. Understood?'

She nods.

'If you leave this room, or wash that off, there'll be trouble.'

After he leaves the bedroom, she stays exactly where she is, up against the mirror, with her back to it. She can't risk moving, can't risk catching a glimpse of what he has written on her. She knows that as soon as she moves, she will look, and she desperately doesn't want to know what word or words he chose. So she must keep her back pressed up against the glass.

It is forty minutes before he comes upstairs again. She knows because she keeps looking at the clock on the bedside table. During these forty minutes, she assures herself, over and over again, that he did not kill or seriously injure her. She is still alive. Definitely. At the moment.

Also, in the forty minutes, she does other things. She urinates in her underwear. She speculates about what Sól Barber has written above her eyes. She decides that it is the word 'bitch'. She can cope with that, as he has already said it to her. That is what she will tell herself it is.

At 2.43pm, he appears in the doorway of her room. He rubs his thumbnail and doesn't look at her. 'Well, I've done my best,' he says. 'You'd have to be really looking, or there's no way you'd see anything now.'

She says nothing. Her tongue sticks to the roof of her mouth.

Finally, he looks up. He meets her staring eyes, then his slide higher and he flinches. It is as if he has forgotten that he wrote whatever he wrote – the word 'bitch' – on her forehead, and is unhappy to have to recall the incident. 'Okay, you can wash it off now,' he mutters, sounding embarrassed. She wonders if it is obvious that she has wet herself, tries to remember what trousers she is wearing.

'Look…,' he begins. It sounds as if he might be about to say something conciliatory. She cannot help him. She is mute with shock and fear. In fact, she can't imagine ever speaking again.

Sol Barber sighs and, without saying another word, descends the stairs slowly and heavily. A few minutes later she hears the front door close – not quite a slam, but an unequivocal thud. He has gone. She is alone in the house.

Now she is truly terrified. She could look at the word if she wanted to. She has the rest of her life to deal with, and she can't; it is too much for her. Even the smallest decision is too much. What did he write? She could find out, by turning round.

She runs to the bathroom, twists the hot and cold taps and splashes water on her face. She squirts liquid soap into one hand and massages it into her forehead, rubbing and rubbing until her skin hurts. Then more soap and more water. The word, phrase or sentence cannot possibly have survived such a frenzied attack.

Eventually, feeling as if she might vomit, she stands in front of the bathroom mirror. Relief floods her when she sees that there is no trace of the orange lipstick left on her forehead, only red, chafed skin. Now she will never know, she will remain blissfully ignorant; it is no longer an issue. It was 'bitch', anyway, in all probability.

She stands back from the mirror to see more of herself. Her trousers are black, thick; they reveal nothing. She winces with relief. Shaking convulsively, she returns to her bedroom and winces again when she spots the large, dark, sodden patch on the carpet in front of the mirror. It is the approximate shape of France. He must have noticed.

Crying, she takes off all her clothes and puts them in a plastic bag. She twists the neck of the bag and ties it in a knot. Then she has a shower, puts on clean clothes and takes the plastic bag downstairs to the outside bin. *I have been assaulted*, she thinks. She considers reporting Sol Barber to the police, but knows she never will. She is too afraid of what he might do to her. There would have to be a court case. She imagines him smirking in the witness box, telling a room full of strangers that she pissed herself, saying aloud the word that he wrote on her face.

She spends the rest of the day bawling like a newborn baby, trying to work out if it is feasible for her to avoid Sol Barber for the rest of her life. She knows only one person who knows him: her friend Olga, for whom Sol made and fitted a wardrobe earlier in the year. It was Olga who recommended Sol to her, as a skilled and reliable worker. She must avoid Olga too, in case the subject of Sol comes up.

She must get on with her life. She hardly knows him. He is only a joiner. A violent, vindictive joiner. He's the unfortunate one, not her.

TWO MONTHS PASS. In flavour and pitch, they have a lot in common with the forty minutes she spent in her bedroom with her back against the mirror, branded with her own lipstick, while Sol Barber was downstairs rubbing at the oil stains on the carpet. She cannot think properly. She barely eats or sleeps. She is afraid all the time. She feels humiliated all the time. She has lost her grip on herself, all her substance. She feels a crippling loneliness, as if she has floated away and noone has cared enough to follow her. Worst of all is her growing suspicion that she deserved what he did to her. She patronised him and, in doing so, invited him to destroy her.

She spends her days and evening, staring at her computer screen, but she cannot work, cannot concentrate on her own words. She avoids all her friends and relatives apart from Olga. Olga she sees much more often than she normally would, and Olga's husband Danny. So far the subject of Sol has not come up. She both wants and doesn't want it to. She would love it if Olga one day told her that Sol had maimed several of the people he'd done work for. Then she could feel lucky. But she would hate it if Olga complimented him, or said how well she got on with him, how mild-mannered and charming he was.

For two months, nothing is said that is of any interest to her, either positive or negative. Then one day she is at Olga's house at the same time as Olga's sister Eve. Eve is leafing through a hard-covered notebook, laughing. Olga and Danny are talking about the company that has been given a government mandate to manufacture the smallpox vaccine; they are debating its competence. Eve interrupts with a question: 'Who's Sol Barber?'

Her heart bucks, like a horse before a wall of flame. 'Sol?' she says casually.

'Our joiner,' says Olga, gesturing around the room. 'All of ours. Why? Oh!'

'He wasn't at your wedding, was he?' says Eve.

'No,' says Olga. 'He must have found that once when he was working here, and added his own contribution.'

Eve frowns. 'Isn't that a bit odd?'

'I suppose. Still, he obviously meant well. It's a nice thing to write.'

'Can I see?' she asks, extending her hand.

Eve shrugs and hands her the notebook. She recognises it as the one that was circulated at Olga and Danny's wedding reception, for well-wishers to write messages in. She remembers that she wrote, 'It's a grand life if you don't weaken' – one of her grandfather's favourite mottos. Not very suitable for a wedding, but she isn't good at gushing exclamations. She told Olga so at the time and Olga said she understood, that it was a good slogan.

She turns to the last page. Sol has signed and dated his addition. The date is six years after the day of the wedding. Above his spiky signature, he has written,

Here in the world, anger is never pacified by anger.
It is pacified by love. This is the eternal truth.
Happy indeed we live, friendly amid the haters.
Among men who hate, we dwell free from hate.
(Dhammapada, 'The Way of Truth')

'I call that vandalising our private property,' says Danny. 'I wanted to sack him, but...'

'...but we'd have been left with only half a wardrobe.' Olga laughs. 'Anyway, I think it's sweet.'

'I didn't know he was a Buddhist,' she says. Her mind struggles with the impossibility of it. Four months before he attacked her, this was what he chose to write. How can the inconsistency not have occurred to him?

'He isn't, as far as I know,' says Olga. 'Maybe he just thought it was a nice idea. Which it is. He's done pretty well, considering.'

'Considering what?' she says. This is why she has been skulking at Olga's house for the past two months, for this moment.

'Well, you know. His background.'

'What about it?'

Olga's eyes widen. 'You don't know?'

'Another good reason to sack the bugger, far as I was concerned,' Danny grumbles.

'His father's in prison for manslaughter.'

'Really?' says Eve. She smiles in a detached sort of way.

'Yup. He was a...what do you call it? Bailiff? He frightened money out of people for a living.'

'A debt collector,' says Eve.

'Beat them up if they couldn't pay. One of his beatings went a bit too far – the bloke died.'

'That's one way to avoid paying your debts,' Danny quips. No one laughs.

'Sol spent most of his childhood in refuges,' Olga tells Eve. 'He was in a young offenders' institute for a while.'

'And this is the guy we gave a key to our house,' says Danny.

'But that's my point,' says Olga. 'Sol's not like that. He's left that world behind. He's a brilliant craftsman, he's got a successful business, a happy family. He's done really well. From what he's told me, his two brothers seem to be going the same way as his dad, but Sol's different. Maybe it's his little…Buddhist words of wisdom that keep him on the straight and narrow.'

She has heard enough. She makes her excuses and leaves.

HER FATHER IS the director of the British Council office in Venezuela. Her mother was a ballet dancer and now teaches dance. One of her two sisters is a cellist and the other is an editor at Faber and Faber. Her brother is an immunologist. They are a happy family; she has always felt loved and looked after.

Sol Barber's father is hired muscle: a debt collector, a killer. And his brothers are 'going the same way', whatever that means. She thinks it means that, in all likelihood, Sol is entirely to blame for what he did to her on that day, and she is not at all to blame. One only has to look at the two families, at the respective track records.

She remembers, often, Sol's shamefaced expression when he said, 'Look…' just before he left her bedroom. Because human beings are basically selfish and self-absorbed, she decides that she can safely assume Sol's thoughts over the past two months have not centred on her fear and defeat and disgrace, but on his own failure to stick to the resolution he must surely have made a long time ago: to prove, with his every word and deed, that he has escaped his miserable, brutal origins, that he is a more enlightened man than his father.

Less comforting is the idea that, in the Barber family, all one needs to do in order to be impressive – a high achiever – is not kill somebody. Among her own relatives, not killing anybody is taken for granted; it is not a matter for pride or congratulations. Not so for the Barbers. How much does it matter that Sol once, when provoked, wrote something in lipstick on a woman's forehead and, all right, got a bit rough with her? He didn't do her any serious harm, did he? And he could have done, he easily could. He restrained himself. For Sol, given his background, this could constitute a significant accomplishment.

Either that or he barely remembers the incident. Most of his relatives probably do more damage daily than he did that one time. He might expect her to be over it by now. If he hadn't mentioned Locke and Rousseau (Marx doesn't count – everyone's heard of Marx), maybe she would be. But he did, and so she cannot dismiss him. The wardrobe he made for Olga and Danny is beautiful, a work of art. She has been attacked by a clever and talented man. This is what she cannot bear. This is why she decides to kill his children.

BECAUSE IT WOULD be pointless to kill him, wouldn't it? To murder an enemy is a dimwit's revenge. If he is dead, he cannot suffer, and if he is not suffering, you've failed. Even if you arrange for him to die slowly and painfully, you know (assuming you do not believe in an afterlife) that his agony will end, he will escape into blissful nonexistence.

She wants Sol Barber to live until he is a hundred and fifty.

She knows where his children go to school: St Anne's Primary, on Glasshouse Lane, in a village that she always suspects will disappear as soon as she has driven through it. Agnes is seven. Wilfred is five. She does not know what they look like but she has seen their mother. Twice while Sol was working in her house Tina Barber brought him things: once some sandwiches and once some jump leads, when his van broke down. Tina is a thin, mousy woman with bandy legs, no waist, and a face like a collie dog.

It is that face that she hunts for in the crowd, sitting in her car on Glasshouse Lane at five past eight in the morning. She has got up especially early to be here on time. Dishevelled mothers, their messy hair stuffed into hoods, haul their offspring around as if they are sacks of soil. Grooves of exhaustion carve the women's faces into defeated chunks. And these are the lucky ones, she thinks. These are the ones whose children will not be killed. Tina has not arrived yet.

She contemplates what she intends to do, the effect it will have. Sol's life will be ruined, which is what she wants, so there is no problem there. But when she thinks about Tina, or the children themselves, she is surprised to find that she feels no anguish, no empathy. Even when she puts the matter to herself in a deliberately emotive way (which she does often, as an experiment), she is unmoved. All she has is a cold sense of necessity. This is what has to happen. She must harm Sol more than he has harmed her. Her heart is a brick; therefore, in order to win, she must turn his into a vast purple lesion, a pulsating carnivorous tumour.

And she can do it, that's the beauty of the scheme. She has the ability. Anyone can harm another person, if they don't care what happens afterwards. She might not be able to fit a kitchen or a carpet, rehang a door or remove an oil stain, but she is confident that she can kill Sol Barber's children.

Not today, though. She will not murder Agnes and Wilfred today. She doesn't even know what they look like, and she hasn't brought an implement with her. As yet, she has given no thought to the practicalities of ending two lives. All she wants, at this stage, is to see the children's faces.

She yelps when she spots Sol walking down the road towards her car. Although there are a few other men in the playground, it didn't occur to her that Sol might bring his children to school. Agnes and Wilfred are on either side of him, holding his hands. He is talking to them, smiling. She draws her knees up to her chest and buries her face in them. A moment ago she was a woman; now she is a ball of fear, rocking back and forth in the driver's seat of her car. What if he sees her? Instinctively, she knows that it would be worse than last time.

A few seconds later, or it might even be minutes, she dares to look up. She sees his broad back. He is kissing his children goodbye. She cannot see them clearly because of all the people, but she notices Agnes's coat. It is brown with a fitted waist, and has a ridiculous collar made of some shaggy, trailing, furry material, as if someone has skinned an animal and draped the scrapings around Agnes's neck.

None of the other girls has a coat like that. It will be easy to spot at break, or lunchtime, when Sol isn't there. She ducks when he turns to leave, keeping one eye half open to check that he doesn't look in her direction. He doesn't. Her body feels as if it has been shaken in a hard box.

Gradually, she recovers her composure. She settles in for the wait, feeling guilty because she could and should be working. She has done nothing, achieved nothing, since Sol attacked her, and she must achieve, substantially and soon. She must prove that she is not worthless. Also, there is something else bothering her. Why are the children called Wilfred and Agnes? What sort of names are those for young, happy, twenty-first-century children?

Agnes and Wilfred. Exploited worker names, victim names, early-tragic-death names. She pictures a downtrodden Victorian servant girl in an apron, curtseying before a tyrannical master; a tubercular chimney sweep or coal miner with a searing cough, broken shoes and a face black with dust from being forced to crawl into holes noone would choose to enter. Agnes and Wilfred. She knows, absolutely knows beyond all doubt, that Sol chose the names. Tina had nothing to do with it. Poor little Wilfred. Poor brave Agnes.

Suddenly, she is crying, gulping, struggling for breath. Why couldn't they be called Francesca and Hugo, or Megan and Josh, or Eleanor and Zachary? It would make killing them so much easier. Sol Barber has ruined everything all over again.

She needs to see their faces close up. It is possible that they will be vivid, boisterous creatures, capable of peeling away from the names Wilfred and Agnes all connotations of shabby pensioners dying alone in cold houses.

She wonders about Sol's real name. Is is bad? Is that why he calls himself after his favourite beer? It occurs to her that she, by chance, shares her first name with that of the lager she usually drinks. She shudders, wanting to have nothing in common with Sol. She will never drink that beer again.

After what feels like an age, she hears the blare of a tinny bell coming from inside the squat school building, and a few seconds later there is a colourful spurt of children into the playground. Carefully, after having checked that she has not had any kind of embarrassing accident (she checks often, these days) she climbs out of the car and walks over to the railings.

She sees Wilfred Barber first and is surprised to recognise him. He looks like Sol but in miniature. She wonders if Wilfred is calmer and kinder than his father, if the Barbers are improving with each generation. Wilfred is with four friends and a football. He speaks and smiles occasionally, but he is not one of the main ones; she can see that straight away. She thinks she can also tell that he wishes the others would pay more attention to him, give him more of a chance to shine. She is sure he could and would shine, if a suitable opportunity presented itself.

Agnes's coat appears, with Agnes in it. She pulls her collar – which, on second viewing, looks like the torn-off scalp of a witch – around her ears. Agnes is alone, standing with her arms folded by the wall of the school building, looking as if she does not expect anybody to join her any time soon. Her skin has a yellow tinge; she is a little tawny scrap, like a doodle Dr Seuss might have rejected as being not quite up to scratch.

Oh, my God, those poor children, she thinks, and begins to fantasise about befriending Agnes and Wilfred Barber. She could be their secret confidante and benefactor. They might grow to love her more than they love Sol. She has seen his temper in action. How many times have the children seen it? How many more times will they see it? She pictures Tina hiding behind an armchair while Sol beats Wilfred with a curtain rail, while he drags Agnes round the house by her hair. Oh, yes, the children are bound to prefer her, almost as soon as they meet her, to their brute of a father.

She closes her eyes, knowing that at some point she will need to draw a line under this sort of behaviour, this sort of thinking. The bell rings again and, when Agnes turns to go back inside, she notices a hearing aid above one of her ears. *So,* she thinks. *So Agnes is partially deaf. That must have made Sol angry, when he first found out. And Tina.*

Agnes is deaf. It is a new detail. It is too much; she doesn't want to know any more about Sol's family. Already, she is too close, close enough to feel involved, confused. She must get away. She cannot, after all, kill

Sol's children. She runs across the road, fumbles with her car door, slams it shut once she is inside and speeds off, feeling chilly, sad and empty.

It takes her two minutes to drive out of his village. It is a nothing sort of place, with an A road running through it, robbing it of any charm it might otherwise have had. The green, a triangle with one curved side, is scruffy and patchy, littered with empty crisp and cigarette packets. Behind it, a sign saying 'Mary's Tea Rooms' is fixed above the door of a detached stone house that, over the years, has been blackened by traffic fumes. There are net curtains in the windows. She hates this place and everything about it. The idea of Sol Barber, the flavour of him, is like a huge, swollen spider, crouching over the part of the country where he lives.

But eventually she is free; she is on a road that seems to have nothing to do with Sol. His domain has an end, and she has passed it. She smiles, feeling better than she has for a while. Because it would be wrong to think she has achieved nothing today. She has taken a form of revenge. If she had children, the thought that somebody she knew, somebody she had once wronged, had driven to their school, stood at the railings and watched them in the playground, and fantasised about killing them, would be too terrible to contemplate. What if the person came back a second time to turn the fantasy into a reality? One might live in fear for ever.

The revenge, she clarifies to herself, is not the killing, therefore, but the thinking about killing. Or the thinking about befriending, poaching. And she can continue to think obsessively about Sol's children in a way that, were he aware of it, would fill him with the worst kind of dread. But never mind the future; this morning, in isolation, is enough. An unbalanced woman has stood and stared at his children, unsure about whether she wants to harm them or not. That is worse than what happens to most people's children, in a civilised society. That is sufficient revenge.

She laughs at herself. So that's it? Some thoughts she had one morning? Big deal, she can imagine Sol saying. Thoughts? Water off a duck's back, oil stains off a carpet. Do you really think you could ever seriously harm anyone, you pathetic bitch?

We All Say What We Want

TOM FOYERS WAS not a straightforward man. He would have liked to be. He admired straightforward people, like his wife Selena, and like Idris Sutherland, with whom he now stood in the lift. They had both got on at the ground floor and would both get off at the eighth. 'How's life?' Idris asked.

'Fine, fine.' Tom smiled. But it wasn't. He loathed his job at Phelps Corcoran Cummings, which hogged about two-thirds of his waking time. He resented this lift that took him up to his office every morning, the way it spoke to you as you ascended – 'floor number three, floor number four' – in a perky, bodiless voice. He detested the building in which his firm was based. It was shaped like a slice taken out of the middle of a cone, glaring white all over, inside and out, menacing in its blandness. It had always reminded Tom of a spaceship that never quite managed to take off. The work itself was boring, and he was treated as a resource, not as a human being. Nobody appreciated his talents or his personality, so he had stopped using the former and hidden the latter. Top of Tom's list of hates was his own office, which was the same size as the coat cupboard under his stairs at home, and had no windows – only a long, thin, glass panel in the door that looked out on to a gleaming white corridor. Idris's office was the same. Inside the building, one was encouraged to believe that there was no outside.

'How are you?' Tom asked Idris.

'Shit. I hate this fucking place. I wish someone'd plant a bomb here. I wish someone would release Sarin gas in the foyer. Sorry, the *atrium*,' Idris added with a sneer.

I'd love to be as straightforward as Idris, thought Tom. He didn't pursue the idea, however, because he knew it was pointless. He had never actively decided on the policy of saying the opposite of what he meant; it was simply what happened every time he opened his mouth. This had been the case ever since he was a child. His mother was prone to hysterical outbursts; she did enough unrestrained reacting for the whole family. At a young age, Tom had learned to tailor everything he said and did to pacify her. As for his own responses to life and the world, these he inspected under the microscope of privacy, like a secret, valuable stamp collection.

Idris was grinning as the lift announced that they had reached floor number eight. He feels better, Tom thought glumly, now that he's got a bit of the poisonous discontent out of his system. 'Have you met our new line manager?' asked Idris.

'Nora?' said Tom. The two men stepped out of the lift and walked along the corridor, swinging their briefcases. Idris swung his higher.

'Yes. She's just like a Nora. A dowdy, mumsy cow. In a meeting last week she showed me photos of her kids. Jesus! Nathan got a look at her CV – she's a complete nonentity.'

'She seems friendly enough,' said Tom, though what he would have liked to say was this: 'She called me into her office last week and introduced herself. She made a point of being very, very nice to me. Instantly, I recognised a fellow non-straightforward person. There must have been an ulterior motive behind her pleasant and confiding manner. She cannot possibly think I'm a good thing, because she's in Gillian Bate's pocket, and Gillian can't stand me because she knows I know that she's a lightweight who doesn't deserve to be high up in any organisation. A suitable job for Gillian Bate would be circus accessory. To be tied to a revolving wheel and have knives thrown at her by a man with an impractical moustache – that would be about the right level for Gillian, given her intellect.' Tom wanted to say all this to Idris, but couldn't, even though he knew Idris would probably have become his best friend on the spot if he had. Tom would have found it easier to do the can-can naked in the atrium than to say what he really thought. Honesty, openness, the direct approach – Tom felt about these the way most people felt about hand grenades.

'She only got the job because she's Gillian's lapdog,' said Idris. 'As Sir Arthur Conan Doyle said, "Mediocrity only recognises itself. It takes talent to recognise genius."

Later, alligator.' Idris unlocked his office and swung into it in one fluid movement.

Tom sighed and carried on walking. Did that mean that Idris was a genius? Or that he thought he was? One advantage of Tom's reveal-nothing approach was that he had an invigorating inner life. He conducted with himself all the stimulating conversations he failed to have with other people.

He emptied his pigeonhole and took the contents to his office to read. He had six letters – two in internal mail envelopes – and two faxes. If he'd had seven letters, or three faxes, there would not have been room for him and all his correspondence in his airless cubicle. As it was, he and his mail fitted snugly.

He tackled the two sky-blue envelopes first. Internal communications were always the deadliest and it was as well to get them out of the way. One was from Imrana Kabir in Human Resources. It told Tom that he was entitled to free eye tests and that he should contact her to arrange one. He balled it up and threw it in the bin. The second was from Nora Connaughton, the new manager. It read as follows:

Dear Tom,

Ruth tells me that you were unable to come into the office last Thursday to collect the Burns Gimblett files and that you asked her to post them to you at home. I do hope you are not unwell. Please let me know if you are, and if there is anything I can do.

Best wishes, Nora Connaughton (cc Gillian Bate)

Tom seethed. Here it was, the first subtle attack. Oh, yes, there was no doubt that Nora was a fellow indirect communicator, an experienced passive aggressor. He knew what she must have wanted to say to him: 'Why weren't you in the office last Thursday? You didn't ask my permission to work from home. Remember, I'm the new boss. Frankly, I doubt you were working at all. I bet you were in the pub playing darts, or having mud and sea-weed rubbed into your back as part of a spa day, cheating the company, you lazy bastard. And, look, I'm telling on you. I'm telling the even bigger boss.'

The inclusion of 'cc Gillian Bate' was the proof. If Nora trusted him, was genuinely concerned for his well-being and had no doubt he'd spent last Thursday work-ing, she wouldn't have felt the need to send a copy of the letter to Gillian. Nor would she have done something so formal as send a letter; she'd simply have emailed him. What did 'cc' mean, anyway? Complete cunt, thought Tom. The company email template offered one the option of 'bcc' as well. Both complete cunts: Nora and Gillian.

The phone on his desk rang. He picked it up, said 'Tom Foyers,' hoping, as he always did, that Jonathan Ross would be on the other end. Jonathan would be phoning from Barry Norman's house. 'Look, Tom, if I don't have a few months off I'm going to go crazy. Barry and I have been having a chat, and we've decided you'd be ideal to present *Film 2005*. You wouldn't, by any chance, fancy it, would you? All you need is a reassuring smile and a stylish yet comfortable jumper to wear.'

It was not Jonathan Ross. It was Selena, Tom's wife. Still, he was reasonably happy to hear from her. Selena was the only person with whom Tom shared some (though by no means all) of his real thoughts. He didn't quite know how this had come about, but he knew that Selena had arranged it. She had constructed a supervised area in which Tom could safely say anything. So could their two children, Joseph and Lucy. Lucy, who was two, had taken to saying, 'For fuck's sake!' every time she encountered a practical difficulty. She said it when she couldn't slot the Piglet piece into her Winnie the Pooh jigsaw, and when her Baby Annabel doll rolled off the changing mat. She'd learned the phrase from Selena, who laughed every time Lucy parroted it. 'That'll give the girls at nursery a shock,' she said. Joseph, who was four, screamed, 'I hate you, Mummy! I hate you, Daddy!' every time he was told that he couldn't have chocolate mousse for dinner and then again for pudding.

'How are you?' Tom asked his wife.

'Extremely pissed off,' said Selena. 'Furious, in fact. Can you come and meet me, now?'

'Not really.' What Tom meant was, 'Not at all.' Selena's current job was to sell eighteen townhouses for Beddford Homes. She worked alone in the sales office, which was the double garage of the show home. This was at least ten times the size of Tom's office, and her bosses, Andrew Beddington and Brian Ford, had installed a fully equipped little kitchen for her at the back. They'd also judged Selena worthy of a carpet, three armchairs, a fan to cool the stifling summer air, and a television. She had already sold four of the houses for them, and they liked and trusted her. They knew she could and would sell the lot. Selena was an extremely persuasive woman. Andrew and Brian didn't even mind that on quiet days she closed the office and went shopping or to get a manicure.

Selena sometimes had trouble understanding the constraints of Tom's working life. 'Why not?' she said crossly.

'Because it's not up to me when I come and go from the office,' said Tom, running amok in this rare opportunity for honesty like a toddler in a Wacky Warehouse ball pit. 'It's up to a fat, snide, glorified tealady called Nora Connaughton.' Last Thursday, Tom had worked at home from seven in the morning until eight in the evening. He had asked Ruth, one of the secretaries, to send the Burns Gimblett files to his house because he hadn't wanted to lose an hour and a half of work time. 'Why, has something happened?'

'Not yet,' said Selena viciously. 'But it will.'

'What? What will happen?'

'Do you remember that…oh, no. There are some people coming in. No, they're not. Yes, they are. I'm going to have to take them round the show home. Just meet me here as soon as you can.'

Tom put the phone down. He turned on his computer and began to draft an email to Nora. What would Selena write? What would Idris write?

From: Tom.Foyers@phelpscc.com
To: Nora.Connaughton@phelpscc.com

Dear Nora, I was not unwell last Thursday. I was at home with an awful lot of work that I was anxious to get through. It seemed sensible to ask Ruth to put the files I needed in the post, as Ruth was already in the office, right next to the post room, in fact. Surely you would agree that for me to drive forty-five minutes each way to collect the files myself would have been an unwise use of my time and therefore the company's time and money. It would also have been ecologically irresponsible. Think of the car exhaust fumes and unnecessary petrol consumption.

Selena or Idris would then almost definitely add, 'I infer, from your cc-ing of Gillian Bate, that you intended your letter as a criticism at best or, at worst, a threat. If you have any reservations about the way I work, please could I ask you to be more direct in future?'

Tom smiled. If only. Then he deleted everything he had typed apart from 'From: Tom.Foyers@phelpscc.com, To: Nora.Connaughton@phelphscc.com'. He kept the 'Compose message' box open, but reduced it to a small square in the corner of his screen so that he could also read his new emails. As soon as he looked at his in-box, he spotted the words 'Staff circular – Idris Sutherland'. He opened this message immediately, half expecting it to be from Gilbert Sparling, the managing director of Phelps Corcoran Cummings, and to say, 'Have all colleagues noticed that Idris Sutherland is much more straightforward, and as a result happier, than Tom Foyers?' But no, the email was from Ruth, informing all colleagues that Idris was to take six months of unpaid leave, starting next Monday, in order to spend some time with his new baby, Oliver.

Tom shook internally. He was not the sort to shake externally. Six months' leave! It was unheard of. Had Nora agreed to this? No, it couldn't have happened so quickly. Gillian must have set it in motion before she was promoted. Right, that's *it*, thought Tom. He often thought this, and nothing ever happened as a result. Several things were immediately apparent to him: Idris was the sort of person who asked for what he wanted, straight out. Therefore, Idris got what he wanted more often than not. Tom would never have dared to ask for six months' unpaid leave, even if he could have managed financially, which he couldn't. If he dared to ask, Gillian or Nora or whichever revolving-wheel-ornament was in charge at the time would say no, without even having to consider it. Tom thought so, anyway. He was pretty sure.

Inwardly, he vibrated at the injustice. He was in a trap and could see no way out. He'd worked for the company for seven years and had never had either a promotion or a pay rise, apart from the minimal, token one that all employees got every year. He knew he ought to try, as Idris had, to improve his situation at Phelps Corcoran Cummings, but once he had tried and failed, what would he have then? Nothing. In realising this, Tom came closer than ever before to identifying the cause of his problem. For as long as he kept his wishes, his fat stack of grievances and his hatred a secret, he still had some power, power he told himself he might one day choose to exercise, even though, deep down, he knew he never would. But the power was there all the same; the sheer force of his illwill towards the company that employed him was awe-inspiring. As long as it continued to grow, Tom was able to feel like a man who could do serious damage if he chose to. He was aware of the steaming bile inside him all the time, energising him, like a hearty dose of steroids. Every time he bumped into Gillian Bate by the water machine and told her he was fine, everything was fine, he felt like David pulling back his catapult, ready to launch a hefty rock at Goliath's head. And not launching it was the whole point, for once the rock lay on the floor at Gillian's feet, once she'd looked down, sniggered at it and stepped over it on her way to her next meeting, it would all be over for Tom.

As he sat at his desk and fumed, he had an unusual idea, the sort of idea that, it seemed to Tom, only a person with some flair would have. He'd had lots of flair once, before his colleagues and bosses at Phelps Corcoran Cummings had underestimated it out of him. Beneath 'To: Nora.Connaughton@phelpscc.com', in the 'cc' box, he entered Gillian Bate's email address, and Gilbert Sparling's. Then, in the larger box below, he typed:

Thank you for your kind letter. I am perfectly all right, and thank you for asking. I was busy working from home last Thursday and I didn't want to interrupt my work, which was why I asked Ruth to send me the Burns Gimblett files. I hope you are not unwell yourself. I noticed that on Monday and Tuesday last week you were out of the office for two hours at lunchtime on each day. Since this was so much longer than the lunch hour we are all in the habit of taking, I was a bit concerned, and then when I saw you at the division meeting on Wednesday, I couldn't help noticing that you were looking a bit peaky. I hope that my concern is unfounded and that you are in good health, but do let me know if there is a problem, as obviously I would be happy to help in any way I can.

All the best, Tom

He clicked on 'Send', then did a little dance of glee. He felt wonderful. Who wanted to be direct and assertive when there was so much fun to be had by being devious and double-edged? But now he had a decision to make: what to say if Gillian asked why he'd copied the email to her. Simple: he would say that, since Nora had sent Gillian a copy of her original letter, it seemed only polite to include her in the reply. Tom was fairly sure he would hear nothing from Gilbert Sparling. Sparling, the MD, was a billionaire who divided his time between Geneva and South Beach, Florida. He was never in the office, and noone Tom knew had ever met him. Hopefully Sparling would be too busy staring at crocodiles through the floor of his glass-bottomed boat, or drinking Kir Royales on the beach with famous fashion designers, to pay any attention to Tom.

Still, if anybody did ask about his email, Tom could dishonestly – and, therefore, all the more convincingly – say that he'd simply been replying to Nora's letter, and had taken the opportunity to raise his concern about her health. Straightforwardness was what terrified him, and this was far from straightforward.

Nora looked rough most of the time. In the meeting Tom had mentioned, when people had disagreed with one another and Nora, as the most senior person present, was expected to take a firm line, she had looked as if she were writhing in pain, as if demons were clawing at the walls of her stomach. To say 'You're right, you're wrong, that's settled' was way too direct for Nora. She wouldn't last five minutes as an assistant at Lucy's nursery, thought Tom. Neither, he conceded, would he.

He pictured the panic on Nora's face when she realised her extra-long lunches had been rumbled, and for an instant his soul was bathed in joy. He tried to focus on the other messages and letters that needed his attention, but it was no use; he was feeling too sprightly and triumphant to sit at his desk and work, so he decided to go to the show home and find Selena. He couldn't wait to tell her what he'd done. If Nora sent him another letter complaining about his early departure, maybe he'd pretend he'd been taken ill. He'd never faked sickness before, but now that Nora had put the idea into his head, it seemed a good one. There were all sorts of things Tom could do that would involve defiance but not directness. He felt dizzy with elation; he couldn't understand why he hadn't cottoned on to this sooner. It had to be because years of working for Gillian Bate had crushed his flair.

As he parked his Citroën in the Beddford Homes development's car park, he allowed himself to hope that perhaps Nora would say nothing about his premature exit from the office. Perhaps she would never dare to criticise him again, now that she knew he was better at the covert digs game than she was.

Selena was in the show home garage-cum-office with her feet up on the desk. She was drinking a mug of tea, and grinned at Tom as he walked in. 'That's the spirit,' she said. 'Leave before midday, teach them not to take you for granted.'

Tom was keen to tell her of his adventure, but puzzled, also, by his wife's change of mood. 'You've cheered up,' he said. 'I thought you were furious.'

'I was, then. But I've dealt with it.' This was the sort of woman Selena was: angry before the event that would make her angry had happened, happy twenty seconds later because she'd sorted out the problem. Often she didn't feel the need to tell Tom what had been wrong, once it was right. Tom was the eloquent and fulsome complainer of the household; ranting to Selena until he'd got it out of his system was the only way he knew to resolve any of his difficulties in the outside world. Until today.

'Tell me,' he said.

'You know that competition I entered, in *Good Housekeeping*?'

'No.'

She sighed. 'You never listen. The luggage company Packed to Perfection ran this competition. You had to write a strapline to promote their merchandise, ten words or less, and the word "suitcase" or "case" had to be in it somewhere. The prize was a long weekend for two at the Hotel Europa-Regina in Venice. Completely free. Anyway, I won.'

'What?' Tom had always wanted to go to Venice. This had to be better than anything that had ever happened to Idris Sutherland. 'But…that's brilliant. What was your slogan?'

'"World open. Case closed."' Selena laughed. 'We have to use their luggage, but that's okay. They're giving us a free set, and our suitcases are knackered anyway.'

'I don't understand why you were angry,' said Tom.

'Because…what were we going to do with Joe and Luce?'

'Hey?'

'It's a weekend for two adults, not for a family. And, quite frankly, I'm glad there's no provision for kids. Joe is four. Do you realise that in four years and four months, we've never – never! – had a night on our own, let alone three.'

Tom saw the problem. 'I'm sure the luggage people would let us take the kids,' he said. 'I mean, we might have to pay for them, but…'

'Tom, I don't want to take the kids. Sorry if that sounds selfish, but I think we deserve a break without children. Clearly Packed to Perfection think so too, and that's why the prize is a long weekend for two, not four. I can't remember the last time we haven't both been up before six-thirty. Can you?'

'No,' Tom admitted.

Selena opened her mouth and an avalanche of names poured out, all friends of theirs, all with children. She told

Tom about the many thrill-packed nights those couples had spent away, alone – at casinos, theatres, nightclubs, artists' retreats, ski resorts, on safari – while siblings, grandparents and godparents had looked after their offspring. By the time she'd finished, Tom was feeling quite resentful. 'Well, I can't think of anyone we could leave the kids with and just…go,' he said.

'Neither could I. That's why I was fuming,' said Selena. She was grinning from ear to ear, so Tom relaxed and allowed himself to assume that a solution had long since been found, that he and Selena would be going to Venice without Joseph and Lucy. A complete rest for three days and nights – it seemed almost too good to be true, even in the new world, the one in which he used Nora Connaughton's own methods to defeat her.

'I started thinking about our support network,' said Selena.

Tom shuddered. 'Don't say that. It's the sort of thing Gillian Bate says.' Last week she had sent a round robin email to all Phelps Corcoran Cummings employees informing them that from now on job interviews were to be known as 'selection events'.

'Okay,' said Selena, 'but you know what I mean. We've both got big families, and yet I knew – I just knew for certain – that nobody would look after the kids for a long weekend, not in the proper spirit, anyway. We've got this amazing opportunity, something we'd never normally be able to afford, and I knew beyond a shadow of a doubt that not one of our parents or siblings would say, "Go for it, have a great time. Joe and Lucy'll be fine with us. Don't worry about a thing." That's why I was so angry. I hadn't even asked anyone yet, but I knew what they'd all say.'

'And?' said Tom.

Selena pulled an A4-sized notepad towards her and began to read from it. She was exceptionally thorough and efficient. Tom would have liked to have a boss like her, someone he could respect. 'Your mum said she could do it if we dropped the kids off no earlier than three-thirty on the Friday, because of her tennis, and came back on the Saturday afternoon instead of the Monday, because she's got bridge on Sunday. She wanted me to ring Packed for Perfection and ask if we could go for just one night – a one-night long weekend! – and donate our other two nights to the runner-up. Stupid old bat. And she expected me to be grateful for her offer, as if she was doing us a real favour. After all the hours I've spent on the phone to her in the middle of the night, when she and your dad have their rows! Do I ever say, "Sorry, Rhoda, but I'd actually like to be asleep now, so can you please shut up?"'

'When are these three nights?' Tom asked nervously, worrying about his annual leave. He'd already taken a lot of it, and there was the camping trip in August still to come.

'Don't panic,' said Selena. 'It's not until next May.' Tom stopped panicking. 'My parents obviously can't do it. My mum's in too much pain from her arthritis, and my dad has to play golf morning, noon and night or the world will end. Bernadette said no because she and Dave fight a lot and she thinks it'd be bad for the children to be in such a combative environment. Tess said no because she hasn't got the room, Anna and James said they weren't sure, that they'd find it very hard and tiring…'

'That's fair enough, isn't it?' said Tom. 'People have got their own lives. Why should they drop everything to look after our kids?'

'That's what I thought at first,' said Selena. 'Then I thought, sod that, sod the understanding approach. They *should* drop everything. Just this once, they should. This trip is something I *won*. It's a *prize*. First prize! That's what makes it different. I've never won anything before, and I never will again. Especially not for something… proper like this, something creative.' Selena's eyes shone with tears at the thought of having to turn down what she had earned, what was rightfully hers. Tom understood. Having to refuse the reward would detract from her sense of achievement. It oughtn't to, but both Tom and Selena knew it would. Another couple would go to Venice, and it would be as if Selena had never won the competition.

'Did you ask Paula and Nick?' said Tom.

'Oh yes! They said no thanks, not while Lucy's still in nappies, but they'll definitely have the kids for a weekend when they're older – yeah, I bet! When they're forty-six and forty-four respectively, by which time we won't have had a break for forty-two years!'

'Can we skip to the part where you solved the problem?' Tom pleaded, feeling faint.

'Not quite yet,' said Selena. 'Good. I'm glad it's not just me. I can see you agree. How do you feel, now that I've told you what everyone said?'

'Well, I hope there's some way of arranging it. I'd love to go to Venice. We could maybe save up and pay for some kind of...I don't know, nanny.'

'Tom, our mortgage has just gone up by two hundred quid a month.'

'It has?'

'Yes! The discount phase is over. We can't afford a nanny. Soon we'll barely be able to afford a pizza. But that's not what I mean, anyway,' said Selena. 'What I meant was: how do you feel about our two large and predominantly able-bodied families?'

'Erm, well...'

'You don't want to sound mean, so I'll say it. You feel as if you might as well not have a family. I mean, all that bollocks about love and closeness and let's-spend-every-Christmas-fucking-day-together. All that hot air from our parents and brothers and sisters about how we don't bring the kids to see them often enough, and they feel they're missing out on Joe and Lucy's childhoods. I've actually lost sleep feeling guilty about it, once or twice! But it's all bullshit, isn't it? We're utterly alone in the world.'

'We've got each other, and the kids,' said Tom, alarmed.

'Of course, but as a foursome we're utterly alone. And four isn't enough, especially when two...' – Selena pointed at herself and Tom – '...want to have eight hours uninterrupted sleep, together, with neither of them having to get up at half six and watch *The Hoobs* and *Peppa Pig* and *Funky Valley* and fucking *Noddy* and...'

'Selena, I've never heard you talk like this before. You love your family…'

'Yes, I know. I'm not saying I don't. You can love people and still be utterly alone in the world, can't you? They probably love me too, and your lot love you, but when it comes to any of them helping us in the way we most need to be helped…forget it!' Selena put on a squeaky voice. '"I think I'd find it very hard and tiring." "Couldn't you go for one night instead of three?" I mean, fuck *off*, the lot of you!'

'Aren't you being a bit unreasonable,' said Tom. 'I mean, if we were both run over by a car, any of our relatives would look after the kids, you know they would. But we don't really need to go for a long weekend in Venice, do we?'

Selena stared at him long and hard. 'I'm going to give you a chance to redeem yourself,' she said, getting up from her chair, her empty mug dangling from her thumb. Tom sighed. Nora Connaughton was a mere shadow in the back of his mind. He had far more serious problems, and, since home misery was worse than work misery, he felt even more dreadful than he was used to feeling. He'd left the house this morning thinking that the Foyerses and the Henshaws were, by and large, two decent and dependable bunches of people. Now Selena had proved to him that his parents and siblings would only put themselves out for him once he had been run over. They would all behave brilliantly, in that circumstance. Otherwise, they would behave selfishly. Which, depending on how you looked at it, could be construed as an incentive to go out and get knocked down by the first oncoming vehicle.

It took only seconds for Tom to arrive at the bitter conclusion that all his relatives wanted to see him flattened under the wheels of a bus, the same ones Lucy was always singing about, the ones that went round and round all day long. 'It's too late to be caring towards somebody once they're dying in hospital,' he said glumly. 'A family shouldn't be like the Samaritans: only there to save you if you're absolutely desperate. They should want you to be happy and…have nice trips to Venice.'

'Exactly,' said Selena. 'And it's not nice trips plural,' said Selena. 'It's one trip to Venice, which I won, fair and square. And they're going to stand by and let us turn it down? Don't any of them care if we both have nervous breakdowns or if our marriage falls apart?'

'But we're nowhere near nervous breakdowns,' said Tom. 'The kids are really easy and good…'

'Not easy and good enough for those lazy shits!'

'…and they're at nursery all week, anyway, and our marriage is absolutely fine.'

'Yes! No thanks to them! Anyway…' Selena held up her hands, fingers spread wide in a 'that's enough' gesture. 'I mustn't get all agitated again. I've spent most of the morning like this.' She exhaled deeply. 'Do you want a drink?'

'No! I want to know how you got round the problem. Tell me we're going to Venice next May.'

'Oh, we'll be going,' Selena said confidently.

Tom's heart plummeted. He didn't like the sound of that. 'What do you mean, "we'll be going"?' As if it were not yet fully in the bag. 'Who'll look after the kids?'

Selena walked over to put the kettle on. When she turned to face Tom again, she had a sly grin on her face. 'I don't know exactly who, but it'll be somebody from our new family.'

Tom shivered. This sounded like a comment of the sort that might first alert a husband to his wife's rankling insanity. 'Our new family?' he echoed.

'Yes. Don't look worried – I haven't gone chicken oriental. I made a simple, practical decision. Nobody should be alone in the world, without a safety net of people to support and look after them in times of need and…offers of free holidays. This morning proved that we haven't got that, and that's not a situation I'm prepared to accept. So I've advertised for new relatives.'

'*What*?' Tom gasped.

'And there's no point trying to talk me out of it. The advert's already up on the notice board at Tesco.' Selena laughed. 'It's brilliant. You wait: once news gets around about what I've done, everyone'll be doing it. Think of all the elderly people who've got noone, or whose kids have cut them off after big feuds. Think of everyone whose loved ones have died, or disowned them because they once got into trouble…'

'Selena, you can't seriously…'

'I'm deadly serious. I'll get masses of responses to my advert, you wait and see. I'm going to hand-pick the members of our new family.'

'What, from the feuders and the abandoned, the disgraced and disowned? These are the people you're going to leave in charge of Joe and Lucy?'

'Oh, you're such a worrier! Listen, I swear to you, if you're not a hundred per cent happy with our new family, we won't leave the children with them. Okay?'

'Okay,' said Tom, though he was far from it. Thinking back over the way Selena had constructed her sentence, it seemed to him that she had snuck in the 'new family' part; there was no suggestion that Tom might be able to veto these solicited relatives, either as individuals or collectively, as a theoretical proposition. He would have a say only in whether or not to leave the children with them. But he knew Selena well and she was not sneaky. She was straightforward. If she made the new family sound non-negotiable, that was because it was. Selena was drawing this feature of the situation to Tom's attention, not trying to disguise it.

He knew there was no point arguing. New relatives would be sought on his behalf, even as he protested. He prayed that everybody in Tesco this afternoon would be too busy to look at the notice board. First thing tomorrow morning, on his way to work, he would nip in and take the advert down.

'So, it'll be fine,' Selena concluded. 'I'm really quite excited about the whole thing. How was your day? Your morning?'

Tom decided not to tell her about Nora Connaughton's memo or his response. It would sound pathetic. Big deal, he'd taken a veiled pop at his boss. Had he really expected Selena to applaud his bravery? She'd spent the morning judging and firing their close relations, and sending out for new ones. She was a woman of action; how could Tom expect her to appreciate the subtle nuances of his way of doing things?

As it turned out, he didn't have a chance to answer. The phone in the sales office rang, and Selena picked it up. 'Beddford Homes, how may I help you?' she recited in a sing-song voice. Then, sounding interested and genuine all of a sudden, she said, 'Yes, it is. Oh, you saw my advert? Brilliant! Thanks *so* much for ringing.'

Tom's gut quaked. The first aspiring substitute relative had made contact.

THERE WAS AN email from Nora waiting for Tom the following day. She made no reference to his enquiry about her health.

From Nora.Connaughton@phelpscc.com
To: Tom.Foyers@phelpscc.com, Cc: Gillian.Bate@
phelpscc.com, Imrana.Kabir@phelpscc.com.

Dear Tom
 In future, please could you let me know if you plan to work from home? It's just that it makes life easier for me if I know where staff are. Last Thursday, for example, Nathan asked me if I knew where he might find you, and I, in all innocence, directed him to your office. Glad to see Burns Gimblett is progressing nicely – well done!
 Best wishes, Nora.

Tom resisted the urge to spit at his computer screen. So now she was copying in not only Gillian, but Imrana from Human Resources, the department that dealt with grievances, internal wrangles, hirings and firings. The subliminal message was unequivocal – it was rather like receiving a message from God, cc The Grim Reaper, suggesting that you might want to visit the doctor for a routine check-up. As for the mock-jovial line about Burns Gimblett – did Nora think Tom was an idiot? Did she imagine that a dollop of praise at the end cancelled out the needling tone of the rest, the subtle bullying, the warning-masquerading-as-humble-request?

Tom gave it some thought and decided that of course she didn't. She knew what game they were playing, and she knew he knew. The email's upbeat last line was not intended to make Tom feel better; rather, it was a shield for Nora, who was evidently too gutless to say what she meant and take the consequences. Part of her wanted Tom to like her, even as she plotted to bring him down. This, he realised, gave him a certain amount of power.

He decided to reply by letter, to make it clear that there was nothing casual about his response. 'Dear Nora', he typed, despising her. Of course, he too was averse to saying what he meant, but for that reason he had always taken pains to ensure that he never became the boss of anybody, never put himself in a position where he had a team of staff to manage. Nora was evidently deluded about her own capabilities. For her to have applied for the job of division manager was as absurd as if Miffy Bunny were to make a bid to replace Orla Guerin as the BBC's Middle East correspondent.

Don't worry about having sent Nathan to my office, Tom typed.

He obviously interpreted, with relative ease, the big sign I'd cellotaped to my door, explaining that I'd be working from home all day and giving several phone numbers where I could be reached. He contacted me immediately and easily, so there was no problem there. Could I just take this opportunity to clarify something? I am unsure of your policy with regard to working from home. Would you a) prefer me not to work from home, but always to work in the office, b) prefer me to ask your permission in the event of my wishing to work from home, or c) simply like me to inform you of the days on which I'll be working at home? No doubt I've mislaid the communication you sent to all staff in which the guidelines were clearly laid out – I'm so sorry for this uncharacteristic carelessness on my part. And, sorry also to create extra work, but could you possibly send it again? I hope I don't sound too pedantic wittering on about efficient dissemination of information. I don't know about you, but I've always found it's all too easy to slip up when you're hazy about what is expected of you. Hope you're making the most of this lovely weather we're having!

All the best, Tom
(cc: Gillian Bate, Imrana Kabir, Johnny Eyebrows)

Tom chuckled. Johnny was a drug dealer who hung around the precinct centre in town. Tom bought a bag of grass from him every now and again. He re-read what he'd written and frowned. Nora would, of course, know that he was taking the piss, but would she do anything about it? Would Gillian, or Imrana, have the guts to demand to know who Johnny Eyebrows was?

Tom decided that one of the three women was bound to, though he wasn't sure which. But questions would be asked, once it was noted that there was no Phelps Corcoran Cummings employee by the name of John Eyebrows. Tom fantasised about how he might reply. 'Oh, yes, didn't I mention it? Johnny's a friend of mine, an artist. He's doing a big installation at the moment on the theme of the language of business, and he's asked me to get him copies of some non-confidential correspondence...' Tom's blood fizzed with glee. He could do it; he could pull it off. All he had to do was say it solemnly, and nobody would be able to prove that his intentions were mocking, anarchic and disrespectful. The worst they could do was ask him, crossly, not to pass on any more Phelps Corcoran Cummings memos to Johnny. In which case he could offer the honest mistake line of defence and promise never to do it again.

Tom sent the letter to Nora, Gillian and Imrana. He did not bother to print out a copy for Johnny Eyebrows, for he was as certain as he could be that Johnny would not appreciate the brilliance of the whole scheme. It didn't matter; Tom appreciated it enough for both of them. His whole body pinged with adrenaline. He spent most of the day humming while he worked and, at five thirty, found that he was less keen than usual to leave the building. The offices of Phelps Corcoran Cummings were no longer merely the site of his suffering; they were the glistening white arena in which he showed a few people a thing or two, people who might say, 'I never thought that mousy Tom Foyers had it in him.'

There was another reason why he wasn't keen to leave work, a reason unconnected to his job. At seven o'clock he was due to drink wine and eat cheese with three strangers who had, on the telephone yesterday and this morning, professed to want to form a family with him and his wife. Tom sighed and pulled Selena's advertisement out of his jacket pocket. He'd removed it from Tesco at five past eight, on his way in, but he'd been too late. At least three people had already seen it, the three who would be joining Tom and Selena at the Beddford development's show home this evening.

Selena had suggested congregating there rather than at home, just in case any of the three applicants for feigned kinship turned out to be mentally unstable. 'We don't want them to know where we live if they're nutters, do we?' she'd said to Tom over breakfast. Briefly, Tom had suspected her of taking this sensible precaution and talking about nutters as a cunning way of presenting herself – by contrast, and falsely – as sane. But then he remembered that Selena did not have hidden agendas. So maybe she was sane; he'd always thought so.

Tom had said nothing. Every molecule of his brain, every atom of his heart was opposed to Selena's plan, but he found it impossible to protest, and this wasn't only because of his usual reluctance to speak his mind. What stumped him was that Selena argued her case so well; logically, he couldn't fault her. His objection stemmed from a combination of two fears: of the unknown (the new relatives) and of the unconventional (the plan to acquire new relatives).

Thinking about it, Tom decided that the latter was the more serious problem for him. 'Nobody does this!' he'd wanted to scream at Selena. 'Not a single person in the entire world has ever done this! I don't want to be a freak!' He could imagine what she'd say: 'Imagine if Noah had been a chicken like you – there'd have been no ark. Imagine if Martin Luther King had said that to himself. Or Emmeline Pankhurst. I'm ahead of my time, that's all. One day everyone'll do it. Real, blood families will be as passé as natural childbirth and breast-feeding – two other bloody stupid ideas!'

He looked again at Selena's notice and shook his head. At the top, in capital letters, she had written, 'DO YOU DESERVE A BETTER FAMILY THAN THE ONE YOU'VE GOT?' Underneath, she'd elaborated. 'Do your relatives continually let you down? Do they fail to meet your needs and support you in the way you'd like them to? Do you feel alone in the world? Or perhaps you really are alone, with no living parents, children or siblings, or at least not ones you're in contact with. If so, then you're in the same position as us. We are Tom and Selena Foyers, a married couple with two children. We have a large extended family but they fall way short of the satisfaction mark, and so we're recruiting for replacements. Reciprocal support guaranteed. If you're interested, ring Selena on 01238554899.'

Tom had felt faint when he'd first read it; he'd phoned Selena at the show home, aghast. 'Couldn't you have put it more diplomatically? What if my mum sees it, or hears about it?'

'Your mum lives in Canterbury.'

'Yours doesn't! Your parents live four streets away! And what about James, who works about two hundred metres from…'

'What about them?' Selena had sounded mystified. 'I'm not scared of them seeing my ad.'

'But they'd be horrified, devastated. They'd never speak to us again!'

'Yes, they would. If any of them sees it, I'll just explain.'

'Explain what? What will you say?'

'That ever since the kids were born we've found their level of support disappointing, and we finally decided to take some action.'

'Oh, that'll really help! That's bound to pacify them!'

'Tom, pacifying our families is not my objective here,' she'd said patiently, kindly, as if he were a bit slow. He gave up. Selena would never see his point; she wasn't like him. Either you were terrified of how everybody might react to everything or you weren't, and Selena wasn't.

THE MOTORWAY WAS particularly clogged that evening, and there had been an accident at junction seventeen. Only one lane remained open, and the traffic crawled along. What was normally a forty-five minute drive took Tom nearly two hours. An hour into his ordeal, he realised he wouldn't have time to go home and change; he would have to go straight to the show home.

The sales office was locked, dark. Tom hovered uncertainly for a few seconds, wondering what he ought to do. The middle floor of the show home was illuminated, the curtains open. Tom heard laughter, some of it Selena's. He wanted to turn and leave, but he wasn't brave enough, and he didn't want to let Selena down. She was doing this for them. For Venice. He rang the doorbell.

The hall light came on, and Selena trotted downstairs to let him in. The show home was arranged on three levels, as were all eighteen houses in the development. On the ground floor there was a long, narrow hall, a utility room, a cloakroom and a large, L-shaped bedroom with a built-in study area. The lounge, kitchen and dining room were on the first floor, arranged around a spacious rectangular landing, where there was also a small bathroom. The top floor comprised an even larger rectangular landing, the main bathroom, two single bedrooms and the master bedroom, which had an en-suite bathroom with a big, round Jacuzzi-bath in its centre.

Most of the houses on the development were empty shells, waiting for new owners to fill them with evidence of good or bad taste, but the show home had been furnished and decorated. Selena had shown Tom round when she'd first got the job with Beddford, saying, 'Don't you wish we could afford one?' All the walls were custard-coloured, all the duvet covers and scatter cushions bright yellow. The curtains in every room were checked – red, orange and yellow – and had belts around their middles on each side that held them permanently open. The carpets were fudge-coloured and fluffy.

Tom would never have chosen to decorate a house in this way, but as he'd moved from one custardy room to another, he'd felt oddly comforted; it was like being inside a big, new dolls' house.

'Sorry I'm late,' he said to Selena. 'Are they...?' He jerked his head in the direction of the stairs.

'Yup, they're all here,' she said. Then, lowering her voice, she added, 'Oh, Tom, they're great. I can't believe how well it's worked out.'

Tom felt frightened. 'You've only known them...' – he glanced at his watch – '...fifteen minutes.'

'No, they were all early. They've been here since half past six. Which is the first thing I realised we've got in common. When aren't I an hour early? Come up and meet them, anyway – they're all dying to see you. Oh Tom, it's so amazing! I feel as if I've known them for ever.'

With a leaden heart, Tom ascended the stairs. His new family was in the lounge, the show home's most impressive room. It was big and square, and had a balcony that overlooked the river. On the yellow leather sofa, an overweight old woman with grey cropped hair and frameless, bifocal glasses was reading a book to Lucy, who was sitting on her knee. The book was called *The Big Red Bath*. Tom had never seen it before. He was about to ask Selena about it when she said, 'Look, Audrey's brought books for the kids.' Tom noticed a pile of them on the floor at the old woman's feet. He took in Audrey's bright-red lace-up shoes with their funny, stitched ridges that reminded him of pastry round the edge of a pie-dish.

Audrey looked up and smiled. Lucy said, 'Hi, Daddy Paddy-whack-whack.' Then they both turned back to the book. 'Water on the floor, bubbles mount, the bath is starting to bob about!' Audrey recited. Joe was lying under the rectangular coffee table, holding an orange plastic gun that Tom did not recognise. Above him were two empty bottles of red wine and three full. Seven cheeses were artfully arranged on bright-yellow plates, which, Tom worked out, Selena must have borrowed from the dining table. 'I'm Butch Cassidy, Daddy,' said Joe. 'And Clive's the Sundance Kid. Bang bang! Bang!'

A round-faced, bald young man in immaculate navy jeans and a white Aran jumper stood up and shook Tom's hand. 'I'm Clive,' he said. 'Twenty-nine, forensic pathologist. Nice to meet you. I hope you don't…you know, disapprove of…pretend shootings.' He nodded in Joe's direction. 'I'm actually a pacifist!'

At that moment, Tom wasn't convinced he disapproved of real shootings. He had himself in mind as his first victim. This was intolerable. 'Clive…?' He prompted, not because he cared what the man's surname was, but because he could see that he was expected to say something.

'We've decided not to bother with surnames,' said Selena, 'since the aim is for us all to be one big family. Actually, we were thinking, if this works out, maybe we should all change our names to a new name, you know, so that we'd all be called the same thing.'

'Kilkenny,' said the third imitation relative, a teenage girl with dreadlocks, two nose rings in her left nostril and a Scottish accent. She was wearing a short leather skirt over patterned leggings, and big black boots. 'I've always liked the name Kilkenny.'

'This is Petra,' said Selena. 'Don't mind Tom being silent and awkward, everyone. This whole thing was my idea, and he's a bit apprehensive. Aren't you, Tom?'

'Well, no. I mean, I'm sure…' Tom began to mumble.

'Maybe we should all introduce ourselves formally,' Petra suggested. 'I mean, so far all we've done is chat. Maybe we should explain why we're all here, why we don't see our own families. Would that help, Tom?'

'Erm, well, I'm fine, really, but, I mean…'

He couldn't concentrate, couldn't finish a sentence. In the background, softly, Audrey was whispering to Lucy, 'Rub-a-dub-a-giggle, rub-a-dub-a-laugh, let's tell Mum about our big, red bath.'

'I see my family,' said Clive. He turned to Selena. 'We don't have to have ditched them, do we?'

Selena assured him, to Tom's relief, that the comprehensive shunning of one's original set of relatives was not a requirement.

Petra looked a bit upset, but said nothing.

'If we start to talk about the various family problems we have, we might get dragged down into a bitchy, negative vibe,' said Audrey.

'Good point,' said Clive. 'I don't really want to bad-mouth anybody.'

'You don't?' Selena grinned. 'I want to badmouth almost everybody.' Audrey, Clive and Petra all laughed. 'And you should hear Tom when he gets going. Who was it at work that you said deserved to have her brain diced and sold as dogfood?' There was more appreciative laughter.

Tom's eyeballs prickled. He felt dizzy, unsteady on his feet. Gillian Bate, and it was fishfood, not dog-food. 'I…could you all excuse me a moment?' he said. He climbed the stairs to the top floor and lay down on the double bed in the master bedroom. When Selena appeared in the doorway, he groaned and rolled himself up in the yellow duvet. 'See what a great dynamic there is between us?' she whispered energetically. 'Do you see how they all totally accept me for what I am?'

'Well, I'm not sure I do,' said Tom through the quilt. 'I can't stand this. Get rid of them.'

There was no response. When Tom finally peeked out from under his shield of bedding, Selena was smiling bravely. 'Look, I know this is weird, but can't you give it a chance?'

'No! Has it occurred to you that you could lose your job? What if Brian Ford drives past and sees you using the show home to host your freakish cheese and wine party?'

'If that happened, I'd just explain.'

'And he'd listen and then he'd sack you!'

'No, he wouldn't. Noone else could sell these houses as quickly as I can, and he knows it.'

'You're deluded, if that's what you think.'

'For God's sake! If I get sacked, I'll find another job. I'll pick up litter at the station with one of those long metal sticks with pincers on the end. I'll become a life coach. I'll start my own telephone sex business, telling lonely men what underwear I've got on. I'm a very resourceful person. We're not going to starve. Is that really what you're worried about? I'll have to get a new job anyway, once I've sold all the houses.'

'You'll need a reference.'

'What, for phone sex?'

'Don't be ridiculous!'

'I'm not. You should applaud me for having ideas noone else would have, not condemn me.'

'You're not being fair. You'd never let me take a mad risk with my job.' Tom shivered, wondering if he had already done so. Johnny Eyebrows. It would be almost impossible to explain with a straight face, he saw that now. What had he been thinking of?

Selena's eyes widened. She stared at Tom as if he were crazy. 'Of course I would, in a good cause. You hate your job. I've always thought you should take more risks.'

Tom sat up. 'You have?'

'Yes,' she said, as if it should have been obvious. 'Now, stop being so unsociable and come and join in.' She swung out of the room.

Tom listened for her footsteps on the stairs. He heard nothing. The house was a new-build; Selena had told him it didn't even have floorboards. It had something more modern than floorboards under its carpets; Tom couldn't remember what, precisely. In his own house, he could always work out where Selena, Joe and Lucy were from the creaks and groans and echoes. Things were changing at a pace that was a little too fast for him. Since when, he wanted to know, had Selena viewed the risking of their respective livelihoods as such a lark, to be dismissed so lightly?

He wondered how much he could earn picking up litter at the station. Or perhaps he could be a gamekeeper, or fight forest fires, or work for the Red Cross. He wondered why he had never, until this moment, explored the possibility of leaving Phelps Corcoran Cummings. Was it because the company was so successful? When Tom told people he worked there, they were invariably impressed.

He heard Selena's voice in the lounge. 'He'll be fine in a minute,' she said. He groaned. For a few seconds, caught up in his fantasy of freedom, he'd completely forgotten the three inconveniences downstairs. 'Now, joking and my bitchy streak aside, I think Audrey's right,' said Selena. 'We don't want to start laying into our blood relatives. They're irrelevant to this. So why don't we approach it from a more positive angle, and focus on us, the prospective new family? What are we each hoping to get out of it?'

Tom, who was hoping for just that – to get out of it, right out, out and away – heard a low, approving rumble from the others. They all liked Selena's idea. 'Great,' she said. 'That's a good way to start. We go round, one by one, and we all say what we want.'

28 June 2005

Dear Tom

There is no company rule that says employees may never work from home under any circumstances. I was troubled by the defensive tone of your last memo. I hope you do not feel that I was attacking you. I merely wanted to make the point that it is helpful to me to know where members of staff are at any given time. After consultation with several colleagues, I am concerned that you do not feel fully and happily integrated into the department. If you are at all discontented, please do come and see me and we'll talk about how we can make things better for you – please don't suffer in silence! Perhaps I am being overly sensitive, but I have noticed that you tend to rush away at five-thirty every afternoon and miss the more relaxed, sociable atmosphere that thrives between, say, six and eight, when the serious work of the day is winding down and people have a chance to relax and chat. Perhaps if you were to stay later occasionally, you would feel more involved.

Very best wishes, Nora

P.S. Gillian tells me that four months ago you borrowed one of the firm's laptop computers. Could you possibly bring this back asap? Thanks! Idris Sutherland is taking six months' leave and has asked to have a computer during that time – I said he could have yours, since you can always use your office computer, can't you?

(cc: Gillian Bate, Imrana Kabir, Alastair Hardisty)

29 June 2005

Dear Nora

    Who is Alastair Hardisty? Is he one of the 'several colleagues' you consulted about my possible unhappiness? Unlikely, as I don't know the man. Is he, then, a street vendor from whom you buy skunkweed? I doubt that too – you strike me as more the gin and tonic type. Therefore I can only conclude that Mr Hardisty is head of Phelps Corcoran Cummings' throwing-people-out-on-to-the-pavement-with-all-their-possessions-in-a-cardboard-box department. Anyway, to answer your various questions: I leave the office at five-thirty because that is the end of my working day. If you look at my contract, you will see that this is the case. Thank you for your suggestion that staying until eight every night might make me happier. I have mulled it over and decided that, in fact, it would not. Yes, I did borrow one of the company's laptops four months ago, but, no, I will not return it asap. This is because I sometimes (see the exchange of correspondence that took place between us a fortnight ago) work from home and need the computer in order to do so.

    My understanding is that Idris Sutherland is taking six months' leave in order to spend time with his son, Oliver. My understanding of the word 'leave' is that it means not doing any work. I can't immediately see why Idris requires a company computer at home, but if he does, can I suggest that a fraction of the firm's

1.3-billion-a-year profits be spent on purchasing one
for him? I have just had a look on ebay, and there
are many excellent models available – some good as
new – for less than five hundred pounds. (Careful,
though – ebay can become addictive!)

Finally, I am sorry if you misinterpreted my last
letter. Yes, you were being overly sensitive (but what
a commendable vice!). I had no intention of being
defensive, and I am not at all unhappy. Perhaps,
as someone who is relatively new to business (isn't
your background in catering?), you are not familiar
with the sort of jokey banter that I and most of my
colleagues take for granted.

Warmest best wishes, Tom

(cc: Gillian Bate, Gilbert Sparling, Johnny Eyebrows,
Imrana Kabir, Audrey Satterthwaite, Clive Winn,
Petra Sargent, Richard Madeley, Judy Finnegan)

TOM WAS RELIEVED to be out of the house. The strain of
pretending that he was still cross with Selena was exhaust-
ing. He drove to the supermarket whistling, smiling to himself, turning up the car stereo's volume louder and louder,
singing along to David Gray's *White Ladder* CD. He felt
better than he had for a long time. Since Selena's cheese and
wine party for the new family, he had entirely lost control
of his own life. Events had leaped out of his grasp and raced
away from him, taking their own (or, to be more accurate,
Selena's) course without paying Tom any attention.

At first he'd been terrified, then irate, and then a
strange sort of calm had descended on him. It wasn't

up to him any more. He had tried to resist and nobody had taken any notice. Everyone – Selena, his children, Audrey, Clive and Petra – had told him firmly that he would get used to the new situation and, though he still vigorously denied it every time Selena interrogated him, it seemed they were right.

Since that night at the show home, the following things had happened: Audrey had persuaded Joseph that chocolate mousse was not the only nice food in the world. In the past two weeks, Joseph had eaten broccoli, spinach, courgettes, fish, porridge, carrots, borlotti beans and raspberries. Petra had potty-trained Lucy, who was now out of nappies apart from at night, and Audrey had taught her how to spell her name, using the magnetic letters on the fridge door. Clive had taught Joseph how to swim, and entertained Tom and Selena with fascinating anecdotes about his work as a forensic pathologist. Audrey, Clive and Petra had undertaken, enthusiastically and without reservations, to look after the children while Tom and Selena went to Venice next May. They would do this not in either of their own houses, nor in the Foyers' house, but in the Beddford development's show home, which Selena would take care not to sell until then. Joe and Lucy had grown very attached to the show home in the past two weeks. It was the place where they had fun with their new grandmother, auntie and uncle; they saw it as a giant playroom on three levels. To stay there for three whole nights next May would be the best possible treat.

Selena had no desire to sell the show home, in any case. Audrey and Petra were both now effectively living in it, a state of affairs that Selena had so far successfully concealed from Andrew Beddington and Brian Ford. Audrey had taken the larger single bedroom with the skylight and the two high, small windows, and Petra's was the smaller single room with the big window and fitted cupboards. Both had insisted that the master bedroom should be reserved for Selena and Tom, in the event of their ever wishing to use it. By unspoken agreement, Selena was the head of the new family just as she had been – though, again, it had never been explicitly stated – head of the old one, the minimal, unambitious, four-members-only one.

Tom had, involuntarily, spent almost all his free time with his new relatives, and had finally admitted to himself (though not to Selena) that he liked them all. He did not love them in the way that he loved his parents and brothers, but he certainly found them less irritating and oppressive. Audrey made excellent cakes almost every day. Clive was a fascinating character. It transpired that he had an untroubled and perfectly satisfactory family situation – he, his parents and his sister all got along fine – but when he saw Selena's advertisement, he'd been unable to resist the temptation to ring up. 'Why shouldn't I have two families?' he said. 'I thought it'd be fun.'

Petra was kind and loyal and did thoughtful things. She praised them all, constantly. She took Tom's car for a service while he was at work one day. 'Didn't you hear the noise the fanbelt was making?' she said. Tom had heard, but hadn't had time to do anything about it. She also did charcoal sketches of Joe and Lucy, which she framed and gave to Tom and Selena as a present. Regularly, she attempted to persuade Selena that they should all change their surnames to Kilkenny, and even that Tom was beginning to find endearing.

The new family spent most evenings in the show home, eating and drinking and talking. They talked about things Tom and Selena couldn't have talked to their real relatives about without risking a row: politics, religion, sex, euthanasia, abortion, capital punishment, the ban on hunting, whether smokers and fat people ought to be treated by the NHS or just left to die slowly by the side of the road. They insulted people they saw on television. They made stupid jokes and giggled. They smoked joints, once the children had gone to bed ('This is heavenly,' said Audrey, after her first few puffs of Johnny Eyebrows' extra-strong skunk), and played phone tricks on unsuspecting strangers whose names they found in the directory. Last Thursday, while Clive's real sister babysat for Joe and Lucy, they all went to the local pub and took part in its quiz. Their team name was The Do Badlies – Clive had thought of it. They did badly in the quiz, but won the snowball question at the end, which was worth two hundred and fifty pounds. To celebrate, they went out for a curry at midnight.

Everything that had happened to Tom in the past fortnight was the sort of thing that couldn't, wouldn't and, some might say – Tom himself regularly did – shouldn't happen. And it couldn't last; things were bound to start to go wrong soon. At some point Andrew Beddington or Brian Ford would turn up at the show home when Selena wasn't there to ward them off, or the Beddford Homes office would receive a worryingly high electricity or gas bill. And there were two real families who could only be kept at bay for so long. Very shortly Tom's mother would demand to know why he had stopped bringing the children to see her, and he would have to tell her that he now had new relatives who took up all his spare time, all Joseph and Lucy's spare time. What would happen then? Would the Foyerses and the Henshaws insist that Tom and Selena make a complete break from the impostor relatives, to prove their loyalty?

On all these points, Tom was clueless, but since nobody in their wildest dreams even entertained the idea that he might be in charge of dealing with any of it, he felt fairly relaxed. It was as if reality had been put on hold and he was living in a fear-free, consequence-free bubble in which anything was possible. Had this not been the case, he would never have dared to send his most recent memo to Nora. It was, he knew, his most extreme communication yet, but he had his defence prepared, should he need it, and he was in no doubt that he would. He would simply say that he had not sent the letter – some practical joker within the company must have taken the original, inoffensive version out of the internal mail tray, substituted this hateful parody and forged Tom's signature. What could Nora or Gillian say? They would not be able to prove that he was lying.

Last night in bed, Tom had nudged Selena and said, 'Why do you think I've stayed at Phelps Corcoran Cummings so long?'

'Because you have a very weak will-to-power,' she'd mumbled sleepily. 'You're a force divided against itself.'

'Oh, right.' Tom was glad to have a firm answer, glad someone was keeping track of things.

'Look at the way you park the car. Miles away from where you want to go, in the nearest big official car park, just because you know there'll definitely be a space and you won't get into any trouble. Whereas I drive to right outside the door of where I want to go and, if necessary, park on a double yellow line. And I don't care about getting the odd fine. It's worth it, for the convenience. I've got a strong will-to-power.'

'You have no respect for the law.'

'Of course I don't. Did anyone consult me about it? I don't see why I should obey a rule I didn't help to make.'

Now, in the supermarket's large car park, Tom remembered Selena's words and drove right up to the shop's automatic double doors. He parked in a disabled space immediately in front of the entrance. If anyone queried his right to be there, he would simply explain that he had a very weak will-to-power. In Selena's opinion, this was a crippling disability, or so she had made it sound last night.

Tom grabbed a trolley and went inside. It took him only half an hour to do the shopping for his new family. In the old days, when there had been just himself, Selena and the children to consider, he'd spent an hour or more, fretting, staring at lists until he was boss-eyed, unable to choose between regular Nescafé and Nescafé Gold Blend, Weetabix and Shredded Wheat. Now he raced up and down the aisles, throwing whatever he fancied into his trolley: Belgian chocolates, Tia Maria, whole dressed crabs, ready-to-roast pheasants. As a result of his new, liberated approach, Tom paid a lot more. This he could scarcely afford to do, not when he risked his job daily with increasingly sarcastic letters to Nora, and not when he and Selena were alarmingly overdrawn.

For the new family had its drawbacks. Neither Audrey nor Petra had an income, and both had lots of irresistible ideas about nice things the Kilkennys ought to do, all of which came at a price. Audrey wanted to make cakes using the best ingredients. Petra insisted that Tom's car had to be serviced at the dealership, because Tom was 'worth it'. Next weekend they were going to Alton Towers and the weekend after to Chester Zoo. Which would mean meals in restaurants, cups of tea in tearooms, souvenirs, train fares. All the days out and treats had to be paid for, and, even though Clive chipped in as much as he could, Selena and Tom still bore the brunt of the expense.

There were also other inconveniences. Audrey couldn't drive and had no car, so Tom had to take her everywhere she wanted or needed to go: to the dentist, to the theatre and cinema, to the post office. Once, after a particularly gruelling day at work, he had arrived at the show home and slumped in a yellow chair with a beer, only to be told by Selena that he had to take Audrey to visit the grave of a famous sculptor who was buried in the next town, ten miles away. He'd had to take her immediately. Selena hissed that it couldn't wait; Audrey had been stuck in the show home all day and needed an outing.

Clive sometimes told excessively gruesome stories about corpses he'd met that day in front of the children, and gave them nightmares. 'When we know him a bit better, we'll ask him to stop,' said Selena.

Petra was at college and often needed help with her coursework. Selena had volunteered to oversee her media studies projects, and Clive was helping her with her IT assignments, but the task of supervising and editing all the history essays had been allocated to Tom. 'But I don't *know* anything about the causes of the French Revolution!' he'd pleaded with Selena.

'Well, find out,' she'd suggested. 'Or take an inspired guess. I mean, they're bound to be pretty much the same as the causes of all revolutions, aren't they? "Let them eat cake", "Can you hear the people sing, singing the song of angry men", that sort of thing.'

'But why can't Petra..?'

'Venice, Tom.' That was all Selena ever had to say. 'Venice, Tom' was synonymous with 'Shut up'.

Tom found, to his utter bewilderment, that he didn't begrudge the extra money and the extra effort nearly as much as he thought he ought to, not only because of Venice but because he genuinely liked having Audrey, Clive and Petra around. He felt bolstered, consolidated. He hurried back from the office to the show home every night, and was greeted with cheers of 'Hey! Tom's back!' And, every time, he felt a proud glow. He doubted very much that Idris Sutherland had complete strangers queuing up to form life-long bonds with him; for the first time in his life, Tom felt like the lucky one. He had an accessory that noone else had: the Kilkennys, a solid band of voluntary relatives.

He loaded the shopping into the back of the car and drove to the memorial hall to collect Audrey from an afternoon event that had something to do with the celebrity chef Amy Dennison. Audrey was waiting for him on the steps when he arrived, wearing a sleeveless denim dress, red sandals and a red shawl. She was holding a Tupperware container.

'Amy's special heart-of-ice biscuits,' she said, as she climbed into the car. 'Joe and Lucy will love them. Only after my lentil and okra casserole, of course – they've got to eat that first.'

'Oh, they will,' said Tom. The children ate whatever Audrey put in front of them. 'So, how was your... thing?'

'Very interesting indeed. I think Amy Dennison must be a lesbian. There was a very pretty young woman in the audience, and Amy kept looking at her.'

'Probably is, then,' said Tom. Because he was in a good mood, he added, 'I was really disappointed when I met a lesbian for the first time. I was quite old, really – in my early twenties. You'd think I might have met one before. But I hadn't. The only lesbians I'd ever seen were in... well, porn films.' He looked at Audrey out of the corner of his eye. She was grinning. 'And, you know – well, you probably don't – but in porn films, lesbians are all slim and blonde and gorgeous and submissive, and only bother sleeping with other women in order to please men.

I kind of liked that idea. And then I met Virginia – this real lesbian I mentioned – and she was all butch and self-righteous, and never once offered to bonk a nubile friend in front of me...'

Audrey began to laugh. She laughed so hard that the biscuits banged against the sides of the Tupperware box on her lap. Tom laughed too, until a frightening thought stopped him: he had said what he honestly thought about something. Surely that wasn't good. When it all fell apart, this new family charade, when Selena was fired and he was fired and they were all turfed out of the show home, he was bound to regret having let a virtual stranger see any part of his true self, even just a tiny fraction, the min-ute segment of Tom Foyers that was dedicated to reacting to lesbians.

'I'm gay, you know,' said Audrey, once she'd stopped laughing.

'Really?' Tom's new sense of freedom expanded even further. He was beginning to feel fluffy-headed, the human equivalent of a meringue. He and his wife were pioneers in the field of experimental living. They had created a new family, and it wasn't the usual con-ventional model – oh no, there was no danger of that. It included an elderly lesbian. When Nora and Gillian at work found out about this (Tom would make sure they did by telling Ruth the secretary), they would see his letters as evidence not of insolence but of a sort of bohemian sophistication. He couldn't wait to return to the office.

4 July 2005

Dear Tom

My background is not 'in catering', as I am sure you must know. I worked in the pharmaceuticals industry for many years as a distribution manager, and have enough experience in the world of commerce to know when an employee is overstepping the mark. I believe that you are doing so, and have been doing so for some time, and I find the situation unacceptable. Please telephone my secretary at your earliest convenience to arrange a meeting with me. I think we need to have a serious talk about your attitude to our team objectives here at Phelps Corcoran Cummings.

Best wishes, Nora

(cc: Gillian Bate, Imrana Kabir, Alastair Hardisty)

5 July 2005

Dear Nora

I tried to ring your secretary to arrange a meeting, as instructed, but she did not answer her telephone. In order to expedite matters, wouldn't it make more sense for us to make an arrangement ourselves? How about next Sunday, 1.30-ish, in Pizza Hut on Albion Street in town? They've still got that great deal on: as much pizza as you can eat for a fiver. I'm sure you'll beat me hands down, but I'll give it my best shot!

Warm and fond wishes, Tom

(cc: Charles Manson, Kofi Annan, Dame Judi Dench, Tinky Winky, Dipsy, Laa-Laa, Po, Donald Rumsfeld, Donald Trump, the Kilkenny family, that BBC1 newsreader with grey hair and a really boring face – can't remember his name, Monica Lewinsky, the Gypsy Kings)

6 July 2005

Dear Tom

Please come to my office at nine thirty on Friday morning. Gillian Bate, Imrana Kabir and Alastair Hardisty will also be present.

Yours sincerely, Nora

(cc: Gillian Bate, Imrana Kabir, Alastair Hardisty)

7 July 2005

Dear Nora

Okay. All my love, Tom

(cc: Marco Pierre White, Condoleezza Rice, Hercule Poirot, Jerry Seinfeld, kd lang, Zola Budd, Trinny Woodall, Susannah Constantine, Ike Turner, David Icke, David Irving, David Dimbleby, Jonathan Dimbleby, Jonathan Livingston Seagull, Oliver Letwin, Morph from that 1970s kids' programme Take Hart, that other plasticine creature from Take Hart that looked exactly like Morph apart from being white, Robert Kilroy-Silk)

TOM STOOD ON the balcony of the show home. Clive and Petra had moved the coffee table to prop open the door and were now sitting side by side on the yellow leather sofa. Selena sat in the big yellow chair. Audrey, Lucy and Joe sat cross-legged on the floor. Even with the door open, it was stifling. There was no breeze, no air, just heavy heat. Other people's noise was all that blew in from outside.

'Do I have to?' said Tom.

'Yes,' said Selena.

The balcony was his stage. All eyes were on him. Everyone expected a performance. Audrey had made some lumpy pancakes, using one of Amy Dennison's recipes. Lesbian pancakes, Audrey had called them, winking at Tom. And Petra had poured everybody a glass of Pimms and lemonade, cranberry juice and lemonade for the children.

'All right, then.' Tom took a deep breath and shuffled the papers in his hand. Then he began to read, starting with Nora's first letter to him. He read it all aloud, the whole correspondence. He read with no expression on his face and no feeling in his voice. He did this because he was embarrassed, not because he wanted to achieve any particular effect or manipulate his audience into having a certain reaction. But after a while he became aware that to read his and Nora's injurious memos to one another in this deadpan way made the whole business seem utterly hilarious, almost clownish in its absurdity. Until this moment, until he heard Audrey, Clive and Petra hooting with laughter, he had taken it for granted that the little situation he had brewing at the office was deadly serious:

a minefield, a catastrophe waiting to happen, a horror on a par with global dimming and the execution of Derek Bentley for saying something ambiguous to a police-man. Tom had felt rather like Dreyfus (about whom he had read in one of Petra's history essays), exiled to Devil's Island for a crime he hadn't committed. The man who had committed the crime was named Esterhazy. In Tom's mind, he had been Dreyfus and Nora had been Esterhazy.

I need to lighten up a bit, thought Tom. I need to lighten up quite a lot.

Selena wasn't laughing. When Tom had finished his recital, she snapped, 'I wish you'd told me about this earlier.'

'Why?'

'All that stuff you wrote – I mean, it's all very enter-taining, but presumably you didn't really send copies to Condoleezza Rice and the Gipsy Kings.'

'Of course I didn't!'

'So it's just a joke. That's her come-uppance, a joke. It hardly hits her where it hurts, does it? And what a waste, when it's such a brilliant idea!'

Tom, Audrey, Clive, Petra, Joseph and Lucy all looked confused.

'She's obviously a total wimp, desperate to have every-body's approval. What better way to get her back than to do properly what you've only pretended to do!'

'What, send all these to Ike Turner and Morph from *Take Hart*?' Tom waved the bundle of papers in the air.

'No. Don't be facetious!' Selena snapped. Tom didn't like the sound of that. Over the past few weeks, he had come to believe that he had a unique talent for being facetious, a talent he'd planned and hoped to nurture, whether he stayed at Phelps Corcoran Cummings or not. He no longer wished he were a straightforward person. Facetiousness was infinitely preferable to straightforwardness.

'What does she care what Morph and Ike Turner think of her?' Selena addressed the room. 'She doesn't know them. Think about it. Would *you* care if Ike Turner disapproved of you?'

'No,' said Tom. Audrey, Clive and Petra also said that they would not.

'But are we saying that because we don't know him, or because he beat up Tina?' asked Petra.

'Look, my point is: Nora would care an awful lot more if Tom wrote a letter that made clear what a complete fucker she is and sent copies to all her friends, her colleagues, her family – the people she knows and cares about. Imagine how embarrassing it'd be for her to have to explain to all of them. And they might pretend to take her side because they're her people, but privately they'd all wonder, wouldn't they? How awful a boss must she be, they'd think, for one of her team to write this about her and send copies to all of them? They'd always wonder. She'd be tarnished for ever.'

Tom liked the idea of Nora Connaughton being tarnished for ever. He liked it very much indeed.

'You've got to steal her address book,' said Selena.

'When, exactly? I'm going to be sacked tomorrow morning,' Tom pointed out.

'Then we'll hire a private detective.'

'Wow!' yelled Joseph.

'That would be quite an adventure,' said Audrey.

'It'll be no problem for a detective to get us a list of everyone who's important to Nora...'

'But what would Tom write, to be sent to all of them?' asked Clive.

'We'll worry about the details later,' said Selena.

'Can we all write it? Can we write it together?' Petra shrieked.

Tom shook his head in mild exasperation. He turned his back on the glee that had broken out in the lounge and stared out over the river towards the hills in the distance. For the first time, he noticed a wind farm. It looked like a group of people, far away, waving. He had only stood on this balcony once before, and on that occasion he'd looked mainly at his feet on the bumpy metal, wondering how secure any such contraption could be; what was to stop a balcony from snapping off the side of the house and plummeting to the hard earth beneath?

Something: that was the answer. There was something in place to prevent that from happening. He didn't know what, but then he wasn't a builder or an architect.

Let other people worry about it.

AT EXACTLY NINE thirty the next morning, Tom walked into Nora's office. Nora sat behind her desk, her hands folded in front of her. She wore the expression of a mortuary assistant, about to open a metal drawer and show somebody their deceased beloved. 'Come in, please, Tom,' she said. But he was already in.

On either side of Nora were Gillian Bate and Imrana Kabir. Tom nearly laughed when he saw their faces, which were even grimmer than Nora's; they looked like two reluctant spectators at a cult slaying. Frankly, it wasn't convincing. Tom was certain that, secretly, they felt as merry and rejuvenated as he did. He noticed that Alastair Hardisty was not present. Why not? Tom had been promised Alastair Hardisty. Where was he? Had Nora made him up? Perhaps he was a tiny plasticine man from an ancient television programme, one Tom had never seen.

Tom sat down on the chair that had been put out for him, opposite Nora's desk. 'Right,' he said, rubbing his hands together to convey enthusiasm. 'What's all this about?'

The Fantastic Book of Everybody's Secrets

1) SOMETIMES I dream about killing myself, just to make people like me more.

2) One afternoon I went to the loo at work. I'm a Business Studies teacher at a grammar school (well, it's not really a grammar school, it's actually a comp but it used to be a proper grammar and it's still called that). Anyway, I knew I was going to be in there for a while, if you get my drift, so I remembered what I learned about what they call 'critical path analysis' when I did my teacher training (basically this means being as efficient as possible by combining more than one task wherever you can – the example most often used is putting the coffee and milk and sugar in the cup while you're waiting for the kettle to boil). So I thought, I'm going to be on the bog for a while, so I'll take some work with me to mark. I took Helen Pritchard's essay,

*and managed to read the whole thing and mark it
before I'd finished crapping. It was pretty good, and
I gave it 68 percent. Anyway, then when I reached
for the loo roll, there was none. I hadn't noticed! I
didn't have any tissues or anything in my pocket,
and the bin (which could well have contained some
old bits of toilet paper) was right on the other side
of the room. So was the sink. It's a disabled toilet, so
it's not small. I couldn't hop across the floor without risking getting my trousers and boxers dirty, so
I had no choice but to wipe my arse with Helen's
essay! I had to pretend I'd lost it and ask her for
another copy, which didn't go down very well, but
I did bump her mark up by a couple of per cent, to
make up for the inconvenience! I never told anyone,
because I was worried I might get sacked!*

I AM THE editor of *The Book of Secrets*. Or I would be, if
I had any decent contributions. These two disheartening
offerings are all I've received so far. The first is intriguing,
but too short. It lacks narrative drive and does not contain enough psychological detail to bring it to life. The
second has detail, but it's crass and essentially boring. It
is early days, however, so I will try not to be too disappointed. And my box isn't the only one. Perhaps when I
speak to Debbie and Lisa, they will tell me that they have
had more promising deposits. You're bound to get a better class of secret in cultured places such as Cambridge
and York than in Loughborough. People will write better
and be generally more insightful.

I don't yet have a publisher, let alone an advance, so at the moment I'm working on the book for free. I'm not too worried about this. It's such an interesting project that I can't see how anyone could resist it. Who wouldn't want to buy it? Eventually there will be plenty of money. Enough for me to give up my job, hopefully. The great thing is, if it works, it will continue to work. There will always be new people, new secrets. *The Book of Secrets* can be followed by *The Book of Secrets 2*. I am hoping that the series will become a talking point, a cultural phenomenon, and the contributions will come flooding in.

Noone is watching me at the moment, so I have stopped working. I am obsessed with getting on with the book and I don't care if I'm caught and sacked. This isn't a job anyone in her right mind would fear losing. I used to have one of those. I was the assistant director of a literature festival. Not in Loughborough; I used to live somewhere superior, the sort of place where, I imagine, the secrets dropped into any box such as mine would be exceptionally entertaining as well as wittily presented.

I'm not sure I'm even going to use the two secrets I've been given so far. I can't work up any enthusiasm for editing the second, and the first is so short that it would need extending, if anything. Since I don't know the situation behind that odd sentence, I am in no position to add to it. Still, there is work I can be getting on with – creative work, I mean, not the demeaning kind the hotel pays me to do. Until now I haven't felt ready to start the introduction, but today, at last, I think I do. I get out my notebook with the soft black leather covers and begin to write:

This book would not exist if I had not met Ian Prudhoe.

I stop and smile. Ian will like that. Who wouldn't? What man could resist the idea that a book existed – a successful, much-discussed book – solely because of him? I chew my pen for a few seconds. I must be careful not to mix up my introduction with my own secret, which of course I am planning to include. There can't be any overlap between these two pieces.

The story of how I met Ian is a peculiar one. It started with a phone call from my friend Debbie. She and I used to work together at the Hathersage Hotel in Loughborough.

I pause here, wondering if I ought to mention that Hathersage have since transferred Debbie, against her will, to their Cambridge hotel. I decide not to. Her move was unexpected and unwelcome, but it is irrelevant. I turn to the back page of my notebook and write a reminder to myself to include Debbie and Lisa in the acknowledgements. At first they both had doubts about collecting secrets for me, but they eventually allowed me to send each of them a box and promised to display it somewhere prominent in their hotels.

Debbie phoned me one night, clearly upset. I asked her what was wrong. 'I'm not sure I should tell you,' she said. 'I'm not sure I should tell anyone.' From the seriousness of her voice, I assumed something awful had happened, and I wanted to know what it was. As someone who had recently survived a shattering experience, I was interested in, shall we say, the genre of ordeals.

I pause again. Does it matter that I have hinted at my own secret? I decide not. Readers are bound to be fascinated by the suggestion that the book's editor is an enigmatic, troubled figure.

It didn't take long to persuade Debbie to tell me. She didn't know what to do, and hoped I would be able to advise her. 'An anonymous letter came in the post,' she said. 'A really nasty one.'

'Someone wrote you a nasty letter?' I was amazed. Debbie is one of the kindest people I have ever met, and I couldn't imagine why anyone would wish to do such a thing.

'No, it wasn't to me. It was addressed to someone called Ian Prudhoe. I know what must have happened. His address is 6 Harrow Square, and mine is 6 The Square.' She sighed. 'I just wish I hadn't opened it. I opened it automatically without even looking at the envelope. Now I don't feel I can send it on to him because he'll know I've read it and… well, I'll feel I'm the one attacking him, by passing on such a horrible letter.'

'What does it say?' I asked.

'It makes no sense. It says, "All good criketers cum over each other. Hope you die a slow and

painful death." Cricketers is spelled wrong, and
cum is spelled c-u-m.'

    'And it's not signed?'

    'It's signed "M8". Whatever that means.'

    I told her it could be text message shorthand for
'mate'. She agreed and said, with a sob in her voice,
'Oh, Tamsin, you're so much better at all this than
I am.'

Because it has no place in an introduction to a work of
literature, I decide not to describe how I felt at this point
in my conversation with Debbie. I remember my feelings
clearly, however, and could describe them if I chose to.
First, I was flattered by her compliment, even though it
was an odd one. What does it mean to say that one person is better than another at receiving and interpreting
wrongly delivered hate mail?

All the same, I knew exactly what Debbie meant, and
she was right. It should have been me, I thought. I wished
the letter were in my hands, in my house. I wished it were
up to me to decide what to do with it. I saw potential
in the situation, while Debbie saw only trouble. I was,
I freely admit, thrilled and intrigued by the mysterious
line about cricketers. What could it possibly mean? I
found it tantalising to speculate about what precise context might have provoked those words in a way that Debbie did not.

There are disadvantages to being the sort of person I
am, one who opts for excitement over boredom every time,
event over non-event. It can mean trouble. Once, when I

was eleven, on holiday, I ignored my parents and sister for three days because they insisted that the car chase I was convinced we'd witnessed was just two unconnected cars driving down the road one after the other.

Luckily, Debbie seemed keen to delegate responsibility. She had considered several possible courses of action and had rejected all of them. She didn't want to go to the police in case Ian Prudhoe found out she had done so and thought she was a stirrer. She told me she knew Harrow Square. It was a dump, an underclass ghetto (this wasn't quite how she put it, but it was the gist), and noone who lived there would be likely to welcome a visit from the law.

'What should I do?' Debbie asked me. 'I think I should just throw it away and forget about it, don't you? I mean, why cause trouble when probably the letter writer's not going to do anything else? People who write anonymous letters are cowards, aren't they?'

She was clearly trying to convince herself, but she failed to convince me. 'You've got to tell this Ian Prudhoe,' I said. 'You can't tear up the letter and pretend it never existed. What if M8 sets fire to his house or something? You'll always wish you'd warned him. If I were you, I'd go round and see him, explain that you opened the envelope by accident, and give him the letter. Then it's up to him to decide if he wants to go to the police or not.'

'I can't do that,' said Debbie. 'I just can't. I don't want him to see me or know who I am. I don't want anything to do with him.'

This puzzled me, and I asked why not. After all, Ian Prudhoe was the recipient of the abuse, not the sender.

'Someone who gets sent a letter like that could easily be – probably is – mixed up in something dodgy. I mean, he obviously knows some bad people, doesn't he?'

Seeing that my friend was in a bind, I offered to help. 'Would you like me to deal with it?' I said. 'I wouldn't at all mind sending the letter on to Ian Prudhoe. He doesn't need to know it went to your house originally. I'll just say I came upon it by accident – I won't say how, he doesn't need to know that – and that I felt I ought to pass it on, although naturally I'd have preferred to destroy it, so that he could decide if any action needed to be taken.'

'Oh, would you do that?' Debbie's voice was full of relief. 'Oh, yes, please. Thank you!'

I stop writing and frown. I am dissatisfied with my introduction so far. Is all this information strictly relevant to *The Book of Secrets*? I may well have to scrap it and start again. But perhaps not. Perhaps I'm wary of it because I know that I am writing it to win Ian over, not for the sake of a wider readership. Still, it's an interesting anecdote, I think, and it does neatly lead in to the explanation for how the book came into being. And I think it's quite well-written, so far.

I wonder, then, if my problem with it is that there is so much I have left out, even at this early stage in the story. My account of events feels dishonest, although I'm not trying to hide anything. I simply want to make the book a pacy read. No, that's not strictly true. I'm also trying to avoid embarrassment. God knows I've had enough of that already, and I don't want Ian to know how keen I was on the idea of him, even before we'd met. It might make me appear rather pathetic.

Debbie's desire to avoid Ian Prudhoe provoked a defensive fervour in me. Because he had received hate mail, she reasoned, he was probably a shifty character. I was astonished when I heard her say this. Yet more evidence, I thought, that one only has to be attacked once – even by a rabid savage, even by a person who can't spell the word 'cricketers' – and other apparently sane, normal people will be queuing up to join in. The moral cowardice of most human beings never ceases to shock me.

Debbie's reaction to the letter brought my own sharply into focus. My instincts were the opposite of hers. As soon as I'd heard M8's letter, I had begun, I realised, to empathise with poor Ian Prudhoe. I wanted to offer him my support. I saw him as the entirely innocent victim of an unhinged persecutor. It also occurred to me that it was not impossible that I might find him attractive. If Debbie hadn't been so keen to give me the letter to do with as I wished, I would have had to resort to underhand tactics in order to seize control, but luckily she wanted rid of it, and by handing it over to me she satisfied both her conscience and her rather squeamish desire to avoid trouble.

I mustn't judge her too harshly, though. She and Lisa are my only friends. They met me here, at the hotel, and liked me in spite of my new, unglamorous job. They also both worked in the housekeeping department, and I miss them now that they've been transferred to other Hathersage hotels. I have never told either of them that I used to help run a literature festival, that I was fired. Would Debbie assume I must have been mixed up in some shady or even illegal activity? That would make me laugh. Nothing could be further from the truth.

Debbie is a gluttonous reader, consuming one novel after another, but she never notices the names of the authors. She reads what we at the literature festival would have called clog-and-shawl sagas. Debbie doesn't call them anything. To her they are simply books, the only kind she is aware of.

Lisa prefers magazines, though she dips into the occasional celebrity biography, and has recently finished Victoria Beckham's. Until she did, she often told Debbie and me that the last book she had read 'all the way through' was *The Twits* by Roald Dahl. I can't tell her, because it would sound patronising, that it amuses me no end to have a close friend who would describe a book in these terms: 'the last book I read all the way through'.

In my old life, I had friends who read Ben Okri and Adam Thorpe and Don DeLillo, but they all lost interest in me after I was sacked.

I needn't have moved to Loughborough. I'm sure I could have got a job in the housekeeping department of the hotel I used to telephone almost daily to arrange accommodation for guests of the festival, but I didn't want to be perceived as clinging on in an undignified way to the life I had lost. I couldn't stand to be seen by anyone who knew what had happened to me. I felt miserable, rejected and ruined, and I wanted to move to a place where, I assumed, many people felt that way. I knew nothing about Loughborough, but it sounded uninspiring and characterless so I chose it, and I haven't been disappointed. It's a horrible town. On some level, I wonder if I am trying to pacify the fates by volunteering to live here. 'You see,' I am saying to them, 'I have no pride left. I have nothing. Look where I live. Look what I do. I cannot sink any lower, so you'd be wasting your time arranging for me to do so.'

When I tried to discuss with Debbie some possible interpretations of the cryptic part of M8's note (I wasn't interested in the second bit – everyone knows what 'Hope you die a slow and painful death' means), I was reminded once again of the differences between us. 'I don't know,' she said. 'It makes no sense.' She was content to leave it at that. Had I endorsed her plan to destroy the letter and forget about it, Debbie would have resigned herself, happily, to permanent ignorance. She would have got on with her day-to-day existence and I don't think she would ever have given a thought to M8, let alone driven herself crazy wondering who he or she was, or about the precise nature of his or her relationship to Ian Prudhoe. Debbie had no burning need to know what the line 'All good criketers cum over each other' meant; she had no inclination to speculate, in the absence of knowledge.

I knew Lisa would be equally indifferent, unless I could prove to her that either Ian Prudhoe or M8 had slept with one of the Beckhams or showed off his (or her) new conservatory in the pages of *Hello!* magazine, so I speculated alone. My best guess was that Ian Prudhoe played cricket and had had some kind of dalliance with another cricketer. M8 was bound to be the wife or girl-friend of this character, the second cricketer, or, if it was an entirely homosexual scenario rather than a bisexual one, his jealous male lover.

I was desperate to have my suspicions confirmed, to discuss with Ian Prudhoe the pros and cons of having an affair with a fellow team member, an attached one at that. I looked forward to demonstrating that I did not belong to the moral majority. I already knew that I would advise Ian to follow his heart rather than submit to the tyranny of M8's emotional blackmail. Marriage is only a piece of paper, I would say. M8 cannot expect to own the sec-ond cricketer, and it is impossible to steal someone from somebody else unless that person wishes to be stolen. Ian would, of course, be impressed by my sophisticated approach to matters of the heart.

I turn back to my introduction, intending to carry on with the story, but am immediately distracted again by the memory of another feature of the situation that appealed to me, at this early stage of my involvement in Ian Prudhoe's life. My downfall, at the literature festival, in the town where I used to live, was brought about by excessive self-absorption. I don't think anybody would deny that. The festival board, the sponsors, the audience who turned up that night to see Ian McEwan – they would all agree that I was obsessed, in those days, with my own selfish concerns. Not so now, in my new Loughborough life. By focusing so avidly on Ian Prudhoe's predicament, by really immersing myself in it, I believed I would demonstrate to whatever authority was watching (I hesitate to say God, but I suppose I had in mind someone along those lines) that I had learned my lesson and now took a whole-hearted interest in other people's problems.

It strikes me, as I sit in the dimly lit, windowless basement of the hotel, that I have failed to convey, in my book's title, my own enthusiasm for the project. Problems, secrets – whatever you want to call them – they amount to the same thing: other people's private business. My working title, *The Book of Secrets*, does not communicate the allure, the enticement, that I need readers to feel if they are going to buy the book in their millions. I, as the editor, have to make contagious my desire to know those very facts and stories people most want to hide. I decide, impulsively, to change the title to *The Fantastic Book of Everybody's Secrets*. I am aware that it is risky to make such an overblown claim, but I think I can get away with it. A few years ago, Tibor Fisher published a collection of short stories called *Don't Read This Book if You're Stupid* and noone thought badly of him. On the contrary, we invited him to the festival.

But I must get on.

I felt it was important to act quickly, for who knew what further assaults M8 had planned, so I wrote Ian Prudhoe a note saying that I had something that belonged to him, and asking him to meet me. I gave him my phone number and he called me straight away. At first he was angry that I refused to

*tell him any more over the telephone, but I felt that,
given the gravity of the matter we had to discuss,
a face-to-face meeting was necessary. He suggested
McDonald's, but I told him Da Tonino's would
be better – it's a nice little Italian, the kind I love,
with dark wooden booths, red and white checked
tablecloths, candles weeping wax down the necks
of plump-bellied wine bottles in straw holders. Ian
wasn't keen, because Da Tonino's is pretty pricey,
but I assured him I would pay. He had no choice but
to agree. I was determined that everything should
be pleasant that could be; everything, in other
words, apart from M8's horrible letter.*

*Ian turned up ten minutes late. He was not at all
physically attractive, as I had imagined he*

Oh dear. I can't say that, can I? I cross it out, scribble on it
until the words are no longer visible. It's a pity people are
so sensitive, because I was going to go on to say that I felt
drawn to Ian despite what many people would describe
as his startling ugliness. My first thought, on seeing his
face, was that it must have been reconstructed after an
accident. Perhaps M8 had already struck. I wondered if
it was acid, broken glass, fire. Ian's lips, nose and eyelids
looked too large for his face, as if they were swollen. Or
rather his face, because of its rough texture, looked like a
weathered stone likeness of a swollen face.

I inspected him more closely and decided that perhaps
the reconstructed effect was a result of bad acne scarring.
Either way – and I know this would make no sense to a lot

of readers, so I will leave it out because I want the book to be a commercial success – I was instantly drawn to Ian, far more than I would have been if he'd been conventionally handsome. His face told me that he had suffered horribly and survived. I wanted to stroke his bumpy cheeks and tell him everything would be all right.

Ian turned up ten minutes late. Very cool, I thought. No woman likes a man who tries too hard, and he hadn't. His fraying jeans were muddy from the knees down, which caused a few noses to twitch in Da Tonino's. Noone said anything, but I suspect they might have done had I not been a regular customer. Lisa, Debbie and I used to eat there every Friday night. Now that they have both deserted me, I continue the tradition alone.

Ian had an interesting face and I warmed to him instantly. He asked me, fairly brusquely, what I had that was his. I told him to relax and sit down, look at a menu. I was going to buy him lunch, after all. I refused to give him any information until we had ordered. I feared that if I launched into the unwholesomeness of M8's letter straight away, the shock might be too much for Ian. Eventually, under duress, he ordered some garlic mushrooms, claiming he only wanted a starter, and I asked him, 'Do you play cricket?'

'No,' he said, as if I was mad. 'Why? What the fuck do you want with me? Just give me whatever it is you've got.' I attributed his hostility to all the suffering he had been through. I could see that *underneath the thin veneer of aggression, he was a kind, decent person.*

At that point I handed over the note. Ian read it expressionlessly. (Stoicism is another of his virtues, as is the ability to keep a cool head in a crisis. How I envy him that!) He said nothing. I explained that the letter had been delivered to my house by mistake, and that I was sorry to have to pass on such a nefarious communication. Still he did not speak. Holding his hate mail, he stood up as if to leave.

'Hang on a second,' I said. 'You can't just go.'

'Why not?'

'Aren't you worried? Is this M8 person a risk? Might he or she try to hurt you in some way? I mean...we need to discuss what to do.'

Ian shook his head and stuffed the letter in his pocket. 'I'd better go,' he said.

'But do you know who M8 is? You must do!'

He shrugged.

'Well? Who is it? Look, sit down. Your mushrooms'll be here soon.'

'No, I'm all right,' he said, and walked out of the restaurant.

I pause to wipe away tears. It is impossible to convey how panicky I felt as he left and I realised there was nothing I could do. Never in my wildest dreams, in my vilest nightmares, had I envisaged that Ian might not want to confide in me. I felt like a total failure. I knew no more than I had before our meeting. I didn't even know Ian's sexual orientation. I told myself that he was sure to be straight, given how surly-verging-on-rude he was. I hoped so. I didn't like the thought of him in the arms of the second cricketer. And perhaps he never had been; perhaps the line about cricketers meant something quite different.

I am debating how much of my reaction to Ian's hasty departure to include in the introduction when my boss appears. June is in her late forties. She looks like a donkey. Her teeth are too long and her tights are always laddered.

'What's that?' She nods at my notebook.

'Nothing,' I say. I let it drop to the floor and quickly resume my work.

'I think we need to talk, Tamsin. Don't you?'

'No. About what?'

'About your level of commitment to Hathersage hotels, and to your work here.'

'I wouldn't have thought it was work that requires a level of commitment, is it?'

June frowns, puzzled. 'A team is only as strong as its weakest member,' she says.

'Yes, but my point is that, however weak and uncommitted I am, surely all that matters is that I do the work. And I do. By the end of the day, all the mess that has spilled into this room has been sorted into the appropriate piles and is ready to go. Well, isn't it?'

My theory is that June would not be so officious if she worked in a better hotel. Being housekeeping manager at the Hathersage, Loughborough, is hardly the most prestigious position. Rocco Forte needn't look to his laurels, put it that way. Hathersages are the same all over the country: flowery, three-star, unjustifiably content to serve watered-down soup. All too often their exteriors resemble multi-storey car parks, which doesn't matter because they cater for people who prize cheapness above all else. I try not to think about the Rembrandt, the literature festival's favoured hotel, with its beautiful Georgian façade, its sleek, modern décor.

'Well, yes, you do seem to work quickly,' June concedes. 'But your attitude isn't quite what I'd want it to be, Tamsin. And I think we both know that.'

'Sometimes I miss my lunch hour,' I remind her. I do not add that this is usually when I want to plan or make notes about *The Fantastic Book of Everybody's Secrets*. Lisa has been in York for two months now, and since Debbie left for Cambridge last week I haven't seen much point in having lunch in the canteen at work. I can manage without it physically, and I'd rather strive to fulfil my literary ambitions than eat cheesy leeks with Dennis and Jimmy the maintenance men. William Faulkner wrote *As I Lay Dying* in only eight weeks, while he was working night shifts at a petrol station.

'It's not good for you to go without lunch,' says June, with her hands on her hips. 'You'll make yourself ill. Everybody needs energy triggers.'

'Do you mean food?' I ask.

'I'm just saying that we have procedures and guidelines in place, Tamsin. Every team member must have an hour's break. Why don't you go now?'

I glare at her, but do as I'm told. I make sure to take my notebook with me.

3) MY MUM and dad turned vegetarian when they were in their fifties, and became really self-righteous about it. It drove me mad. I mean, if they'd never cared about animals before, why now, all of a sudden? The worst thing was that I hate vegetarian food, and I had to eat it, not only when I went to their house but I also had to cook it when they came to mine. In other words, every time we got together to eat, we had to have the food they chose, and never the food I chose. They called it vegetarianism, but I called it selfishness. So, I planned a little revenge. Every time I cooked them a meal, I would sneak some bit of a dead creature into it. I started off small – a pureed prawn in a vegetable chilli, that type of thing. But then a prawn started to seem too insignificant. Gradually, I became more daring. I cooked them a chilli using half beef mince, half Quorn. My moment of glory was when I pureed a whole venison steak (I'd diced it first) and put it in a lentil and pasta bake I made for them. They asked me what the strange flavour was and I said fenugreek! Now I love having them round for dinner, because I always play one of my little tricks and they never suspect.

PS I don't know if this counts as a secret or not, because I have told one or two of my friends. Some of them have said what I do is really awful, but I've never fully got over the immature teenage urge to rebel against my mum, who was very strict and would never let me out, etc.

PPS Do I get any royalties if this goes in the book?

Now we're talking. I feel like singing and dancing for joy when I read this. In the time it took me to eat my lunch, somebody has dropped this into the box and, in doing so, rejuvenated my ardour for the project. That PS says it all; clearly the sneaking of meat into her parents' food (the author has to be a woman – such finely tuned passive aggression!) is about far more than a disagreement over animal rights. And that maddening 'etc', which makes one wonder what else the strict mother would not allow her to do. I have in my hands a potentially (because it needs a bit of tweaking) heart-breaking tale of parental oppression and daughterly retribution. The aspect of the story that I love most is that the revenge is located inside the parents' digestive systems. They tried to control her, as a teenager living in their house. She goes one better and tries to control them inside their own bodies, by tricking them into eating food they are violently opposed to. It's fantastic.

I am also indebted to my third anonymous contributor for reminding me that I need to grapple with the tricky task of defining what exactly a secret is. Must it be something you have told nobody, or can you have told everyone you know apart from one crucial person? Perhaps this issue could be dealt with in the book's foreword, if the story of me and Ian Prudhoe is the introduction. I could ask an intellectual to write the foreword. He or she could praise both me and the book before getting down to providing a sound definition of the terminology. I turn to the back page of my notebook and write 'Alain de Botton? A C Grayling? Tom Paulin?'

I am in a jolly mood after reading the carnivorous submission, and the prospect of returning to my introduction fills me with gloom. I will tackle it again tomorrow morning. This afternoon, I'll set myself a task that is lighter, more fun. I will write my acknowledgements. The acknowledgements page is a genre I know well. I always read them, and feel cheated if a book does not contain one. One learns so much about how the author wishes to be seen. The crucial things an acknowledgements page should communicate are: a) that the author is sensitive and warm, and has lots of fulfilling personal relationships, b) that the author is on intimate, private-joke terms with some household names, and c) that the author is modest and fully aware that, without the half-hearted, patronising, Sloaney platitudes of a selection of blonde ex-boarding-school girls in London, she could never hope to be anything more than a dinner lady.

Buoyed up by the 'energy triggers' June forced me to consume, I begin to write:

ACKNOWLEDGEMENTS

I would like to thank my bestest, bestest pals Debbie and Lisa, for believing both in this book and in me right from the start, before anybody else did. Words cannot express my gratitude to my two Ians: Ian Prudhoe, for your inspiration, for being you, and for the wonderful challenge, and of course to Ian 'let's-not-mention-the-dressing-room-incident' McEwan. I'm also hugely grateful to Philip 'Dwekkie' Dwek – he knows why.

Philip Dwek is my landlord. I am not grateful to him for anything, but I have just remembered that an acknowledgements page also needs a pointless mysterious allusion. The aim, undoubtedly, is to make the reader feel isolated and inferior. I know it is immature of me to indulge myself, but for once I am on the inside, and I don't see why I shouldn't make the most of it.

> *Last but not least, my wonderful agents and publishers*

(I leave a gap here, into which I will later insert the names of some blonde, patronising Sloanes who will ring me up infrequently and who, when they do deign to ring, will say simply 'Tamsin!', as if I should know who they are instantly, from their posh voices. A famous author who once came to the festival told me her agent did this and it drove her mad.)

> *without whose tireless, dedicated and painstaking work on my behalf, I would still be working in the housekeeping department of a hotel in Loughborough. And thanks to June Skelly, my ex-boss at the hotel, for advice about team spirit and energy triggers that sustained me while I was working on the book!*

I decide at the last minute to mention June, because a lot of authors, I have noticed, also use an acknowledgements page as an opportunity to demonstrate that they have not been spoiled by success and are still on thanking terms with a few genuine proletarians.

Just after I have written this line about June, she leans into the room, flashing her donkey teeth. 'Tamsin, I don't want to have to tell you again,' she says. 'Put that bloomin' notebook down and get on with your work.'

I sigh heavily. 'There was an item on *You and Yours* about bullying at work the other day,' I tell her. 'Do you know what counts as bullying? Constant criticism, undermining an employee's confidence...'

'I'd like to see you in my office first thing tomorrow morning,' she says.

'Why not now? It's because you haven't yet decided what you want to say to me, isn't it? You're trying to make yourself feel important by picking on me.' But I am talking to June's back as she marches out of the room. She's lucky I don't instantly delete my faked gratitude to her from my acknowledgements page.

My cheerful mood is ruined, so I decide I might as well turn my attention back to my introduction – the difficult and, at times, agonising story of my relationship with Ian Prudhoe.

After Ian walked out of Da Tonino's, leaving me alone with all my unanswered questions, I went home and tried to forget about him, M8, the second cricketer, and the whole nasty business. I found that I couldn't. Whether he realised it or not, Ian needed my help. Our uncaring society encourages us to feel that we can manage on our own, when the truth is that for most of us this is simply not the case. Ian was embarrassed to fill me in on what had been going on in his life because it is not the done thing to talk about such personal matters with a stranger. I reflected upon the sadness of this social convention, for how can a stranger ever become a friend unless secrets are shared?

The following evening, I called round at Ian's house, a small terrace with rotten, splintering window frames. (Ian is refreshingly unmaterialistic.) I also noticed what could only be slug trails in the hall, behind him. 'What the fuck do you want?' he said when he saw me. I suspect that, like many men, he is afraid of intimacy.

'Come for a drink with me. Please,' I said. 'I've got something really important to tell you.'

'Another letter?' he growled.

I didn't contradict him, and eventually we went to Mad Ma Jones, the pub at the bottom of Harrow Square, where he lives. I'd never been inside it before and hoped not to have to again. It's the sort of pub inside which life seems thinner, quieter, darker than it does outside. Even the pool table wasn't a properly vibrant shade of green. I bought a glass of dry white wine for myself and a pint of bitter and a whisky for Ian – he asked for both.

'Well? Has she sent another letter?' he demanded, as we stood at the sopping wet bar.

She. So M8 was a woman. 'Who is she?' I asked.

'Mind your own fucking business! Just tell me: is there another letter?'

'Ian, let me tell you something about me, something I haven't told anyone before,' I said. I realised that my mistake up to this point had been to expect Ian to confide in me without indicating that I was willing to give anything in return. 'I used to be the *assistant director of a famous literature festival,' I told him. 'I lost my job, in extremely humiliating circumstances, and I now work in the housekeeping department of the Hathersage Hotel.'*

'That's got a twenty-five-metre pool, hasn't it?' Ian asked.

'Yes. It's a bit grubby around the edges, though. It's only a three-star hotel.'

'Do you get to swim in it for free?'

'I could if I wanted to, but I can't swim.'

'Still. That's pretty good.'

I was stunned. Ian was impressed by the job that had always been a source of shame to me. It still was, but I felt slightly happier about it after he said that, because I realised that, however awful it was, it did at least have a perk. I was allowed to use the grimy pool. My inability to swim was neither here nor there; the only salient point was that the perk existed. 'I work in laundry, specifically,' I told Ian. I was narrowing it down, zooming in, getting perilously close to telling him what I did.

He looked interested. 'What do you mean, "specifically"?' he said. Looking back, I suspect he didn't understand what the word 'specifically' meant, but given my own embarrassment about my job, I interpreted it as an enquiry about the exact nature of my work. I decided to trust him and hope that fate would reward me by making him trust me. 'I work in the towel room, in the basement,' I told him. 'All the used towels from the hotel and the health club get brought to me, and I have to…sort them out.'

Ian shrugged and sniffed. I had been evasive, half hoping I would get away with it, half wanting him to force the whole truth out of me. 'I'd better go,' he said again. He had dealt swiftly with his two drinks; each one disappeared in a gulp. 'Have you got another letter for me or what? If not, I'm going.'

I blurted out the truth then, desperate to maintain the tenuous closeness between Ian and myself. 'I have to sort them all into two piles,' I shouted at him. 'Those that can go straight into the wash, and those that need to be treated for stains. And the ones that need treating, I have to treat. That's my job. I used to virtually run a world-renowned literature festival and now I'm director of the blood- and shit-stained towels department of the Hathersage Hotel! So…' I shrugged at him.

I don't know quite what I was hoping he'd say. Whatever it was, he didn't say it. All he said was, 'Right, then. I'm off.'

'Wait!' I begged him. 'Who's M8? You have to tell me!'

He sneered. 'No, I don't.'

'But you do know who it is?'

'I reckon so, yeah.'

'What, you mean there's more than one candidate?'

'Hey?'

'More than one person it could be.'

'Maybe.'

'But surely for the line about cricketers to make sense, you must know who wrote it.'

'I don't know what that cricketers shit's about.' He scratched his ear with his index finger, which he then put in his mouth. He seemed to be telling the truth. After all, he could easily have admitted that he knew and still refused to tell me.

'*What*? What do you mean, you don't know? "All good crikeers cum over each other" – come on, it's pretty specific. It must mean something to you.'

He shook his head. 'Nah,' he said.

'But…well, surely you should contact whoever you think wrote the letter and *ask* them what they meant.'

'Nah, I'll probably just leave it,' said Ian. 'Get the fuck off my case, will you?'

'Wait, come back!' I yelled after him. 'I have to tell you why I got fired!'

'Fuck off!'

I am crying again as I remember all this. I wipe my eyes and am startled to realise that I somehow imagined I was still writing when in fact I have stopped. How much of what I have just recounted in my head should I put in the introduction?, I wonder. I definitely don't want readers to know what I do for a living. I know Faulkner worked nights in a petrol station, but hunting for patches of blood and shit in a pile of white towels and then scrubbing at the stains, day in, day out, is, let's face it, a bit worse.

To cheer myself up, I decide to leap ahead and start writing the part of the introduction where I describe how I came to have the idea for *The Fantastic Book of Everybody's Secrets*. I can always fill in later the many failed attempts I made to persuade Ian to talk and listen to me.

After a lot of soul-searching, I had to stop and ask myself why Ian was so determined to resist my help and friendship, why he often appeared almost repelled by me. Eventually I worked it out. My attempts to tell him my secret alarmed him. Not many people are as brave as I am about confronting and sharing the aspects of my life that show me in a less-than-favourable light. I am a sufficiently evolved creature to know that secrecy, in the end, equals loneliness, and my efforts to reach out to Ian were a very positive step for me. I wanted the same positive development for Ian, but I could see that that would never happen, because he was utterly unwilling to take me into his confidence. His reluctance to 'own', to own up to, certain facts of his life, was preventing him from expressing himself, and therefore impeding his recovery. And then I had a brilliant, compelling idea. What if there were to be a book of secrets, I thought. What if I were to edit such a book, and ask for anonymous submissions. That would enable people to unburden themselves entirely, to burst a hole in the dam built from years of restraint and repression, without having to put their names to what they had written and risk unwelcome consequences. If I were to edit a book like that, I realised, Ian and I could both purge ourselves of all the things we had bottled up for too long. And so could hundreds of other people, perhaps thousands. And so, without further ado...

How DOES ONE end an introduction: without further ado, here's the book? No, that sounds absurd. I read mainly novels for pleasure, and most don't have introductions. Never mind. Perhaps I'll wait until I have a contract before I worry about the more difficult details. Maybe for the time being I'll just copy-edit the carnivore's confession, secret number three.

What June doesn't realise, what the festival board, the sponsors and Ian McEwan never realised, is that I am a pretty shrewd character. I have my setbacks like everybody else, but I always bounce back. You see, I knew (the knowledge was hard to avoid after Ian Prudhoe had told me to fuck off for the tenth time) that I had made a bit of a fool of myself by pursuing him so fervently. I needed to save face, and to make him see that I was not someone to be dismissed lightly. The one time he had looked at me with something akin to respect had been when I told him I was allowed to use the hotel's pool without paying. Surely, I reasoned, editing a prestigious book is even more impressive than free use of a malodorous leisure facility.

See? I'm not stupid. What chance is there that someone as unrefined, morose and yobbish as Ian Prudhoe will ever make it into a published book without my help? None, I would say. And he will know that. So when I tell him about *The Fantastic Book of Everybody's Secrets*, he will realise how much he needs me. He will write the story of himself, M8 and the second cricketer (if this mythical figure even exists) and he will submit it to me.

'TAMSIN, I'M AFRAID we've had some complaints about you,' says June. It is the day she called tomorrow yesterday. I am happy to be in her office receiving a ticking-off. It is preferable to wrestling with a giant mound of soggy whiteness, looking for spots of red or brown. On June's desk are two framed photographs, each of a different pudding-like child, a girl and a boy. The word 'lumpen' springs to mind.

'Complaints from whom?' I mutter sarcastically. 'Noone ever sees me. Unless some of the towels have complained.'

'Christine says you forced her to put this on reception.' She produces my box from under her desk. I read my own handwriting on the label: 'Coming soon from a major UK publisher: THE FANTASTIC BOOK OF EVERYBODY'S SECRETS. Anonymous contributions welcome! See your own deepest, darkest secret in print!' I made the box out of an old cereal packet.

I want to snarl at June to give it to me. There might be some new offerings inside it. Actually, part of me can't believe how few people have contributed so far, given how many pass through the Hathersage, Loughborough – hundreds every day. And my box has been around the hotel for nearly a month. Is it possible that some people wouldn't want to publish their secrets, even anonymously? I suppose it must be, although, hard as I try, I cannot get inside the mind of such a person.

'Tamsin, why do you think Debbie and Lisa asked to transfer to other hotels?' says June. 'And even then you didn't get the hint. Apparently you've given them each a similar, er, contraption, and they're not at all comfortable with that. They're worried about you, Tamsin, and so am I.'

I do not want June's concern, only Ian Prudhoe's. I care nothing for anybody else. Even the news of Debbie and Lisa's betrayal doesn't hit me as hard as I would have expected it to.

'Surely, as a caring employer,' I suggest, 'you shouldn't stand in the way of employees' creative projects.'

'It's not real, though, is it? It's a silly game you're playing. You must know this book of secrets is never going to be published, even if you do manage to collect enough secrets to make a book. And…well, you must know that's never going to happen.'

'I know no such thing,' I assert calmly. 'I've put serious time and energy into this project. I certainly wouldn't have bothered if I didn't believe the end result would be worth it.'

'Why would anyone want to buy a book of secrets? Why would anyone want to put their secret in a book? What's the point?' June says impatiently, revealing her philistinism.

To tell her even a fraction of what I know and she doesn't would take too long; I can't be bothered. Would she have said the same to Nancy Friday, about *My Secret Garden*? 'Who'd want to read about strangers' sexual fantasies? Who'd want to send in details of their own sexual fantasies to be included in a book?' Plenty of people, actually, June. That's why there have been two sequels; that's why all three books have been international bestsellers.

It would be pointless to talk to June about the huge popularity of confessional and misery memoirs. Equally pointless to explain that secrets – which often are basically misery with the added bonuses of suspense and intrigue – might have an even wider appeal. What could be more fascinating than to read about the things people find it necessary to conceal? What greater insight into the minds and hearts of others could there possibly be? It would be – it *will* be – a book not only about secrets but about psychology, the human condition, morality and social norms at the start of the twenty-first century. And the relief of finally being able to express yourself, within the framework of a safe, anonymous community of fellow secret-sharers. To get it off your chest, without having to suffer the consequences in your daily life: the suspicious looks, the sarcastic comments…To take what has been festering inside you and make it part of something constructive, something *in*structive…

I realise I need to write an advance information sheet for the book to send to publishers, highlighting the project's unique selling points, where exactly in the market *The Fantastic Book* would fit. Why haven't I done this already? I also need to make a new label for my secret-collection box, one that's worded less lasciviously. It was a mistake, I realise, to dumb down in order to appeal to the Hathersage's clientele. My box will attract more deposits if I highlight the social science aspect of the project. These days everyone wants to appear clever in front of their friends, especially people who aren't.

'Anyway, you can't keep that box in the hotel,' says June. 'If you want to…well, you'll have to do it in your own time and on your own premises.'

'I need the hotel,' I explain. 'I need a constant supply of new people. If I put the box in my bedsit, noone will see it except me.' June has no faith in *The Fantastic Book* because it is my idea, and she thinks I am just a towel-scrubber. If she knew about my literary background, would she change her mind? One thing's for sure: if the idea were not mine but Elaine Showalter's, or Natasha Walter's, or Susan Sontag's, if June saw any of those women talking about it on *The South Bank Show*, she would be visibly impressed.

'Tamsin, I think you're ill. I think you need medical help.'

I find this notion interesting. 'Really?' I say. If I am ill, then a whole range of things might not be my fault. 'How long might I have been ill for?' I ask, wondering if I could find a doctor who would certify that my disease, whatever it might be, started long before the Ian McEwan incident.

'I'm afraid I'm going to have to let you go, Tamsin.'

'What? But you just said I was ill! That's discrimination! I should be off work on full sick pay until such time as I'm well enough to resume my shitty-towel-scrubbing career.'

'I've never liked your sarcasm, Tamsin.'

'I've never liked *you*, June. Your skirts are ridiculously short for a woman your age. You think you can get away with it because your legs are long and slim, but you've obviously never seen the cellulite on the backs of your thighs. I, on the other hand, see it every day, through your laddered tights. And you have a face like a donkey.'

She shrieks, then begins to cry. I try to enjoy the spectacle, but find I cannot. Perhaps I am sicker than even June imagines.

4) *MY HUSBAND doesnt know our babys not his. Shes Gary from works. Now I cant tell him or hed walk out on us both, so I have to lie for ever and its doing my head in.*

5) *I am nothing. I used to manage one of the world's leading literature festivals almost single-handedly, until I was fired. After that, I worked in the laundry department of a hotel. My job was to sort out the bloody and shitty towels from the unblemished ones, and apply stain remover before throwing them in with the rest of the washing. I was fired from this job too. As I write this, I am sitting on a bench on the top of Ludlum Hill. It is the middle of a January afternoon and my hands are numb with cold.*

My secret is the incident that led to my being fired from the literature festival. It is an odd sort of secret, because it is known by almost everybody who considers themselves part of the literary scene. However, it led to my moving to a new town to start a new life, and in that new life it has remained a secret. I did once try to tell someone – a man – but he told me he wasn't interested. So I will tell the readers of this book instead, because I have to let go of the past and this is the only way.

It was the 2001 literature festival. Ian McEwan was about to read to a full house at the Maltings, and I was hosting the event. I arrived late, a little flustered. You see, I'd had another of the phone calls that had been plaguing me for some time, and I'd found it difficult to tear myself away from the phone, even knowing Ian McEwan was waiting, in case it rang again.

Two years earlier, I had split up with my boyfriend. To be more specific, he had left me. One day I returned from work and he and all his possessions had vanished. He refused to meet me or talk to me, and used his sister to relay the message that I was not to try to contact him at any time in the future. His sister said that she knew his reasons, but that she was not allowed to tell me. It was baffling, because the day before he vanished he asked me to marry him and I said yes. Later, in bed, when he kissed me goodnight, he said, 'I can't believe I have to waste eight hours sleeping before I can see you again.' I'm sure I don't need to explain to readers why I was so dumbfounded when he chose the very next day to disappear without a trace!

I coped extremely well under the circumstances – everyone said so – and was able to run the festival perfectly adequately (with aplomb, even), despite my unhappiness. As time went on I realised that I could live without him, but not without his reasons.

I needed to know why he had deserted me, and he refused to tell me, which left me in a terrible bind.

Approximately three weeks after he went, I started to get nuisance phone calls. The phone would ring, I would answer, and there would be a brief silence, or sometimes background noise, before the caller hung up. When I dialled 1471, I found that the number had been withheld. After this happened for the twentieth, or perhaps the thirtieth, time, I began to wonder if it was my ex-boyfriend. I recalled what he'd said about having to waste time sleeping before seeing me again, and grew more and more convinced that, whatever happened afterwards, he must have loved me when he said those words. And if he loved me that much the day before he ran away, it wasn't inconceivable that some of that love survived his hasty departure. I thought it entirely possible that he was torn between his love for me and, perhaps, a fear of commitment, and that, while it was the scared part of him that ran, it was the loving part that kept ringing me and then slamming the phone down.

I became obsessed. When other men asked me out (even a famous one, a Booker Prize nominee who shall remain nameless), I felt I had to say no. If the nuisance caller was my ex, then in some ways he had not completely gone from my life and I felt I owed him some loyalty. If he was still persistently telephoning me, I concluded, then that had to mean that at least on some level he wanted us to get back together, and was simply having trouble plucking up the courage to say so.

I stopped going out, apart from to work. My social life came to consist of nothing more than sitting in my lounge, tensely waiting for the next nuisance call. Some evenings I would get nine or ten – that would make me happy. But other nights there might be only one, or, God forbid, none. I was inconsolable when he didn't phone at all, and prayed that he hadn't decided to move on and forget me. None of my friends knew about my obsession, and I didn't dare tell them. I knew exactly what they'd say – 'you've no way of knowing it's him and it may well not be' – and I couldn't have endured that. I wanted it to be him. I needed it to be.

Earlier in this account I wrote that these calls 'plagued' me. I suppose it would be more accurate to say that my uncertainty was the truly pestilential aspect of what was occurring, not the calls themselves. Was it him or wasn't it? The anonymous caller was depriving me of the means to interpret my own life story and make the choices we all need to make in order to feel wholly human. For as long as I believed it might be him, I was stuck, blocked, doomed.

So, as a result of my mental imprisonment I was late for Ian McEwan's event, which was a disaster because I was supposed to be introducing it. As I ran to the Maltings, I feared that they might have started without me, that Ian McEwan might have had to be introduced, in an emergency, by Barry the sound engineer or, worse, by himself. Luckily, I arrived to find that everything was running half an hour late because the writer who had been on before Ian had refused to stop talking.

I found Ian McEwan waiting in the wings, in the darkness. I introduced myself and apologised for my lateness. He told me not to worry about it. I felt I owed him a fuller explanation, so I said, 'I've been getting nuisance calls. For two years.' I told him the whole story. He didn't say much, which I took as an invitation for me to elaborate. I think he intuited that listening without interruption was the best thing he could do for me. I had never spoken about the matter before, and I found that I was suddenly eager to share my turmoil with somebody.

'The thing is,' I said. 'I'm always scared to speak, even though part of me wants to say something significant, quickly, before he hangs up. Perhaps he's waiting for me to make the first move. I want to ask if it's him, but I can't risk it, in case it isn't and the person speaks and says no, and I discover it's not him after all. But until I'm brave enough to ask, I will always assume it's him, and there's a danger in that too. Can you imagine how frustrating it is for me, not knowing whether I'm still having a relationship with him or not? To be forced to listen to silence, in silence, over and over?' I was proud of that line. I think I even repeated it: 'to silence, in silence'.

'Mm,' said Ian McEwan.

'I mean, it must be him, mustn't it? Who else could it be? Evidently it's not just some random sex pest, because there are never any questions about what colour knickers I'm wearing or anything. There isn't even heavy breathing. And the timing is too much of a coincidence. As I said, the calls started three weeks after he disappeared. I suppose you think I ought to forget about him, don't you? Put the past behind me?'

'Well...'

'Or contact the police. But, if it is him, I don't want to get him into trouble. I have a really strong sense, you see, that it's him, and that has to mean something. Do you believe in non-verbal communication? In telepathy?'

'Well...' McEwan mumbled.

'I never used to, but I think when two people love each other enough, a form of psychic communion might be possible, don't you? And there's another weird thing. His name is Ian. And here I am talking to you, and I've got this really strong, strange feeling of rightness, of everything fitting together.'

'I see,' said McEwan.

'Do you think it is him that's phoning me?'

'I don't know.'

'But if you had to make an educated guess?'

'I really don't know. Shouldn't we…?' He pointed towards the empty stage.

It was probably selfish of me, but I wasn't yet ready to share him with an audience of three hundred people. I decided to approach the matter in what I thought was a tactful way. 'I tell you what,' I said. 'I'll take you to one of the dressing rooms, and then I'll go and find out what's holding things up.' Ian McEwan seemed to be satisfied with this suggestion, and followed me to the theatre's smallest, most inaccessible dressing room. Noone would think to look for us here. The room contained only a mirror, a table and two chairs, and was a little chilly. 'Have a seat,' I told McEwan confidently. 'I'll go and investigate, and I'll find you a drink while I'm at it.' I closed the door, and made my way as quickly as I could to the stage. I wasn't nervous, that was the strange thing; I was simply doing what was necessary. It didn't feel wrong.

I strode towards the microphone. 'Ladies and gentlemen,' I said. 'I'm afraid there will be a delay to the start of this evening's performance. Ian McEwan is feeling slightly unwell, though he assures me he will be fine in due course, if he is allowed to rest for a while. So, can I suggest that you go and have a drink at the bar, and we'll reconvene in exactly an hour? Thank you very much for your patience, and I'm sorry for the inconvenience.'

I raced back to the little dressing room. Thankfully, Ian McEwan was still there. He looked concerned when I told him that the event had been put back an hour. 'Sorry,' I said. 'The sound engineers are sorting out a few technical problems. So, where were we? Oh, yes. One thing that I keep coming back to is the contradiction between him – my ex – saying that he didn't want to waste eight hours sleeping before he saw me again, and him disappearing the very next day. When a person's words and actions can't be reconciled, what do you do? Which do you believe – the words or the actions? Presumably you, as a writer, would plump for the words, wouldn't you?'

'Erm…you mentioned a drink,' said Ian McEwan.

We got no further than that. Ruth, the festival director (in name only, I should point out), burst into the room, followed by McEwan's agent and his wife, and of course my little white lie was exposed. I hadn't adequately thought it through; I can see that now. I suppose I assumed that, once Ian McEwan's event had been a roaring success, as it was sure to be, noone would have any interest in discussing the late start to the evening, let alone its causes.

I have to say, though I still love his books, McEwan's lack of support shocked me. I expected him to write to the board and insist that I be reinstated, but he didn't. Neither did his agent or his editor, with whom I had always been on excellent terms. They all betrayed me. My parents, who read about

*my disgrace in Private Eye, wrote to Ian McEwan
and apologised on my behalf. My mother sent me
a copy of the letter, in which she told McEwan that
she was 'thoroughly ashamed' of me. I haven't spoken to my family since.*

*I moved away, far away, shortly afterwards. Now
nobody telephones me and I'm grateful. I'm glad I
have no friends. I couldn't stand to pick up a ringing phone and hear a voice on the other end instead
of silence. I mourn the loss of my mute caller every
second of every minute of every hour. It is only now
that I realise – way, way too late – that I loved him. It
no longer matters whether he was my ex-boyfriend or
not. I miss him in his own right. What we shared was
beyond words.*

When I finish writing this, I am shaking and I feel sick.
The facts remain unpalatable, even so many years later.
Still, I believe I am making progress. For example, earlier
I was convinced that my downfall was a result of excessive self-absorption. Now, reading through what I have
written, I realise that it was confiding inappropriately in
the wrong person that ruined me. I should not have told
Ian McEwan about my personal problems; I should have
allowed him to go ahead and do his reading, as planned. I
resolve not to try again to tell Ian Prudhoe my secret. It's
in the book; that's good enough for the time being.

I close my notebook and walk down to the main road,
where I catch a bus to Harrow Square. A few minutes later
I am knocking on the door of number six. Ian Prudhoe

opens it, wearing a green tracksuit top and grey sweatpants. It is three fifteen in the afternoon. He obviously doesn't have a job either.

'Fuck! Not you again,' he says.

'I'm editing a book,' I tell him. 'I was wondering if you wanted to be in it, to write something for it.'

His eyes narrow, as if he is either suspicious or concentrating really hard. 'A book? What, a real book? Will it be in shops and shit?'

'Of course. It's going to be a bestseller. It'll be in service stations and airports and supermarkets all over the country. It'll be one of the three books in the buffet-shop cars on Virgin trains.'

Ian looks dissatisfied. 'But what about bookshops?'

'Yes, there too. But all the most successful books these days are in service stations and supermarkets. That's more important than bookshops.'

'So, are you, like, a writer?'

'No. I'm an editor.'

'Will I get any money?'

I don't want to lie to him, so I say, 'I can't be specific at this point about how much money the book'll make. I'm hoping lots. But I promise you that, whatever I make from it, you can have fifty per cent.'

'Hey?'

'Half. I'll give you half the money.'

'Cool,' he says. His thick, bumpy lips form a grin.

I smile. There will be plenty of time later for me to tell him my name, and that I want him to write the unabridged story of his liaison with M8. 'How about a drink?' I say.

'Are you buying?'

'Of course.'

We set off to the pub together. 'How do you feel about festival appearances?' I ask him.

'Hey?'

I can see it now: Ian and me, on stage at the Maltings, talking about how we met, the unusual start to our friendship. They don't know it yet, those dullards who sacked me, but I am on my way back.

Twelve Noon

IT WAS AS if the sign knew more than I did. I stared in
disbelief, wondering how I could have failed to notice it
before. It was square, blue with white writing, attached to
a slim grey pole that disappeared into the pavement in a
raised hill of concrete.

If I'd spotted it I would have parked elsewhere. There
was a single yellow line across the street. Ron's disabled
badge was stuck to the windscreen of our car, but I was
alone, unsure of the rules, and queasy with nerves after
my first attempt at driving in nearly ten years.

I read the words again. 'Maximum stay 2 hours. No
return within 2 hours.' I looked at my watch. Half past
ten. I had set off from home at nine thirty, and the drive,
which as a passenger I'd done many times, took about
half an hour, so I must have parked at ten o'clock. Morrison's was less busy than usual, and I'd been so distracted
that I'd managed to buy only two things: a jar of coffee

and a packet of spaghetti. These I succeeded in obtaining only because they were the items Ron had reminded me about. I couldn't make any decisions: lager or wine, chips or potatoes. I tried to plan the week's meals in my mind, but my head reeled with thoughts of the other task I had set myself for this morning, the one I still hadn't done and might never do. Yet it was so important to me that I'd refused Ron's offer of a lift, in spite of my phobia. As recently as half past nine this morning, I had intended to honour the deal I had made.

I decided that, instead of allowing the sign in its entirety to baffle and intimidate me, I would break it down into its two parts and consider each one separately. This calmed me somewhat. The first restriction – 'Maximum stay 2 hours' – presented no problem. It was the second limitation that bothered me: 'No return within 2 hours'. Taken together, the sentences were confusing. If I was not allowed to return to my car for two hours, that meant that I still had an hour and a half to use up. But if I also wasn't allowed to park for longer than two hours, then surely the sign as a whole meant to say that I must come back at precisely twelve noon.

I was an English teacher before I retired, and I imagined what I would say to the grey pole with the blue square head if it were one of my pupils: 'If "You may park here for exactly two hours, no more and no less" is what you mean, why not say so?' I hid behind this surreal fantasy for a few seconds. If the sign had been merely inefficient, I would not have been trembling on the pavement, unable to take a step in any direction.

'No return within 2 hours.' I tried not to leap to any sinister conclusions, but I could see no sense in this instruction. What if all one had to do was nip into Boots? Surely the sooner each space was available for another driver's use, the better. I shivered, feeling my skin prickle. The second prohibition made sense only in one context: if you were me, in my present predicament, with my particular dilemma.

The sign knew. It stood there, impassive on its one cylindrical leg, for me.

I hovered outside Greggs bakery, with my Morrisons carrier bag in one hand and my handbag in the other. I forced myself to focus on my physical surroundings, to combat the unsettling sense I had that I was the only real component in an unreal scene, a breathing colour figure pasted on to a still, monochrome backdrop. Blood drummed in my ears. I tried to disregard it and listen outside myself, to the humming of car engines, the chinging of the till through the open door of the bakery, carefree conversations that hurtled towards me then left me, as suddenly, standing in their wakes. Fine rain settled on my face like mist. The sky was greying at the edges, darkening the morning. I tried not to take this as an omen of what might happen to me if I disobeyed.

For it seemed indisputable that the sign was ordering me to keep my promise. I had exactly an hour and a half, ample time. All I had to do was go to the Halifax, withdraw two thousand pounds and donate it to a charity. Simple. Why, then, were complications already tugging at the corners of my mind? I had never taken out so much money before. I had never had so much. The two thousand pounds was the result of six years of saving. Would notice be required for such a large amount? Would the people in the Halifax let me have cash or would it have to be a cheque? If the latter, I would need to decide upon a charity in advance, unless I asked them to leave the top line blank, which I wasn't keen to do. The staff would be bound to eye me suspiciously: *Two grand and she doesn't even know who it's for?*

My heart began to beat higher and faster as I realised that getting my hands on the money, in whatever form, was only the first challenge. What ought I to do with it then? Could I walk into one of the charity shops in town and hand it over without explanation? I doubted it; I was too polite to refuse to answer a reasonable question. I was also a hopeless liar. A fluttering sensation in my throat interfered with my breathing. I needed to sit down, even more so when it occurred to me that I ought not necessarily to restrict my choice of charity to those that had shops in town. In order to do justice to my promise, my decision had not to be based solely – or even at all – on my convenience.

It was all becoming too difficult. Waves of panic threatened to force all rational thought out of my mind. I dropped my handbag and my shopping on the pavement. This was the same feeling I had when I drove, the one I'd struggled with all the way into town. 'Are you sure you're up to it, love?' Ron had asked. 'I'm happy to take you in. It's no trouble.' Ron's kindness made my task so much harder. I would have to explain to him why the holiday that we had been planning for so long was now out of the question. That I knew he would forgive me made it worse, not better.

With a shaking hand, I reached for my car keys, thinking that if I could only sit down for a few moments, I might regain my composure. I was about to press the unlock button when it occurred to me that this could constitute returning to my car within two hours. Certainly sitting in it might. The immobile sign stared at me, each of its white letters an eye. Here, on the pavement, what if I was too close already? Would a traffic warden believe that I meant no harm, that I was only standing here in a sort of desperate paralysis?

It must be because these spaces were so few, so precious, I deduced. Evidently the council wanted to ensure they were only used by those whose business in town was substantial, taxing, and would take longer. The most deserving.

If I kept my promise to myself and gave the two thousand pounds to charity, that category would include me. I picked up my handbag and shopping and stumbled along the road, stopping when I reached a small, empty café called Mario's. I didn't want to be near people.

I ordered a pot of tea and sat at a red, Formica-topped table with a scratched surface, counting in my head. When did I become so frightened of everything? It was difficult to pin down a particular moment; it had been gradual, like my aversion to driving. I would have found it easier to understand if, the day after Katie walked out, I had woken up terrified, doubtful of my ability to control either myself or the car. But it didn't happen that way. My problems began several months after I last saw Katie. One day, when I was driving to work, I was careless and mounted the kerb. The following week I lost a friend's birthday present. It was around this time that I began to doubt my ability to cope. Ron started to have to make allowances for me, or 'take special care' of me, as he put it. 'I don't mind,' he said. 'You've looked after me all these years.'

He must have meant financially. His disability was not one that required physical care. Ron suffered from tinnitus. He had worked in a factory until his condition made it impossible. He hadn't had a job for fifteen years. I was the one who took care of our material needs. Not for long. Guilt made me wince. Yet a far worse guilt awaited me if I left the two thousand pounds in our holiday fund.

A young snub-nosed waitress brought over my tea. I pulled a notebook and pen out of my handbag, wrote 'Possible Charities' at the top of a blank page and underlined it. I must have looked intelligent and organised. At work, I had had a reputation for exceptional efficiency. Colleagues referred to me as 'a stickler'. Pupils did the assignments I set before those set by other teachers, knowing who would give them the sharpest telling-off if the work wasn't done. I reminded myself of this now, to bolster my confidence.

Choosing a charity was harder than I'd anticipated. The act of bestowing the money had to be utterly unselfish, with no benefit to me, not even a potential future benefit. This, I reasoned, would make my task even more agonising. Cancer Research was ruled out because I might one day be diagnosed with cancer, and, as Ron and I would soon be pensioners, Age Concern was a non-starter. I wrote 'NSPCC', then crossed it out when it occurred to me that Katie was bound to have children one day. And if she stayed with that awful man…

My heart, shrivelled from years of anguish, shrank still further. I would probably never see Katie's children. I could live with that, in the way that people learned to live with crumbling hip joints and debilitating migraines. What was intolerable was the thought that my unknown but nonetheless beloved grandchildren would grow up in the house of Toby Rollinson.

'Why don't you like him, Mum?' Katie had asked me, on what I now called the worst day of my life. It was the nineteenth of January, 1994. Every nineteenth of January since had been a torture to live through. I often wondered why anniversaries were so dreadful. It wasn't as if one avoided the pain for the rest of the year; it was there all the time. 'If you're worried about me not concentrating on my university work…'

'It isn't that,' I said.

'So it *is* something?' She knew she'd trapped me; I used language with more precision than most.

'Katie, I'm worried. You are…taking precautions?'

'Of course!'

'No, I mean…what contraception are you using? It's not pregnancy I'm worried about.'

She frowned. 'Oh. Well, you don't need to worry. We use condoms. And Toby hasn't got AIDS, if that's what you mean.' It was at this point that she had begun to sound indignant.

'I'm sure he hasn't,' I said quickly. Katie and I had always got on so well. I wanted to hear her usual happy voice again, but now that I had started I knew I had to continue. Keeping it from her wasn't an option. Even Ron agreed, and he hated discord. He even worried about offending people he disliked, an attitude I had never been able to understand. 'But it isn't only AIDS you need to think about. There's herpes, chlamydia…'

'Mum!'

'I'm sorry. Katie, there's something I have to tell you. About Toby. You're not going to like it.'

'What? Tell me.' She wanted it over with quickly. So did I.

'He has sex with prostitutes. Young ones.' I could have said children.

Katie's face paled.

'I've known for five days. It's taken me this long to think it through. I needed to be absolutely sure that—'

'You're lying!' She had found her voice, a shrill wail. 'You've always hated him!'

'That's not true.' Though I'd had my reservations. The presents he bought Katie were never ordinary nice things. Without exception, they were brilliant ideas that made people comment on Toby's cleverness. A reproduction of the *Mona Lisa*, but with Katie's face. 'How did you do it, Toby?' everybody asked.

'One of the girls he…pays is a pupil of mine. She saw the photo of you in his wallet when he opened it.

She'd seen you with me in town and knew you were my daughter.'

'She's lying! Maybe she knows Toby from somewhere else. Maybe she's obsessed with him and she's trying to wreck our relationship...'

I shook my head. 'I don't think so. It was very difficult for her to tell me. She made me promise I wouldn't tell anyone. Apart from you, and she said I had to keep her name a secret. She's one of my cleverest girls, Katie. She likes me.'

Lindsay Carter. Very bright and very poor. I sipped my tea, saying her name inside my head. I had kept my word and told noone. I'd lied to Katie slightly. Lindsay had told me it was her friend who slept with men for money, but I'd known instantly that it was her.

After Katie stormed out, I was calm. I washed the dishes, expecting her to be back as soon as she'd confronted Toby and found out I was right. I should have anticipated no such thing. How complacent must I have been? That day was the last time I saw her.

She ignored all my pleas, even the letter in which I wrote that I had been mistaken and I was sorry, so sorry. I would have said anything. I went, several times, to the house she shared with three other students, but she refused to see me. Obsessively, as if I were in court in my own mind, I interrogated myself about how this could happen to a bond as strong as ours. When I thought back over the history of our relationship, I found no precedent, no tensions beneath the surface. We were about as close as a mother and daughter could be. Years later, I read about her engagement to Toby in the *Daily Telegraph*. His parents were just the sort who would waste money on that sort of nonsense.

Having crossed out 'NSPCC', I was at a loss. Amnesty International was a worthy organisation, but I couldn't be absolutely certain that I would never need its help. What if I were kidnapped by terrorists? One read about such things more and more these days. It was highly unlikely, I knew, but not impossible. Eventually I settled on the RSPCA. I had no pets and did not particularly like animals. To have to take my precious money and give it to an organisation that would spend it on dogs and rabbits would make me want to do someone an injury. It was ideal.

I paid for my tea and hurried to the Halifax before I lost what little nerve I'd mustered. When I reached the counter, I asked for a cheque for two thousand pounds to be made out to the RSPCA. I was astonished when the man behind the window said, 'RSPCA? Not time to book the holiday, then? Or is it already paid for?'

'Pardon?'

'I'm Terry, remember? Ron and I play bridge together.'

'Oh…of course.' My fingers gripped the desk. I would have to tell Ron straight away; otherwise this man might. I would have to tell him straight away, because my nerves would not permit me to keep it from him.

'Ron showed me the brochure. I've never stayed in a five-star hotel.' His voice was full of admiration.

'Neither have we.'

'Ron says it's got three swimming pools.'

'Yes. I'm actually in, er...' I looked at my watch. I couldn't bear to hear the details of the treat we would have to forego. Furious with myself for the ridiculous bargain I'd made and now had to honour, I allowed a voice in my head to say, *It's not worth it*. Then I feared I would be struck down. What sort of mother would have such a thought, even fleetingly? I didn't mean it, of course, but Terry's musings on the Grand Hôtel des Iles Borromes forced me to remember all those weeks in cold caravans, on sagging mattresses.

I was probably rude to him in my desperation to escape. Once I had the cheque, I went straight to the phone box outside the library and rang directory enquiries. Another call and I had the RSPCA's address. Before I had time to change my mind, I marched to the post office like a robot, where I bought an envelope and a stamp and did what was necessary.

Once the two thousand pounds was in the post-box and out of reach for ever, I felt the full horror of what I had done, what I could so easily have avoided doing. Only I would ever have known. I had told nobody about the deal, not one single other living soul, and the chances were my breach of it would have made no difference whatsoever. I believed in the notion of tempting fate enough to sacrifice our holiday, but not enough to be able to take even a grain of comfort from the idea that, having sacrificed it, I would be rewarded.

I staggered outside, weeping. People stared at me, but I found it hard to believe they saw anything but a shadow. Now everyone else existed in the realm of colour and sound and I was grey, silent, unreal; misery had made me invisible. I walked back to the Halifax and pressed my face against the window, wetting the glass. Beside me, a woman who was using the cashpoint shifted to the right to put some distance between herself and the distraught lunatic. She completed her transaction and hurried away.

So eager was she to flee that she forgot to take her money. Time seemed to slow, as if the world needed winding up. I stared at the wavy edges of the notes poking out of the slot. Again, I had the sense that I was being shown something that was there for me alone. How could I be so superstitious when I was known for my rationality? I was a stickler. Everybody who knew me knew that I didn't watch horror films because I couldn't believe in ghosts or monsters, not even for two hours.

I reached out and grabbed the cash, noticing from the thickness of the bundle that it was quite a lot – certainly more than ten or twenty pounds. The woman was still visible. I watched her rush down the high street. She stopped when she got to Dandylion, a designer clothes shop for children. The incorrect spelling irritated me. I could have followed her and given her the money. Instead, I walked in the opposite direction, towards my car.

The sign was still there. It still said 'No return within 2 hours.' I looked at my watch. It was eleven ten. Fifty minutes to go. I stopped before I got too close and counted the notes in my hand. A hundred and fifty pounds. Disappointment wrapped itself around me. This would make no difference to anything. And I had done a terrible thing. I had deliberately stolen money and it wasn't as if I were starving. I had robbed a young woman I knew nothing about for the sake of a luxurious holiday in the Italian lakes. Did this make me as bad a person as Toby Rollinson? I nearly vomited on the pavement.

But there was still time. The difference between a good person and a bad one, I used to tell my pupils, is that a good person tries to make amends. I crossed the road and ran towards the police station. I needed to get there quickly, in case the woman from the cashpoint saw me. I didn't want to be caught by her before I'd done the right thing. How would I be able to prove my good intentions?

I had never been inside a police station before. The reception area was bland, beige. The woman behind the desk was not wearing a uniform. If it hadn't been for the police logo on the posters pinned up behind her, I would not have been able to guess where I was.

'I've stolen this,' I said, dropping the money on the counter, not wanting to touch it. 'From a woman, at the Halifax cashpoint down the road. I can describe her in detail. You'll be able to get it back to her, won't you?'

'What do you mean, you stole it?'

'She walked away without taking it. She was in a hurry. I picked it up...'

'When was this?'

'Just now. Five minutes ago.'

'But...you said you *stole* the money. When, actually, you brought it straight here.'

'No. I stole it. I was going to keep it. I could have run after her, I...It was only later I changed my mind and decided to hand it in. I'm a thief.'

The woman sighed. I might have been crying. 'Not much later. Five minutes. Look, you've handed it in now, so there's no harm done.'

'There is! Theft is still theft, whatever the thief does afterwards. I should be charged just the same as any mugger would be.'

'Do you want to be charged?' She gave me a quizzical look.

'I...yes.'

'Why?' She leaned her elbows on the desk, slumped a little: plenty of time to listen to the confessions of a whimpering middle-aged oddball.

'I don't want to tempt fate by getting away with anything.' I was definitely crying by now. 'My daughter...' I wanted my daughter to forgive me.

'The woman was your daughter?'

'No, no...I...' I was too distressed to speak, and missed what happened next. The scene broke down into particles. I couldn't process anything properly. I had a vague impression of another woman appearing behind the desk, of being led into a room by the first woman, of being alone for a while. A warm Styrofoam cup was placed in my hands.

Following instructions, I sipped strong, orange tea. That helped. I took deep breaths, also to order. 'I'm listening,' the policewoman said. 'You need to get it off your chest, whatever it is.'

'I need to be charged with robbery.' My words were slow and tentative, as if I'd never spoken before. If I were to be sent to prison, however briefly, this woman would have to tell Ron what I had done and why. She could show him my statement. I wouldn't have to watch his face become a collage of crushed hopes when I explained that I'd thrown away our savings. And then Ron would have to tell Katie.

He hadn't tried to speak to her since the rift, not once. It was understood, assumed, that I would be the spokesperson for both of us. I was the one who dealt with words. My parents hadn't thought Ron was my intellectual equal. He was the one who did the driving. He should have forced me to get behind the wheel when I least wanted to. If he had, perhaps I wouldn't have been here now.

I would make him tell Katie, if he didn't think of it himself. 'Your mum's in prison. Because of you. Because she loves you so much.' It might make all the difference.

'Why did you steal the money?' asked the policewoman.

'My husband and I are supposed to be going on holiday in the summer. We'd saved two thousand pounds. It took years. We...we haven't had a night out or bought new clothes for longer than I can remember. The holiday was more important.' I cleared my throat. 'Anyway, today I withdrew all the money and gave it to the RSPCA.' A piercing laugh escaped from me. My account sounded so absurd. I half expected to realise, suddenly, that I hadn't done it, that it was a hallucination.

The policewoman didn't smile. 'Why?'

'My daughter. She hasn't spoken to me for ten years. I tried everything, but...in the end there was nothing I could do apart from...what I did. Have you ever made a deal with fate?'

'How do you mean?'

'If this happens, I'll do that – that's the form they usually take.'

'Oh. You mean like, if I get this job I really want, I'll give up smoking?' She blushed. 'That was the only time I did it. I didn't get the job and I still smoke.'

'Yes. Well, I vowed to myself that if Katie – that's my daughter – that if she ever got in touch, I'd…give some money to charity. At first it was only a hundred pounds. The amount went up as the months passed, then the years. I thought that the more it was, the greater the chance she'd contact me. You know, because I couldn't bear to part with such a large amount…' Discussing it for the first time made me curious: what exactly was the rationale behind pacts such as mine? I had never examined this before; it had all been intuitive, almost organic. I hadn't asked myself *why* I would give money to charity if Katie got in touch. It seemed obvious. It went without saying. 'I suppose we make these bargains because we so fear that we won't get what we want, we feel a need to set up a consolation for ourselves. *At least I can keep my money. At least I can still smoke.* Or maybe it's an attempt to bribe the gods.'

'So your daughter got in touch, then? If you say you've already given the money away.'

'Yes… Yes.'

'Well, then.' She smiled, but I saw doubt in her eyes. I knew she didn't dare ask me why, then, I wasn't elated, full of joy and relief. Why was I stealing paltry sums from innocent passers-by instead of celebrating?

I couldn't tell her. To say that Katie had got in touch was a better way to finish the story. It was the right ending: Katie wrote to me, finally, we were fully reconciled, and I handed over the two thousand pounds as promised. I was ashamed to admit to this well-meaning stranger that fate had made a fool of me. After all these years, the communication I received from my daughter was an article from the local newspaper, about her husband. He had become a managing director. His company had raised a large amount of money for a children's hospice. The story was accompanied by a photograph of a smug, bloated Toby passing a cheque to an elderly woman, his arm round her shoulders.

Katie hadn't sent a note with the clipping. If she had, it would have said, 'See how wrong you were about him?'

I knew perfectly well, and fate knew, that this was not what I had meant when I prayed for Katie to contact me. But I was a person who valued precision; I couldn't pretend that I didn't recall the terms of the deal, word for word: 'If Katie gets in touch, I will give two thousand pounds to charity.' I inserted no sub-clause about hostile, defiant communications.

The injustice was hard to stomach: that I should lose all my money in exchange for this. I tried to believe that Toby himself might have sent the cutting, not Katie, but I couldn't know for sure. And I couldn't risk trying to cheat. Fate would not catch me looking for a loophole.

I told the policewoman none of this. I feared I might disintegrate completely if I made it too vivid by saying it aloud, so I drank my tea in silence and listened as she told me that I would not be charged, that I should write to the RSPCA and ask for my money back, that I should be happy.

As far as I could see, I had only one thing to be happy about: I was doing the best I could to meet the demands made of me, as I understood them. I had given away our savings; we now had only three pounds and sixty-seven pence left in our holiday fund. I had handed in the money I stole and tried to secure a punishment for myself. I had not returned to my car within two hours. A reward for all this good behaviour might still be forthcoming.

I said thank you and goodbye to the policewoman and walked out of the building, trying and failing to feel free. I looked at my watch, saw that my time would shortly expire, and began to run. Then, because I'd sprinted too fast, I slowed down as I passed the bookmaker's and the bakery. I read the sign again. 'Maximum stay 2 hours. No return within 2 hours.' I had done it, complied with both requirements. I hoped this had been observed by the relevant authorities. As I pressed the button on the key fob to unlock the car, it was exactly twelve noon.

The Nursery Bear

THE CAR WAS outside the garage. All four of the Devines were in it. Mark was in the driver's seat, his face pale, eyes closed. One of his hands was in his lap, the palm facing upward, the fingers slightly curled. I couldn't see his other hand. His body was exactly in the middle of the seat, as if he'd measured the distance between each of his arms and the relevant edge before assuming his position. His head completed the straight line of his body, making him the neatest of the four.

Kay, his wife, was slumped to one side with her shoulder pressed against the front passenger window, her head inclined in the direction of her husband. Her eyes were also closed. Mine took in the twist of green hosepipe on the ground behind the car. I gripped the window sill. Behind Mark and Kay were the girls. My mouth opened, but no breath came out. The girls: Anya and Celia. Anya's head drooped forward, as if too heavy for her neck.

Celia's eyes were open, staring straight at me. Tight red straps held her in her toddler seat, a Y-shape against her chest. I called out, 'John!', forgetting that he wasn't home; he was collecting Matthew. Noone answered. Something inside me speeded up.

I stumbled to the front door and threw myself against the glass – all the time seeing the girls, the red straps, the curl of green hosepipe – thinking that there might still be time, they might still only be unconscious. How long does it take to die of carbon monoxide poisoning? Why didn't I know? I pulled at the door handle, my hands slippery. Nothing happened. 'Come *on*,' I hissed, grasping the stubborn metal with both hands as if I were trying to wring someone's neck. Then I remembered it was locked. It was always locked, even when we were in. Basic security, John said. What if the children wandered outside without us knowing?

The key. Where was it? Why wasn't it in its usual place, on top of the burglar alarm box? Where else could it be? Sweat poured out of my skin. It wasn't in the keyhole. It wasn't on the carpet. Emily. It had to be Emily.

I ran to the lounge. She was crawling across the carpet, chasing her bash'n'go UFO. 'Emmy, what have you done with the front door key?' I forced myself to separate the words.

'Rabbit noo,' she said. She nodded solemnly, as she always does when she is telling me something she thinks is important.

'Yes, there's a rabbit at nursery, isn't there? Em, where's the front door key? Quickly. You've put it somewhere.

Where have you put it, darling?' I must have left it in the
door this morning by mistake. *Idiot*. Em was tall enough
to reach up and grab it.

'Bear noo.' More staccato nods.

'No, there's no bear at nursery. Emily, give Mummy
the front door key. Key?' My voice cracked on the last
word.

Emily pointed at herself. 'Emmy bear noo. Emmy
have.' She hit her UFO with a flat palm and it jerked
across the carpet, bleeping.

'Where's the key?' I wailed. Too loud. Mistake. Em's
face turned red and folded in on itself: the prelude to a
screaming bout. 'Emmy bear noo!' she shrieked back at
me. 'Want bear home!'

I stifled a howl and raced to the kitchen. The back
door key was in the lock. I turned it and ran out into
my garden. 'Hello!' I shouted. 'Help!' Outside, I was still
trapped. Our garden was separated from those belonging
to our neighbours by three solid fences, all too tall for me
to climb over. I might have been able to do it if I'd stood
on a chair, but I wasn't sure and, even if I'd succeeded, I
would only have been trapped on somebody else's property. *How long, how long does it take*? The only way out of
any of the gardens was to go through the attached house.
All were enclosed on all sides; there was no independent
access to the street. Burglars never bothered with us. We
lived in a very safe neighbourhood – everyone always
said so.

I ran inside, crying, back to the kitchen window. The
Devines looked the same. In my panicked state, I couldn't

decide whether it was too late, whether it had been too late all along, or if they still had a chance, one that was narrowing towards blackness as I crashed from one side of my house to the other like a wasp in a jar. I couldn't reach them. I had to summon somebody who could: an ambulance. The police.

I grabbed the phone and stabbed the '9' button three times. A patient female voice told me to calm down, and asked for basic details, which I provided: the car, the green hosepipe. As I said it, I saw it. I feared I would see it clearly for ever. Then I ran back to the kitchen, and, without looking, lowered the blind. I was panting; I couldn't stop. Emmy was still crying in the lounge. *Anya's bent head, Celia's open eyes...*I couldn't sit. I was here, at the scene. The police weren't here yet. I had to do something.

I ran back to the hall and forced myself to look more systematically for the front door key. On my hands and knees, I patted the hall carpet. Nothing. Should I try the lounge? The Devines called their lounge 'the best lounge', even though they only had one. John and I mocked them. I shuddered. The Devines were a tragedy, not a comedy. I had misjudged their essence, looked at them and seen something that wasn't there. This thought brought ghosts to mind, made me pat the carpet harder, until the skin on my palms stung.

As my head jerked from side to side I saw something glinting inside one of John's walking boots. The key. I felt the shock of seeing it all over my body. Only once I'd touched it did I believe it was there. Arranged around it were three pieces of fuzzy felt furniture: a sofa, a lamp and a chest of drawers.

I unlocked my front door and ran out into the drive, seeing the police car at the same time. I heard the screech of its brakes, watched the two uniformed officers, both male, run to the Devines' car faster than I'd ever seen anyone move in real life before. I stood, frozen, behind my front garden wall. Two cops. Like on television, I thought numbly, my brain on automatic pilot. One with a failed marriage behind him, who both loves and is awkward around his kids, who likes country music or jazz. One who eats, drinks and smokes too much, ignoring his doctor's advice, and has dysfunctional relationships with women who sometimes turn out to be the murderer.

The ambulance turned into our road. I saw one of the policemen put his hand out. Stop. He shook his head. *No. No.* I closed my eyes. It was too late.

I heard a clash of voices, car doors opening. I opened my eyes gradually, squinting at first. I couldn't see properly because the policemen were between me and the car. Then my knees nearly gave way as I saw, and heard, Mark. Upright, alive. His voice was loud and strong. Next I saw Kay, heard her laugh. I scrunched my eyes shut, and when I opened them Anya was stepping out of the car, looking bored as she usually did. I couldn't believe what I was observing. How could they even stand after all the carbon monoxide they must have inhaled? I thought, What about Celia? As if she were reading my mind, Kay Devine lifted her younger daughter out of the car at that moment. I watched Celia wriggle and moan in her mother's grasp.

A brief conference of whispers took place between the Devines, the police and the ambulance staff. Then all heads turned towards me. I stared at my neighbours, at the strangers in uniform, who had begun to process solemnly towards me.

Mark and Kay wore concerned smiles like masks, masks one might put on to visit the local invalid. 'Hello, Ruth,' said Mark.

'But…you…' *Were dead. You were dead.*

'We were having a nap.' Mark tried to laugh heartily. It sounded false.

'Aaah!' Kay tilted her head to one side as she often did, indulgent and sympathetic. 'The girls both fell asleep in the car, and…'

'…We didn't want to wake them when we got home,' Mark took over.

'You'll probably think we're silly, but…'

'…Kay and I were pretty exhausted ourselves, so we thought we might as well have a little siesta in the car.'

Celia stuck her thumb in her mouth and stared impatiently at her own house as if keen to be inside it, resentful of being outside mine.

'Right,' I said. When Emmy was a baby and Matthew was going through his wakeful-at-night phase, I had once fallen asleep on my feet in the supermarket, leaning on my trolley.

I felt horribly and visibly foolish. There had been no disaster after all. Embarrassment was all over my skin like a rash, making me hot and uncomfortable. My head was still jangling, my nerves clenched. How long would it take my body to realise that everything was all right? Because it *was* all right, however humiliated I was; the Devines were alive.

I felt angry with Mark and Kay, newly suspicious of them, though I knew this was irrational. Did it make sense to say that you were suspicious of someone unless you suspected them of a specific thing? And what could that be, in this case? I had suspected them of one thing and one thing only – being dead in their car – and now they had proved quite adequately that they were not. That should have been the end of the matter. So why did I feel that Mark and Kay had outwitted me? Kay was wearing an identical skirt to one I owned. I decided never to buy anything from Next again.

Mark was generously telling the police officers and ambulance men that they should not resent the waste of their time, that mine was an easy mistake to make, anyone might have done so, that his family and mine were not merely nextdoor neighbours but good friends as well, that I was a writer and therefore could be expected to have a vivid imagination (I write user manuals for food processors and other kitchen equipment). Kay nodded her agreement to all of this.

'Shall we all come in and have a cup of tea?' Mark suggested, looking past me into my hall. 'It's quite funny, really, isn't it, when you think about it?' Anya sighed and wrinkled her nose, as if the whole matter were beneath her. I had always found Anya a little frightening, I suddenly realised. She was only nine, but that didn't stop her from exuding dismissive authority with all the complacency of a Tudor monarch.

I was beginning to feel more normal, my mind cooling down after the hot panic.

'Milk. Milky!' Celia whined.

I wondered if it was natural that Mark and Kay weren't at all cross with me, given what I'd done, that they were being so good-humoured about it. What would Mark expect in return for his leniency? A cup of tea, to start with. 'Now's not really a convenient time,' I said. 'Sorry.' I needed to be alone, to compose myself. I still felt horribly embarrassed, and couldn't bear to be observed by anybody.

The police and ambulance staff looked relieved. They didn't want tea, didn't want to extend this pantomime. Perhaps they had never before encountered an obsessive socialiser like Mark, someone who makes you feel that ending a phone call with him, a chat, an evening together, is something you need to prepare for and rehearse, otherwise you will never achieve it. Whatever the occasion, Mark always wanted it to go on and on. 'Because he always has more to say,' said John. 'He loves the sound of his own voice. And he's not happy. You can't tell me he's happy, a guy like that. His ho-ho-ho act's a sham. He can't stand silence, or his own company. Or his own house, come to think of it. He prefers our house! It's like a stage for him. That's what it is: he needs to be performing all the time.'

The last time the Devines were due to come round for dinner, John issued me with a warning: 'I really mean it this time. If that guy's not gone by half eleven, I'm bringing my pyjamas down to the lounge and changing into them right in front of him. Maybe then he'll get the hint!'

Both policemen looked bored and anxious to get away – after all, crimes were no doubt being committed

– and it was only this that enabled me, finally, to close my front door with Mark and Kay Devine on the optimum side of it. I couldn't have explained why, exactly, but I knew that, without the officers' presence, I would not have succeeded in fending off Mark's suggestion that I should offer refreshments to him and his family.

I shuddered and groaned in the hall for a while after they had all gone, cringing at the huge obviousness of my mistake. I wished it hadn't happened with a pointless desperation that made me feel faint. I should have listened to John last year and been more reserved, instead of rushing into a friendship with our new neighbours. John had never been keen on the Devines. Even before we knew them, he was not comfortable with them as a concept. 'It's embarrassing,' he said. 'There's four of us, and there's four of them. Their eldest goes to Matthew's school, their youngest goes to Emmy's nursery. Mark leaves the house every morning in a suit, like I do. They probably get the same bloody newspaper as us. Don't invite them round for any drinks or meals! I'm not socialising with them!'

John had never liked people who reminded him of any respect in which he was not unique. He refused even to read about people like himself. I was the one who read about the domestic and romantic lives of the English professional classes; I liked the familiar, the easily recognisable. John read about driven fools with spikes sticking out of the front of their boots who were obsessed with reaching summits (but only if they were summits not previously reached by other driven fools) and who invariably ended up clinging to fraying ropes with their frost-bitten teeth, wondering which of their legs to cut off with a pocket knife and eat raw first. That's what's wrong with the Devines, I thought, as I leaned against my front door, feeling as if there was something I needed to work out: they're not familiar, but they think they are. They try to be.

I had ignored John's insane embargo, as he always expects (and secretly hopes, even as he rants) that I will, and within a few weeks of them moving in our two families were on friendly terms and saw each other socially once every couple of weeks. Mark Devine irritated John profusely by beginning too many of his sentences with the words 'If there's *one* thing I'm good at, it's...'

'It's so dishonest!' John fumed. 'It's the double-bluff aspect that pisses me off. You know, the upfront boast, but it's not really a boast, because it's as if he's saying, "Look, I might be an essentially talentless underachiever but I do have this *one* small area of prowess", but actually it *is* outrageously fucking boastful, because he says it every five seconds about every single topic that arises. It isn't one thing he's good at, it's five hundred things: chess, fixing cars, DIY, maths, running – everything!'

It was true, I had to admit. Mark Devine thought he was 'the donkey's bollocks' – another of his favourite phrases, though he was careful never to say this directly about himself. He merely reported it when other people said so. So, we discovered that, whereas Mark thought his boss, his firm, his chess teacher as a child, his personal trainer at the gym, were the donkey's bollocks, they (trainer, chess teacher, boss and firm) thought Mark was the donkey's bollocks. 'And, of course, as the most donkey's-bollocksy people Mark's ever met, they must be right!' said John.

I half smiled as I remembered this; I was so used to thinking of the Devines as comic extras in our lives. Mark wasn't the only member of the family with funny behavioural tics; Kay Devine had a habit of saying 'Aaaah' all the time, in the tone of voice people adopt when they say, 'Bless!', as if whoever she happened to be talking to had just said or done something impossibly cute. So a typical conversation with Kay might go like this:

Me: Hi, Kay. I was just about to take Emmy to the
park, but it's started raining.
Kay: Aaaah! We're on our way to the Wacky Warehouse, if you want to come.
Me: I don't know. I might take the opportunity to
nip to Sainsbury's, actually.
Kay: Aaaaah! All right, then. See you soon.

And I would walk away puzzled, wondering if, without being aware of it, what I had actually said was, 'Two little black kittens with white paws and pink ribbons round their necks.'

I'd always felt sorry for Kay, mainly because when Mark was around she didn't get to speak. Her brief, it seemed, was to listen proudly to her husband, which she did with gusto, even when he was talking the most puer-ile nonsense, as he often was. If Kay got carried away and attempted to speak while Mark was speaking (which was all the time), she rarely got further than 'Aaaah' before being cut off by his rising voice.

How John and I laughed, delighted that our new neighbours had provided us with so many snide giggling opportunities. First there was their fear of the sun, and their insistence that Anya and Celia wear factor fifty sunblock all year round ('because cloud cover isn't infallible' – Mark). Then there was the best lounge, with its curtains that were always closed. When I was feeling mischievous and wanted to bitch, I mentioned the lounge to John. It always got him going.

'They say it's just the children who aren't allowed in, but when they had us for dinner that time, Mark kept making excuses to keep us in the kitchen! I don't reckon they even let themselves go into that room. I bet it's like a museum, the museum of their own lives, all their best stuff locked away in glass-fronted cabinets...'

'...huge, hideous studio photographs of themselves in their smartest clothes on the walls,' I contributed.

'...immaculate carpets that no foot has ever touched. It's pathetic! And, I mean, their house is an exact copy of ours, so we know they can't spare a room. I tell you, it's typical of Mark Devine, to want his own museum...'

'You don't know it's that,' I said, laughing. 'You just made that up!'

'...like the fucking Brontë parsonage! I bet he imagines that in years to come people will travel from miles around to look at Mark Devine memorabilia, except – oh, sorry, Mark, didn't anyone tell you? – noone does that with accountants, irrespective of whether they're the donkey's bollocks or not! And I'll tell you another thing: noone would be remotely interested in that guy if his name wasn't Mark Devine!'

I stared at him, puzzled. 'What do you mean? Noone *is* interested in him, are they? Except us, when we want to have a bitch.'

'If his name was…' John wagged his finger in the air.

'Duncan Pilkington,' I suggested.

'Exactly! Noone would give him a second thought!'

'Noone *does* give him a second thought. Anyway, I think you're wrong about the best lounge,' I told him. 'I reckon they use it, Mark and Kay. But only them. I don't reckon they ever take friends in there, or family. Maybe it's their special bonking room, full of sex toys. That'd explain why the curtains are always shut.'

'They're shut because of Mark's sun phobia. Even so, he probably sits in there with whale blubber smeared all over his face, just in case cloud cover and curtain cover aren't infallible!'

And then another memory. Not a funny one this time: Kay telling me how pleased I must have been to have a girl, finally, when Emily was born. Matty standing next to me, hearing every word she said. Me saying, 'I was happy to have both my children.' Her saying, 'Aaaah. But girls are much better. I only ever wanted girls. Girls are nice and clean!' Matty unusually subdued that evening, despite my reassurances.

Emily appeared in the hall. The sight of her, with tears still visible on her cheeks, broke my train of thought. 'Ganny Bapa?' she said hopefully.

'No, darling, not today.' I bent down to hug her. 'We'll see Granny and Bapa at the weekend.'

'Good boy, Mummy,' she said, wriggling free, running back to the lounge.

I rubbed my forehead and sighed, knowing my ordeal was far from over. I would have to tell John about my hideous error. Mark would certainly mention it, and if John hadn't heard about it from me first, he would be understandably puzzled and perhaps even angry. My marriage to John – its success – was based to a large extent upon our ability and desire to keep one another fully informed of everything we needed to know and an awful lot of things we didn't strictly need but would undoubtedly prefer to know. The efficient and enthusiastic transferral of vast amounts of necessary and unnecessary information was our strength.

This was the first thing I had ever wanted not to tell my husband, the first story I would have to relay to him that showed me in an unflattering light. *How sane and sensible I usually am*, I thought. It made this one lapse all the more humiliating. I told John about it as soon as he walked through the door, to get it over with. I'd been dreading his reaction, imagining the baffled, concerned look in his eye as, privately, he questioned my sanity. I needn't have worried, since he opted to question it in a more public, overt manner.

'Is there something wrong with you, mentally?' he demanded. 'You see them in their car and assume they're *dead*?'

'There was a hosepipe on the ground behind the car,' I said wearily. I had no energy for an argument I couldn't win. Clearly I was not going to succeed in proving that I was right to think the Devines were dead, so what was the point of saying anything?

'It's often there, if Mark's been cleaning the drive. Haven't you ever noticed it before?'

'No. I don't know…They looked dead, John. You didn't see them. Mark and Kay had their eyes closed, Anya's head had fallen forward. Celia's eyes were open but just sort of staring emptily…'

'She's a toddler! What do you expect to see in her eyes: anxiety about the world's dwindling oil reserves? She was probably daydreaming!'

'Look, it's embarrassing enough without you going on about it!'

'Are you cracking up? Okay, let me try to put myself in your position. No, I still don't get how you could look at our neighbours, asleep, and assume they were *dead*.'

'Because it's not normal for an entire family to have a nap in their car, right outside their house!'

'Oh, and I suppose it's much more normal for them to gas themselves with a hosepipe. That's an everyday occurrence in our neck of the woods, isn't it? You're losing your grip on reality! You'll end up one of those fragile housewives, the kind everyone tactfully refers to as 'sensitive', monged out on Valium, with lipstick the colour of dried blood running into the wrinkles around your mouth, shuffling around in a houseoat!' John had never been one to shy away from a potential problem.

I changed the subject as soon as he allowed me to. I hoped I had concealed from him the extent to which the incident had crushed my confidence. It was stupid and embarrassing, yes, but it was more than that. When, one by one, the Devines had stepped out of their car, loud and full of life, I had been genuinely frightened.

Absurdly, over the next few days, a faint trace of that fear lingered. Every time I saw Mark leave the house with his briefcase in his hand, every time I saw Kay drop a bulging white bin liner into the green wheelie bin outside their house, I shivered as if I were looking at the undead. A stubborn part of my brain still refused to accept that I had been wrong. Alongside my mild dread was an equally mild irritation. Mark's smile now looked to me like the smile of a man who dared to defy the most fundamental natural law, knowing he would get away with it.

I shared none of these thoughts with John. For the first time in our marriage, there was an obstacle to the effective flow of information both relevant and irrelevant.

The following week, the doorbell rang one day while I was alone in the house. It was Kay. 'Aaah!' she said. 'I just popped round to check Matthew and Emmy are still coming to Anya's birthday party on Saturday.'

'Of course,' I said, thinking again about Kay's bizarre opinions on boys and girls. She always abbreviated my daughter's name – to Em or Emmy – but never my son's. He was always Matthew. His birthday card had been six days late. Em's birthday was a month before Matty's. Her card had arrived on time, with a present attached to it.

'Aaaah,' said Kay. 'And obviously you and John must come, too. There'll be plenty of grown-ups there.' She was still wearing my Next skirt.

'Great,' I said. The prospect of the party made me feel tired in advance, and I couldn't even rouse myself to pronounce my consonants properly. My words slurred into each other as I murmured, 'I'll mention it to John.'

Foolishly, I did. 'In the old days,' he ranted, 'parents used to drop their kids off at parties and pick them up, along with a bag of goodies, at the end. Now, though, we're not allowed to make any distinction between children and adults, are we? Oh, no – because that wouldn't be politically correct. Now grown men like me are expected to want nothing more than to spend our precious Saturday afternoons pinning the tail on the donkey with the chocolate-smeared offspring of people we don't even *like*!'

I also didn't want to go to the party, but I felt that I had to, to make up for my faux-pas. Just this once, I said to myself, just this one concession, to atone for my mistake, and then no more. I would not socialise with the Devines again. They made me feel uneasy; I wasn't even sure that the horrendous episode with the car and the hosepipe had been the beginning of it.

On the relevant day, at the appropriate time, I left the house with Matthew, Emily, and a card and present for Anya, feeling that a messy and disturbing chapter in my life was about to close. 'Aaah!' said Kay. 'You didn't need to bring a pressie! Just having you all here is enough.' She's probably a very nice, friendly woman, I thought.

She's probably got nothing against Matthew; I'm bound to have imagined the whole thing. I should like her. At the same time, I realised I never had. Certainly I had never warmed to her pompous, loud-mouthed husband. I had maintained our friendship with the Devines first out of curiosity, a desire to investigate the new neighbours, and later because it was satisfying to watch them acting so much like themselves.

'Girls' toilet upstairs, boys' downstairs,' said Kay, shaking her finger at Matthew, mock-strict. 'Don't forget, Matthew.'

The best lounge was, needless to say, out of bounds. I tried the door at one point, knowing John would be disappointed in me if I didn't, and found it locked. There was enough room in the large kitchen for most of the partying children, and those that didn't fit roamed the hall, stairs and landing. At one point I was shoved out on to the porch armed only with a slice of Anya's birthday cake, and bumped into Sally Henney, the mother of one of Emmy and Celia's nursery contacts. She pushed her daughter into the throng of children. 'Aren't you worried about your weight?' she asked me, nodding at the crumbs in my hand.

'Should I be?' I said.

'Actually, my sister's much fatter than you. She's really obese.'

'Is she?'

We appeared to have run out of things to say to one another; that, at least, was my hope. Then Sally leaned towards me and whispered, 'Has Emily ever had the nursery bear?'

'The what?'

'The nursery bear. Oh, come on! You must know about it.'

I didn't.

'God, what planet are you on? It's big and brown and it wears a yellow T-shirt with a big "M" on it, for "Moorlands".' This was the name of the nursery our children attended. 'The children take turns to take the bear home with them for a week. It's, like, a treat. You must walk around in a world of your own! Haven't you seen the photos?'

I remembered Emily screaming, 'Emmy bear noo! Want bear home!' I hadn't understood. Guilt began to prickle inside my mind. 'What photos?' I asked.

'Of all the adventures different children have had with the bear! The child who gets the bear has to take a photo to bring in, for the display. They're up all over the wall, just when you come through the door. Honestly, you working mums! You're so busy trying to do everything, you don't notice anything! I'm glad I'm not a career woman.'

I don't know what came over me then, but I grinned at Sally and said, 'It's okay, you don't have to pretend. I *know.*'

'Know what?'

I lowered my voice. 'That you fly all over the world with plastic sacks full of heroin stuffed up your bum. That you're a *drugs mule.* Kay told me.' Sally's mouth fell open. Before she could say anything, I elbowed her in the ribs and began to giggle. 'Only joking!' I said brightly. 'No, Emily hasn't had the nursery bear.'

Sally eyed me suspiciously. Her face was post-box red, but she gave me another chance. 'Neither has Lauren,' she said. 'It doesn't seem fair, really, does it? I mean, for Celia Devine to have the bear, when she's only been at Moorlands a few months.'

'What's the bear's name?' I asked.

'Its name? It hasn't got one. It's just called the nursery bear.'

This struck me as unsatisfactory. I felt sad on Em's behalf. She clearly wanted the bear, and she had never had it. And I hadn't understood what she was talking about, why she was upset.

Sally Henney, though wrong about a wide range of topics, from the validity of horoscopes to the dangers of child vaccination, turned out to be right about the present whereabouts of the nursery bear. I saw it later that afternoon. It was wearing a party hat, sitting on a high shelf in the kitchen, a blob of pink jelly on its otherwise immaculate yellow T-shirt. I hoped Emmy wouldn't see it. She didn't, thankfully, but I was tense until we left the party, in case there was some sort of scene. Seeing that a friend of yours has something you want is hard enough for an adult; for a child of Emily's age, it is unthinkable torment.

The following Monday morning, I had a private word with Jacqueline, the manager of Moorlands, who appeared to know that Emmy wanted the nursery bear and had wanted it for some time. My guilt thickened – why hadn't I known? On the wall beside us were all the photographs Sally Henney had told me about, of the nursery bear on his many outings: with Owen at the Saturday market; with Harry at the swimming baths; with Eliza at a barbecue. I asked Jacqueline on what basis the nursery bear was allocated, not caring if I sounded as petty as Sally Henney. Jacqueline told me Emily could have it the following week. We stared at one another, both aware (and aware that we were both aware) that she had not answered my question. She was probably thinking, *pushy parent*. I was thinking *perpetrator of injustices, however small-scale*. I said, 'Good, because I know Celia Devine's got it this week, and she's not been here as long as Emily. Is there…How *do* you decide which child gets the bear?' I presented the question as if it had just occurred to me.

'Emily'll have him next week,' Jacqueline repeated cheerfully. We both pretended that we had not been through the same question-and-lack-of-answer process twice.

That afternoon, John came home ashen-faced. He'd caught the train home with Mark. 'Did you know the Devines had a son, Brendan, who died?' he demanded, as if it were my fault for not telling him.

'No,' I said.

'I didn't know what to say. I just muttered, "Bloody hell". *Bloody hell*! How could I have said that? What a dick I am! Mark must hate me.'

I told him everyone said tactless things in moments of stress, and that Mark must be used to it. Anyone who has suffered a tragedy must be used to it. 'What did Brendan die of?' I asked. 'How old was he? Did you get the details?'

'The *details*? Jesus, it's not like getting a brochure off an estate agent. The *details*!'

'It's not crass to be interested and want to know a bit more,' I told him crossly. 'Sometimes people who've been through something awful prefer questions to an embarrassed silence!'

'Oh, so you *do* think I reacted like a dick, then?' said John angrily. I decided not to pursue the conversation.

I wondered if Brendan's death was the key to Kay's horrible comment about boys being less clean than girls. Competitiveness, John and I had often agreed, was one of the Devines' main characteristics. If they had no boys, if their boy had died, girls had to better. They might have tried hard to make themselves not want what they no longer had. It was an odd reaction, true, but people responded to grief in all sorts of ways. Aaah.

The next day – John had, thankfully, just left for work – I was looking out of the kitchen window and saw a red-faced, quivering-jawed Kay Devine marching towards my house. My first thought was: Brendan. She's upset about the way John reacted. Then I saw that she was holding the nursery bear. I wilted inside, knowing that Jacqueline had been indiscreet and that, as a result, some sort of confrontation was heading my way. I reminded myself that appearances could be deceptive, particularly where the Devines were concerned. On this occasion, however, they turned out to be spot-on. I am always right when I least want to be.

'Here!' Kay thrust the cuddly toy towards me, holding it with both hands. She didn't say 'Aaaah'. 'In future, if you've got a problem with me and my family, talk to me about it, don't go behind my back!'

'Kay...'

'They gave the bear to Celia because she's always so *bloody* miserable at nursery, and they thought it might cheer her up and make her feel part of things, but if you're going to be funny about it, here! Have it!'

'Kay, I didn't say I...'

'No! You have it! Even though Emily's *absolutely fine* at nursery, really happy there, no problems at all, you have it, because, after all, you were here *first*, weren't you?'

I felt awful. She was right, I knew. When I collected Emmy from nursery, Celia was invariably crying on someone's knee, or skulking, hollow-eyed, in a corner, not seeming to be part of things. Anya, also, never seemed happy. I didn't think I'd ever seen her smile. Was it because they had lost their brother?

'Did you tell Sally Henney I said she was a *drug dealer*?' Kay demanded. 'What the hell's the matter with you? Are you some kind of lunatic?'

'Oh, God. Look, you've...it was a joke...' I mumbled feebly, but Kay didn't stay to listen to my excuses. She dropped the bear at my feet and marched away. I picked up the cuddly toy. One of its eyes was missing, and there was a black patch that looked like a burn mark on its right arm. It didn't look nearly as desirable and appealing as it had at the party.

I couldn't wait to return it to Kay. It was, I told myself, the right thing to do. After I'd dropped Emily at nursery the following morning, I took the one-eyed bear and went round to see Kay. 'Look, I'm really sorry,' I said. 'I honestly didn't want to take the bear away from Celia. I just wanted to check Emily would have a go with him at some point. And, no, I didn't tell Sally Henney…you know.' I felt myself blushing. 'I made a silly joke, and she misunderstood it.'

Surprisingly, Kay seemed ready to forgive me at once. 'Aaah,' she said. 'I'm so glad you came round. I've hated us not being friends, haven't you?' She took the nursery bear. I didn't know what to say. Our not being friends had lasted for less than twenty-four hours. I made what I hoped was an all-purpose soothing noise. When Kay invited me in for a cup of tea, I felt I could hardly refuse. Glumly, I followed her into her kitchen, which looked as if it had been devastated by an act of God. There was no paper or paint on the walls, only plaster. The lino had been half ripped off the floor. I inhaled dust and began to cough.

'Aaah, have a seat,' she said. 'We're decorating. It'll be like this for a while. Bit of a pain!'

'I expect you'll just use the lounge more,' I said pointedly.

'Exactly!'

'Shall we…?'

'No, let's park ourselves here. The best lounge is a bit formal. So, tell me all your news.' Kay dashed round the kitchen banging utensils together. The best lounge, I thought scornfully. It's the only lounge, you fool. Typical Mark, to spawn an affectation like that and inflict it upon his wife, condemning her to sound like a prat every time she said it.

I began to talk about my work. Kay oohed and aahed (especially the latter) at my relatively dull anecdotes involving juicers and microwaves. As I spoke, I noticed that the wall next to me was covered in graffiti, and remembered that Matty and his friends had done the same to our lounge walls when we'd decorated last year, while the plaster was exposed and awaiting its new covering. I began to read the slogans: 'Westlife', 'I hate skool'. Anya. To my surprise, I saw more grown-up handwriting as well. Had the Devines turned defacing the kitchen walls into a family activity? 'The Tories are the cream of Britain: rich, thick and full of clots', somebody – either Mark or Kay – had written. Whichever of them hadn't written that had scrawled, lower down the wall, 'Military intelligence is a contradiction in terms'. An interesting insight into their politics; I had assumed Mark and Kay were Tories. Wrong again.

I was about to ask Kay whether she ever thought about going back to work when I noticed, in black capital letters, the words 'BRENDAN POOEY MONSTER'. I froze, my mouth half-open. Kay said something, but I didn't hear it. Quickly, I scanned the rest of the wall. In blue biro again, further up and to the left: 'Brendan pooey monster'. I felt dizzy as my eyes whizzed from left to right. Cursive writing. Lower case. How many were there? Three, four, five. Six. Seven. The wording exactly the same each time. My heart leaped up to my throat.

'Are you all right?' Kay asked me.

'No. No, I…I'm sorry, I feel a bit ill. I'd better go.' She tried to keep me there, of course, offering first tablets, then her and Mark's bed for a lie-down, but I pushed past her, mumbling apologies.

I phoned John as soon as I got in and asked him to come home from work immediately. He agreed. He has the sort of job he can abandon instantly at any point in the day without anybody noticing or caring; John couldn't stand to do anything that mattered to anybody. The less people focused on him, the happier he was. I said nothing about the nursery bear, its new injuries. I knew he would be scornful.

When he got back, I told him about the writing on the Devines' kitchen wall. I didn't need to explain its significance, and he didn't call me a nutter or bring up the matter of the Devines' non-suicide to damage my credibility. 'Christ!' he said. 'Fuck.'

I had a list of questions prepared. 'Are you sure their dead son was called Brendan?'

'Was that what I said?'

'Yes.'

'Then yes.'

There was a brief silence.

'Could there be an innocent explanation?' I wondered aloud.

'No!' said John. 'What sort of people write nasty things about their dead son or brother on the kitchen wall?'

'Remember that thing Kay said to me, about girls being better, girls being nice and clean?'

John growled. 'What exactly are we saying here?' he asked.

'I don't know!'

'This is grim!'

'So what do we do?' I asked.

'I don't see that we can do anything. Except fucking avoid them like the plague. I don't want our kids having anything to do with theirs.'

'Right.'

'Right!'

For the rest of the afternoon and evening, John and I forced ourselves to sit and do nothing, even though John wanted to ring round estate agents and see how quickly we could move, and I wanted to go back to Mark and Kay's to see if the graffiti was still on the wall, or if Kay had quickly painted over it, hoping I hadn't spotted it and drawn sinister conclusions.

In principle I agreed with John that we should have nothing more to do with our next door neighbours, and I was almost mystified to find myself, the following morning, walking in the direction of the Devines' house, just seconds after John had left for work. I say almost because, deep down, I had a clear motive and aim, though I had deluded nine-tenths of my brain into believing that it was a sort of irresistible natural force that drove me towards Kay's door, pulled my finger towards the bell.

Behind the glass, I saw her running down the hall to let me in. 'Aaaah! Are you feeling better?' she cooed.

'Yes, thanks,' I said. My dread from the previous day had dissipated and I was back, an information-gathering machine. The more you know about anything, the less spooked you feel. I wanted to collect a few facts to keep my fear at bay; this technique had always worked for me in the past. It had something to do with the prosaic nature of facts. A fact was an innately pedestrian item, which was probably why it was always comforting to have the full story, however gruesome.

The Devines' kitchen was still a hard-hat area, the graffiti about Brendan still clearly visible. Had it not occurred to Kay that I might have read it? This struck me as distinctly odd. Whatever her and Mark's crime, whether they had merely hated their son or done something worse, why didn't they care if the neighbours knew? It made no sense.

'John told me about…about Brendan,' I said. 'I'm really sorry.'

Kay turned to face me, her eyes round with surprise. 'Yes,' she said distantly. 'Well, so were we. We were sorry too.'

'How old was he?' I asked.

'Brendan? Only four months.'

Was it my imagination, or was the 'only' said with a dismissive slant? Or was it anger, because Brendan had had so little time? 'How awful. And how…was it…I mean, was he ill, or…?'

Kay frowned and stood up straighter. 'Why do you want to know that?'

I found that I was completely unable to form an opinion about whether her question was a normal, natural one. It depended, I had to suppose, upon whether mine had been normal and/or natural, which I also couldn't judge.

'Kay, you've got "Brendan pooey monster" written all over the wall here,' I said, thinking *John will kill me. He will absolutely kill me.* I do not usually behave in a rash and unwise manner, but I was having trouble keeping my mounting desperation at bay. I felt as if I were travelling towards something, and needed to get there as soon as possible. I had to make things happen, if they didn't happen of their own accord.

Kay's eyes widened. 'You think *I* wrote that? That wasn't me!'

'Who was it, then? Mark? Anya?'

'No! How could you think that? I was a bit upset when I saw it too. It must have been the people who lived here before us. It's not about our Brendan.'

I felt my eyes narrow. 'Really?' I said. 'Well, that's... Isn't that a bit of a strange coincidence?'

'Yes!' said Kay. 'It is! I'm not sure I want you in my house. I think you've got it in for me and my family, that's what I think. First you call the police and say we're dead, then the business with the nursery bear, and now this!'

If she was lying, she had a talent for it. And, looking at her wobbling mouth and moist eyes, I suddenly feared she was telling the truth. 'Look, what was I supposed to think? I mean...'

'I don't care,' said Kay, who had started to cry. 'I just want you to leave. Please.'

I sighed and did as she asked. I phoned John at work and told him what had happened. To my surprise, he didn't berate me for breaking our agreement to avoid the Devines. 'She's lying,' he said. 'And we can easily prove it. We can ring the Dysons.' These were the people who had owned the house before Mark and Kay.

'What if she's telling the truth, but it wasn't the Dysons?' I said. 'It could have been the people before them.'

'Westlife haven't been around for that long,' said John. 'I'm going to phone Greg Dyson now.' He was eager to seize the reins. Things were getting serious.

I sat on the sofa, waiting for him to ring me back, wondering how the children would feel about moving to another street, or another town. Why shouldn't we do it? I worked from home and John could easily manage a slightly longer commute. I had always loved our house – it was a happy, relaxed home that, everyone agreed, had an air of holidays and fun about it – but now I felt as if it had fallen under a shadow.

The phone rang. 'You've really done it this time, you idiot!' John yelled at me.

'What?'

'Kay was telling the truth. I've just spoken to Greg Dyson. Their kids were bullied by a lad called Brendan at their school.'

'But…So they wrote the graffiti?'

'Well…look, I didn't want to interrogate the guy! He sounded quite upset when he said about the bullying.'

'Oh, God!' I should have known, I thought, from the other things that I'd read on the wall, about the Tories and military intelligence. Of course. The Dysons were ardent lefties; we'd always known that about them. They had sometimes had posters up in their window announcing an imminent revolution. They thought that the Labour Party was too right wing. I remembered Greg telling me this at the time of the last general election. He had made a point of voting, instead, for a solitary eccentric in an unravelling jumper whose party had an implausibly long name, 'on principle', he said. 'What principle's that, then?' John had sneered. 'The principle of treating real life as if it's just another jolly evening at the public school debating society? The principle of wasting your vote, instead of actually using it to stop the Tories getting in? Stupid tosser!'

'The Dysons don't know the difference between socialism and imbecility, that's their problem,' I joined in. 'Like, have you noticed, they *will not* send a Christmas card? I mean a proper one, with a Santa or a snowman on or anything. Nothing Christmasy. Instead they send some sort of handwoven picture of some South American peasants...and it's the same with birthdays!'

'That's their stand against the crass commercialism of the card industry!' John laughed. 'It's all part of the struggle. It's sure to bring about global equality!'

As John yelled at me, I remembered this conversation from several years back and felt sad. We used to turn on our acquaintances together. Now John was turning on me. 'You fucking dolt!' he grumbled. 'We'll have to move! I can't face them ever again. We'll have to move *today*. Why couldn't you just keep your mouth shut for once? I can't believe you accused Kay like that. I can't *believe* it!'

I was glad I'd never told him about the nursery bear. I didn't have the energy to defend myself, or to point out that, until he'd spoken to Greg Dyson, John had agreed with me. I was thinking, instead, about Kay's reluctance to tell me how Brendan – *her* Brendan – had died, even before I said anything about the graffiti. I was thinking that I had never seen a smile on Anya's face, or Celia's. 'I'd love to move today,' I told John. 'But we can't, can we?'

'No, we bloody well can't! So you'd better go round and grovel and get her to forgive you!'

'Why? You don't even like them!'

'Because, if you don't, Mark'll come round and stick an axe in my skull! He's exactly the sort of guy who would! Just think of his insistent heartiness, his donkey's bollocks attitude.'

'What about it?'

'Well, it's all a bit...feverish, isn't it? Imagine him putting the same amount of zeal into a grievance...'

'All right, all right!' I shivered. 'I'll go and apologise.'

'Good. And then try not to do any other stupid things before I get home.'

I put the phone down and cried a bit. John's view of me, our relationship, had fallen under the shadow cast by next door and I didn't know what to do about it.

I felt numb as I left the house again and walked up the Devines' drive. Which was lucky, because underneath the numbness lay, I suspected, fury and resentment. I *knew* that I was basically right, yet thanks to the Devines I had been made to feel wrong three times. Right about what, though? What exactly was my contention about them? I still needed to work that out.

This time Kay walked slowly down the hall to open the door. Through the frosted glass panel, I tried to see her hands, to check she wasn't carrying any sort of weapon, but all I could see were two pink blobs. 'I'm here to apologise,' I told her. Mercifully, she was empty-handed. 'I shouldn't have...'.

'I bet you went and phoned the people who used to live here, didn't you?' she demanded.

'I...Yes.' There seemed no point in denying it. You can't lie and apologise at the same time.

Kay's eyes seemed to bulge a little in surprise, but she recovered quickly. 'So you didn't trust me. You had to check out my story.'

I shrugged. 'Look, what can I say apart from I'm sorry? Brendan is an unusual name. It *seemed* too much of a coincidence.'

'Well, coincidences happen, don't they?' Her voice was bitter, the words clipped.

'Kay, I really am truly sorry.' *Please don't get your husband to put an axe in my husband's skull.*

'Fine. Well, let's not discuss it any more. But...Mark thinks it's better if we don't see you.' She looked vaguely guilty and afraid as she said this, as if she expected me to challenge her.

'That's understandable,' I said. Relief seeped into my bones. Maybe we wouldn't have to move after all. Plenty of people had nothing to do with their neighbours. We could be like them. The shadow might lift, disperse. And if nothing *else* happened, if an absence of noteworthy events became the norm...Kay and I exchanged sombre half-smiles full of wisdom and suffering. She closed the door. I imagined she felt shielded by the barrier between us, as I did.

I was about to turn and make my way home when I registered something green on the edge of my vision.

I looked to my left and noticed that the curtains of the Devines' best lounge were not quite pulled shut; there was a multicoloured sliver of space bisecting the beige velvet.

My feet propelled me in the direction of this tantalising gap. I recalled what I had said to John about a room full of sex toys, and wondered if I was about to see something disturbing: chains, vibrators. Not that a vibrator was particularly disturbing, I corrected myself, embarrassed by my own prudishness.

I peered in, cupping my hands over my eyes and against the glass to get a better look. The first thing I saw was the Georgia O'Keeffe print on the wall, *Black Iris*. In a black frame. I began to shake as my eyes completed their inventory of the room: green sofa against the wall under the O'Keeffe, opposite a silver flat-screened television. A red chair and a blue chair. Behind these, a whole wall of shelves. A white rug on the beige carpet. A Kasimir Malevich print, *Red House*, directly above a green-glass-topped Ikea coffee table. Two cacti in clay pots in the corner. Everything was there. Everything.

I was looking at a replica of my own living room.

I gasped and staggered back a few paces. I was too shocked to move effectively in any particular direction and, although I was desperate to be back inside my own house with the front door locked, my legs wouldn't do the necessary work. I closed my eyes and leaned against Kay's wall, breathing and counting as I had in labour. It had helped then.

I heard a noise and jumped. It had come from the window. I turned, but saw only beige fabric against the glass.

Kay must have yanked the curtains properly closed. The idea that she might have seen me, might have worked out what I had seen, got me moving, finally, and I sprinted back home.

When John returned from work that afternoon, I tried to open my mouth to tell him what I had seen, but the words wouldn't come out. 'What's wrong with you?' he demanded angrily. 'Try to be more normal.' He would have said I'd imagined it, just as I had imagined that the Devines were dead in their car. 'Perhaps their lounge is a *bit* like ours and you got carried away. As usual!' That's what he would have said.

But I knew I had seen only what was there. I could prove it. Not factually, which would be the only sort of proof John was interested in. I could prove it psychologically. The green sofa, the red chair and the blue chair had not been identical to ours. Nor had the cacti. The wall of shelves hadn't been stuffed full of books, videos, DVDs and photograph albums, as ours were. They had been empty, totally bare. The carpet was a lighter shade of beige, the rug more cream than white.

Oh, yes, there had been differences. There would have to be, I reasoned. Mark and Kay would not have been able to replicate our lounge with total accuracy, not without asking us where we'd got certain items. And of course that would have given the game away. The things that were easy to come by were exact replicas: the prints (mass-produced, available from any decent art shop catalogue), the television (in every branch of Comet in the country), the stupid Ikea coffee table that had always wobbled because John had assembled it in an impatient mood and thrown half of its components away, claiming they were 'spares'.

That's how I knew I was right. If I had been hallucinating, why wouldn't I have seen our lounge as it is, in every detail? Why would I have seen this subtly altered version?

I tried again to tell John that evening, but as I began to speak he started to check the washing-up I had just done. He found some salmon still stuck to a pan. Then he rearranged all the kitchen cupboards, replacing my haphazard system with a superior one of his own devising. He went to bed at ten, without asking me if I was coming too.

After he was asleep, I drank three glasses of wine and wondered if I should risk talking to anyone else, any of my friends, about what had happened. Would I alienate them as I had alienated John? I could imagine people laughing about the non-suicide and even the nursery bear, but not the Brendan business. I knew I would get nothing but sharp intakes of breath if I confessed fully, and a partial confession would be pointless. And nobody would believe me about the Devines' best lounge.

And even if it's true, so what? They've done up their lounge like yours – what's so terrifying about that? That question was one I couldn't answer – not because I didn't know, but because the knowledge was so instinctive, so deep-rooted, that it would be impossible to explain. Only I will ever know how I felt when I saw that room. I will always know, but I will never be able to paraphrase it, summarise it away.

That night I lay awake in the spare room and began to doubt the very things I had been so positive about earlier. The sofa and chairs *had* been different. And most people have some shelves in their living room, and a television, and plants. If it hadn't been for the two prints…and perhaps I *had* imagined those.

In the morning, I lay in bed in the hope that John would come and find me, but he didn't. I heard him whistling in the bath, signalling his intention to punish me for a while longer. 'Okay, then,' I imagined myself saying to him, next time he deigned to speak to me. 'You tell me: why didn't the Devines paint *over* that graffiti, that coincidental graffiti? How could they live with it in their kitchen, even for a second? And why don't they talk about Brendan more? Most people who lose a child mention them occasionally, as a way of keeping their memory alive.' He would see my point instantly and I would be the one to receive an apology for a change.

Or I could smash the Devines' front window and show him the best lounge. Then he'd see that I wasn't crazy. But the more I considered the options, the more certain I was that I didn't want to say or do anything about the Devines any more. All I wanted was to move house. This was more than an idle wish; I knew that I would have to do it, however upset the children might be at the prospect.

Eventually I got out of bed and began to fold clean, dry clothes into piles: me, John, Matt, Em. Through the open curtains, I saw Celia Devine playing in the garden. She sat cross-legged on the grass. She kept trying to bend the nursery bear in the middle so that it would sit up. It was missing its yellow Moorlands T-shirt, I noticed. Today it was wearing some sort of sleepsuit – blue with little white sheep on it. Anya appeared behind Celia, holding a large, maroon school bag, and leaned against the back wall of the house for a few minutes, watching her sister, not saying anything.

I closed my eyes, pinched the back of my hand hard and looked again. Yes, the scene was exactly as it had been. Still, who could say how long a delusion might last? A ghostly tremor passed through me as I wondered if I had misjudged my own underlying essence all these years. Had I looked at myself in the mirror every morning and seen a rational, sane woman who did not exist?

I was about to retreat when Anya suddenly ran on to the lawn and snatched the bear out of Celia's hands. Celia called out 'Mummy! Mummy!' Anya laid the bear down flat on the grass. I saw its single eye, the black scar on its arm: two things I hadn't imagined. Anya took her school bag and pressed it down on the bear's face, holding it there. I could see the energy vibrating through her body as she pushed and pushed the bag, as if trying to drive it, and the bear underneath it, into the ground.

'Mummy!' Celia wailed. A few seconds later, Kay came outside. She stopped when she saw what Anya was doing. I knew what was going to happen. I actually saw it in my mind, plain as day. This time I knew I *was* hallucinating; I was seeing the very near future, the events that would take place only a few seconds from now, maybe sooner, less than a second. And it unfolded precisely as I had foreseen. Kay didn't hurry over to rescue the bear from

Anya, as Celia had clearly expected and hoped that she would. Instead, her first reaction was to turn and stare at my house. I saw her eyes, nervous and sharp behind the lenses of her glasses, dart from window to window until, finally, they landed upon the small one at the top, and met mine.

The Tub

I AM STANDING in a room that has a low ceiling and smells faintly of stale cigarette smoke and the cage of a rabbit or some other small animal – a guinea pig or a hamster, perhaps, though no such creature is visible in the surrounding greyness. I am standing in the lounge of Edwin Toseland's parents. They don't know I'm here. They are fast asleep in their bed, or so I'm told. When I first walked into the lounge, I trod on something soft that turned out to be a pair of tartan slippers, each one with a thin, crumpled sock inside. It is half past midnight. I am about to spend the night with Edwin Toseland, a man whom I have heard described, diplomatically, as 'not universally liked'.

Sleeping with Edwin will no doubt turn out to be a mistake. Not because he is Edwin (although that feature of the situation is bound not to be without its drawbacks) so much as because he is – to me, at any rate – a symbol.

He is almost more a symbol than a person. One should never copulate with one's symbols. It invariably disrupts their imagery; often they come to signify something far less welcome.

So, a mistake, then. Still, if I know that in advance, perhaps I am armed. And it isn't as if I've never made a mistake before. Mistakes are survivable. Mostly. And it might be comforting to do the wrong thing deliberately, rather than to try to do the right thing, only to have your attempts end in catastrophic failure. In any case, there's no point ruminating on the matter, because the tiny, shadowy, calculating part of me that makes all the decisions without ever consulting my brain is dead set on the plan. Tonight, it tells me, I will sleep with Edwin Toseland.

The hall light illuminates drifting motes of dust in the doorway. The lounge is dark, apart from the computer screen's square of radiant blue, with a column of icons, smaller squares of different colours, arranged down each of its sides. I stick my head round the door. 'Can I check my emails?' I call out as quietly as possible. Edwin is in the kitchen making coffee.

'Sure,' he shouts back. I wonder why he isn't worried about his parents waking up and finding us together. Of course, he's a grown man, and only staying here tonight because his parents are going on holiday tomorrow and he's cat-sitting, but still…for them to discover us would be embarrassing, I would have thought, especially for Edwin. But then he has never given a toss what anybody thinks of him. That is one of the reasons why he is not universally liked.

My mind is not really on my emails, but I need an activity. I don't want Edwin to return and find me standing here, unoccupied. I feel that would give him the advantage, somehow. I do not know him particularly well.

He comes in holding two cups of coffee and puts mine down on the table in front of me. Then he rests his head on my shoulder, not as a gesture of affection but in order to read the message on the screen. It is from my mum, asking if I would like anything special for lunch on Sunday. 'Fascinating!' says Edwin. 'Your mum's obviously a scintillating woman.' I sign out of my Hotmail account and turn to face him, smiling.

Edwin is a small, skinny man with bad posture. His blonde hair is greasy enough to be mistaken for mid-brown. He has high cheekbones, a sharp nose with a bumpy bridge that brings to mind the word 'corrugated', and full, pouting lips. He looks like a cross between a pretty girl and a ferret. The sight of him, dressed in a suit that's made of some sort of furry maroon material, reminds me that I prefer tall, big men. This leads to an area of thought into which I am determined not to stray, and solidifies my resolve to have sex with Edwin. I need a night off from all that. And Edwin is the opposite – physically, symbolically, in every possible respect. He can help me to fend off the feelings that would lay into me if I were alone.

I smile when he insults my mother. I cannot afford for this night to end badly, and it won't, as long as I decide right now that I will accept whatever Edwin says or does.

More than that, I will welcome it. I will make a success of this venture, so that when I look back on tonight it will be as a fond memory.

'I've got something to show you,' says Edwin, taking the mouse from my hand and jabbing me with his elbow. 'Shift!' I allow him to push me off the chair. As he clicks, I stand behind him, sipping my coffee. It's too strong and the rim of the cup is slimy. I rub my lips together and it is as if I am suddenly wearing lip balm. I turn away, pull a tissue out of my handbag and wipe my mouth until it hurts.

Why does Edwin want to sleep with me? I cannot possibly be a symbol for him in the way that he is for me. Nobody's mind works in the same strange way that mine does. When I figured this out, I stopped explaining my behaviour to people. Nobody's understanding is enhanced by an explanation, I realised, unless it is one they themselves might give.

My eyes are beginning to adjust to the darkness. I notice that there are three walking sticks in one corner of the room, leaning against the wall behind the sofa. Two have smooth sides. The other has a rough, gnarled look, rather like an enlarged pretzel.

'Here we are!' says Edwin proudly. The computer screen fills with a picture of a sweaty, naked couple having sex.

'What about it?' I ask, not understanding, wondering if I'm supposed to recognise one of the people.

Edwin tuts. 'It's meant to make you feel horny. Doesn't it?'

'No.'

'Oh. Well, it does me.'

'That's probably because you can see everything the woman has to offer and very little of the man. As with most pornography.' I fall silent, cringing at my own words. I sound like a prig, or a feminist.

'Right. Close your eyes,' says Edwin. 'Avert thy gaze.' I have heard him do this before, call people 'thee' and 'thou', so I don't worry unduly or take it personally. I think he does it so that everybody remembers he works in a library. 'Okay, you can look now. This'll be more up your street.'

I turn to face the computer screen. The big picture of the copulating couple has gone, and in its place are six smaller photographs, laid out neatly in three rows of two. I inspect them carefully, one by one. The first is of an erect penis poking out of a pair of blue checked boxer shorts. The penis itself is orangey-brown, the colour of fake tan. I raise my eyebrows; time to move on, I think. The next photo is much the same, except this time the penis is paler and has one or two pimples around its base. Beside me, Edwin rocks back and forth in his chair, impatient for me to show signs of enthusiasm. 'Well?' he says.

'Er...yeah!' I try to sound appreciative. All the pictures belong to, shall we say, the same genre, though the details vary. One phallus has a peculiarly jaunty-looking head. Another nestles in an absurdly large, purple scrotum. In one photograph, the pubic hair looks tired and colourless, like grass around the central reservation of a motorway.

'What do you reckon?' says Edwin.

'Well…they're a bit gross.' I laugh, to soften my criticism.

'There's no pleasing some people,' he mutters. 'You're not into porn?'

'Er…no, not really. But…I mean, I've got nothing against it.'

'Look, I thought some dirty pictures might help us get in the mood, that's all. Forget it.' He sounds irritated. He switches off the computer with a sudden poke of his finger. The room is even darker now, and I am relieved. Edwin takes his coffee over to the sofa and sits down. 'So. You're not into porn,' he repeats.

'Are you?'

'Yeah. Course. I'm a pervert,' he announces cheerfully. I note his quick recovery from disappointment, his ability to switch back to a good mood as if the bad one never happened, and am pleased, once again, by his oppositeness, his symbolic value. 'All men are.'

'Oh.'

'Why not, anyway?'

'Why aren't I into porn?'

'Yeah. Do you think it's sordid, or something?'

'Erm…' I do, but I don't want to say so in case it damages my credibility. I couldn't stand it if Edwin laughed at me or thought I was silly. I am also aware that it is absurd for me to be worrying about this. After all, Edwin has just, out of the blue, presented to me six photographs of hard, veiny erections, so strictly speaking, and by any objective assessment, I am by far the least ridiculous person in the room. 'I think men tend to be more into pictures than women,' I say. Women prefer to know and, ideally, like the man whose pimply prick they're looking at, I don't add.

'I know lots of women who are into porn,' says Edwin.

'Not me. Sorry.' Things mustn't go wrong. 'But…I don't need anything to get me in the mood, so don't worry. If I wasn't in the mood, I wouldn't be here, would I?'

'Fair enough.' He grins and slurps his coffee.

The truth is, my head is in the mood, and on this occasion I am allowing it to ride roughshod over my body, which is lagging behind by some considerable distance. When I bumped into Edwin in the pub this evening, I was filled not with desire but with a different sort of urgent need.

I was with my two best friends, both of whom are called Susan. Edwin was alone. Drinking on his own on a Friday night. I began to wonder if his unpopularity went further than I'd suspected. Perhaps he wasn't even locally or narrowly liked. I introduced him to Susan and Susan, and, with great energy, he set about ridiculing them for having the same name. When I told him the three of us had just been out for a Chinese meal to celebrate Susan's birthday, he put on a stupid mock-oriental accent and said, 'Sucky fucky Yankee dollar.' He kept saying it.

In the ladies' toilets, where we went at one point to get away from him, I told Susan and Susan that Edwin wasn't racist, but that he did like to annoy people. As the evening progressed, Edwin began to flirt with me more and more, probably because I was the only person at the table who wasn't staring at him as if he were a seeping boil. At one point he said to me, 'I bet you taste nice. I can tell from your colouring. I could go into more detail, but I don't want to embarrass Sue One and Sue Two.' He guffawed at his own joke. 'You know, as in *The Cat in the Hat* – Thing One and Thing Two.'

Edwin invited me back to his parents' house for coffee. Only me, not Susan and Susan. Not that they would have wanted to go. 'I won't bother inviting you two,' he said. 'We aren't exactly hitting it off, are we? And me and Joanna have got a lot of catching up to do, haven't we, Jo? We go back a long way. We have a shared past.' He mimed inverted commas as he said these last two words.

Susan and Susan looked at me as if I too were a pustule. A shared history, their eyes said, with this specimen? I shrugged at them apologetically and went home with Edwin.

I don't know what I'm going to say to them tomorrow. I would have no objection, in theory, to telling the truth, but I know that they would find it implausible. Then, once I had persuaded them to believe me (for why would I pretend to be as reckless and unhinged as I, in fact, am?), I would have to devote almost as much time to comforting them, like children after a night terror, because they would surely be unsettled by their brief foray into my thought process, which, I freely admit, is a strange land by any ordinary person's standards.

Susan and Susan are nice, normal people. I fear that they are friends with me because they believe I am too. I'm very convincing, most of the time. I am usually smart, fragrant and articulate. I am frequently funny. They are entertained by me, which is gratifying. I enjoy their company, and only occasionally come away from our evenings together feeling like a sociopath who has successfully deceived her host group, whom she needs for camouflage purposes.

'Your friends are prudes. Dullards!' Edwin said, on the way back to his parents' house. I smiled and said nothing. He was rude – deliberately, in a premeditated way – and I made a point of not taking offence. I relished the opportunity to embrace his unappealing qualities. It was all symbolic, all meant to be, all totally the opposite of the other business, the one I wasn't thinking about because it was my night off suffering.

And even if I weren't determined to like Edwin, however unlikable he is, I would be forced to acknowledge that his impoliteness is intended at least partly, at least some of the time, to make others laugh. He is one of those people who confuses rudeness with a sense of humour. You hear men in pubs doing it all the time. One says, 'You fucking cunt', and the other laughs uproariously and replies, 'Suck my dick, shithead', and then they both laugh until they cry. I think that is the sort of thing Edwin is aiming for, except he makes two fatal mistakes: he chooses the wrong audience (middle class women instead of working class men) and he sometimes inserts a little too much erudition into his foul-mouthed-thug behaviour. In doing so, he reminds listeners that he is a chartered librarian with several degrees and not at all the sort of man people have in mind when they talk about 'widening participation'. Therefore, everyone imagines, he should know better.

'So, if you aren't into porn, what are you into?' he says now.

I am standing in the middle of the room, sipping my drink like a mayor at a civic function. Edwin hasn't asked me to sit down. It dawns on me that that isn't all he hasn't done. Oh no, I cry inside my head. Things are terribly amiss. Things are going wrong already. He hasn't even kissed me. We are on opposite sides of the room, and he is chairing a panel discussion on my sexual preferences. That's how it feels to me, at any rate. 'What do you mean?' I ask.

He sighs. 'You must be into something.'

'Well...like what?' I have no idea what he expects me to say. Does he want me to name my favourite position, or my preferred type of man? Or would either do?

'I don't know. Oral, anal, girl-on-girl?' he suggests. 'Whips and leather? Something must turn you on!'

I panic. Clearly, a response is required. I wonder if he has asked anybody else the same question. Have other women stood here, exactly where I'm standing now, and, in reply to interrogation by an impatient Edwin, come out with lines such as 'I like to have my breasts stroked' or 'Well, actually, I'm rather partial to having my clitoris rubbed'? I conclude that it is an indication of my sexual unadventurousness that these are the hypothetical answers that spring to mind. Perhaps Edwin is right to be disappointed in me.

More panic. No, he can't be disappointed – that can't happen. It would ruin the oppositeness of everything, if disappointment were to be involved. (On his side, I mean – it's fine for me to be disappointed. Which, as long as Edwin isn't, I won't be. What matters to me is not that I should enjoy this but that he should. I am desperate to make Edwin Toseland happy. I am the only person in the world who is. Mine is, indeed, a minority position.)

'Golden showers, master-slave, swinging, cross-dressing…' Edwin continues to list sexual practices in the hope that I will plump for one of them.

I ransack my mind for something impressive to say, but can think of nothing with enough sparkle or wit. Total honesty is my only option. 'Individual people,' I say eventually.

'Hey?' He looks puzzled.

'I just like to have…well, relatively normal sex, I suppose, with people I fancy. There, will that do?' I cannot help the confrontational edge that creeps into my voice. 'And something I don't like is too much talking, too much analysis. I've always thought that if you're going to talk during sex, it has to be pretty good, exactly right, or it's better to keep quiet.' I regret this as soon as I've said it. I don't want to fight back, I want to please Edwin, and appease him, as a symbol, place offerings at his pointy-booted feet.

To my amazement, he grins. 'That's more like it. That's the Jo I know.'

He is referring to our shared past (mimed inverted commas). The way he said this to Susan and Susan made it sound darkly intriguing, whereas in fact our history, our back-story, such as it is, is rather silly. Four years ago,

Edwin accused me of stealing a book from the library. I had done no such thing, and took exception to being branded a thief on the basis of no evidence. Edwin responded by calling me a 'shrew-bag'. When he found the book in question, he thought it was hilarious, and rang me to tell me. He giggled a lot, didn't apologise, and used the word 'misunderstanding' rather too many times for my liking.

For three years, I ignored Edwin. I made a point of going to the library and cutting him dead whenever I could spare the time. Then, one day last year, as he was stamping my book and we were not speaking to each other as usual, something strange came over me. Edwin was shooting regular hopeful glances at me, as he had taken to doing, and I heard myself say, 'Edwin, this is daft. It was ages ago. Shall we call a truce?'

His smile appeared straight away, as if he'd had it ready and waiting just in case. 'An end to hostilities!' he said. 'Yes, why not? Long as you promise not to purloin any more vols.'

And that was that. Friends. I even laughed at his little joke, irritating though it was. As I left the library that day, I felt a calm, happy feeling spread through my whole being. I had taken something horrible and destructive and extracted an upbeat outcome from it. I was not the stubborn, harsh, unforgiving judge I'd always thought I was; I was a peacemaker. It sounds absurd to say it – which is why I never have, not to anyone – but it was my relationship with Edwin Toseland, its trajectory, that made me think things could improve, wounds and scars could disappear, the world was not necessarily past its peak. Previously, I had been a sort of cheerful cynic, non-chalantly and wittily expecting the worst, and not really caring either.

Every time I saw Edwin after the day we cemented our entente cordiale, I felt a warm glow deep inside me. Redemption suffused me, and my thoughts invariably turned to hope and salvation and mercy and kindness and innocence and essential goodness. I was full to the brim of benevolent abstract nouns, quite the most jolly person in the library. As the only adversary, in my long history of bickering and brawling, with whom I had ever sorted things out, Edwin had come to symbolise the possibility of a better future.

Oddly enough, I wasn't tempted to try to make peace with anyone else I had fought with over the years. That wouldn't have been at all appropriate. The decision was made, in the control room of my being, that Edwin was to be the only one. Of this I was convinced, and my certainty was unflagging. There could be only one Edwin, just as there could be only one God (whether one believed in Him or not).

It's no surprise, really, that when the thing I prized most in my life turned to sludge and slid away greyly, decomposing as it went, Edwin sprang to mind in a consolatory capacity. I started to go to the library more often, to be close to my symbol of redemption, but for the first time it didn't make me feel better. I thought nothing would, because of the severity of the problem. Until this evening in the pub, when he started to flirt with me, and it occurred to me that perhaps what I needed was greater proximity – greater sexual proximity, to be specific – to my salvation icon. I needed more than Edwin's smile and blithely offensive banter over a library book. I felt driven to internalise his essence, which would then cure me from within. This is not, of course, compatible with safe sex, but one has to prioritise.

'You say it's better to keep quiet during sex,' he says now. 'But we're not actually having sex yet, are we?'

'No. Your pedantic questions are holding us up, that's why.'

Edwin squawks with laughter and sounds like a parrot. I am relieved to see that I judged the situation correctly. He prefers it when I give as good as I get. It's that rudeness-as-sense-of-humour thing again, and I am heartened to discover that Edwin does not have a double standard about this; it is not one law for him and another for me. In this respect too, he is the opposite. He sees us as equals. I am pleased and offended.

'I've noticed an interesting thing over the years,' says Edwin. 'All the women I've ever done the deed of darkness with, without exception, have made a hell of a noise. Screaming, moaning, wailing. All faked, of course. Do you think it's true in general that women make more noise in bed than men?'

'Yes,' I say at once. It *is* true, although it has never occurred to me before.

'So what is it with you women, then? Why do you all make such a bloody racket?'

I laugh. I cannot answer, because I am experiencing a moment of pure joy. Everything is totally fine between

Edwin and me, as good as new, couldn't be better. We are sharing new insights. We can say anything to one another.

'What?' he says.

'I was just thinking, it's weird that we fell out and now everything's really good between us. That hardly ever happens, does it? I mean, normally, even after you've patched things up with someone, that's all they ever are – patched. It's almost impossible to be as fallen out as we were, and then make up again so…properly, so that no lasting damage has been done.'

Edwin shrugs. 'I don't know. What's the point in making up if you don't do it properly? I never hold grudges.'

'It's different with members of your immediate family: husbands and wives, parents and children, siblings. But there are very few people you can have a full-scale fight with, knowing everything will definitely be fine again soon.'

'Stop banging on and take your clothes off,' says Edwin. 'Some of us are yearning to ogle thy bod. Come on.' He stands up and taps his hand against his thigh. 'The bedroom's through here.'

I follow him, thinking about what I've just said. I'm right. But why should it be the case? Why shouldn't friends – lovers – be the same as family in this respect? Why is it so hard to put unhappy, troublesome shared experiences behind us, even when all the right words are said, the correct procedure followed? Even after apologies and acceptances of apologies. 'If I knew that…' I whisper to myself.

'Stop mumbling, loon,' says Edwin. We are in a bed-room. The smell of rabbit cage is stronger here. There are two white fitted wardrobes, with pink lines around their edges. They look like wedding cakes stuck to the wall. On a matching white-and-pink bedside table there is a ball of cotton wool, a brown scratched glasses case and a bandage that might be used or unused. 'This is my mum's room,' says Edwin. 'She's had to go in with my dad tonight, because I'm here. His lucky night!' He chuckles.

Somehow, we end up standing on either side of the bed, which slots neatly into the space between the two wardrobes. Everything is covered in white hairs about an inch long: the flowery duvet cover, the pillows, the pink carpet. I remember Edwin mentioning cat-sitting. I haven't seen a cat, but there must be one around some-where. As I arrived, I pulled a similar short white hair out of my mouth, unsure how it got in. I was still only in the porch at that stage.

'Go on,' says Edwin. 'Get undressed.'

He still hasn't kissed me. If my flesh had a mind of its own, I would suspect individual skin cells of trying to slide towards the door, desperate to escape. I feel awk-ward and self-conscious but I do as I am told. Edwin watches carefully. I have no idea whether he approves of my body or not. 'Lie down on the bed,' he says. I obey. It is easier to follow instructions. As long as Edwin is happy, I'm happy. Once I am lying down, Edwin removes his clothes (thank God – that awful furry suit) and climbs on to the bed. I find that his appearance is less disturbing when he is nude. His legs and arms are muscly, tubular.

I am fairly sure that none of the six pictures he showed me earlier was of him, and am relieved that blatant self-promotion is not among his flaws.

He plants his knees on either side of my legs and kneels over me. 'Right!' He rubs his hands together. 'Let's see what turns you on.' I remind myself that this is an important ritual, and try not to think about how ridiculous the scene would appear to an outside observer.

Edwin puts two of his fingers inside me, then three. He then commences an activity which I can only describe as rummaging around. There is a distracted, straining expression on his face, as if he thinks he might have left his car keys somewhere near my cervix. It is so absurd that I cannot even scream or moan convincingly, so I remain silent and just stare at him, bemused. Can he really believe that this is what one is supposed to do?

After a while he gives up rummaging (no car keys – oh well!), extracts his hand, leans back and sighs. 'That didn't seem to be going anywhere,' he says. Then his eyes light up. He bounces off me and lands cross-legged to my right. 'I know,' he says. 'Do you masturbate?'

Marvellous. Absolutely bloody marvellous. If I say no, he will attribute it to spinsterly frigidity. He will begin to wonder if I collect lace doilies. If I say yes, he'll think I'm a sex-crazed nymphomaniac who doesn't get serviced often enough by real men. I opt for what I hope is a compromise answer. 'Sometimes.'

'Go on, then,' he says.

'*What*?' Oh, shit.

'Masturbate.'

'Er…no!' I sit up.

'Why not?'

'Because…Look, no offence, Edwin, but I hardly know you.'

'So?' He smiles at me indulgently, as if he might be thinking that I am charming but difficult. 'All right, you don't have to. Why don't you tell me what your favourite sexual fantasy is and we can act it out, if you want.'

'I *don't* want.' Heat behind my eyelids tells me that I might be about to burst into tears.

'What? What have I said?'

'Nothing, it's just…Look, you're probably going to think I'm a prude, but I don't care! The whole point about masturbation is that you do it *when you're on your own*! And the whole point of sexual fantasies is that they exist in your head *and nowhere else*! If you start trying to act them out it turns into a pantomime. It's ludicrous!'

Edwin looks peeved. 'Okay,' he says. 'I've done my best with you, but…I'm going to have to ask you: what's really going on here?'

'What?' This I was not expecting.

'You're tense as fuck, and you seem determined to… close down all the avenues of possibility. I'm going to have to go to the bog for a sly wank at this rate. What the fuck's the matter with you? Come on, out with it.'

I stand up and dress as quickly as I can, my skin buzzing. Edwin doesn't bother. He puts his hands behind his head and leans back, stretching out like an artist's model. Once I have the protection of clothing, I sit down on the bed beside him. 'I had a…bad experience recently,' I say.

It is true, and I suppose there is no reason why I shouldn't tell Edwin, but I am alarmed by how low I am prepared to sink. Do I really intend to use the most terrible trauma of my life so far (and hopefully ever) as a way of getting Edwin off my case, rather than admit that, even in a brilliant mood and in the best of all possible worlds, I am simply not the sort of person who masturbates in front of live audiences and/or turns my sexual fantasies into am-dram productions?

'What, were you raped or something?' Edwin asks.

'No,' I say crossly. 'Why does it always have to be that?'

'What do you mean?'

'Everyone is always getting raped! Any time someone has some bad event in their past, it always turns out to be rape. It's such a cliché. It's almost like, if you haven't been raped, shut up – you've got nothing to complain about.'

Edwin shakes his head. 'You're a real nut case. You sound as if you're jealous of rape victims.'

'No, but at least their trauma is all in one…register. It's horrible and grim and vile and nothing else. Whereas what happened to me is too ridiculous to be considered properly tragic. Except for me it *is* tragic. And if I tell you, you'd better not laugh.'

'Tell me, tell me!' Edwin rubs his hands together. The prospect of hearing about my misery has cheered him up.

I know I should be offended by his manifest glee, but I'm not. Rather, I am encouraged by his eagerness to hear my story. He wants to join in, which pleases me. The worst thing about suffering is the loneliness of it. Noone ever seems to care enough. 'There was this man. We were…

going out, I suppose, although the relationship hadn't got very far. Everything was fine, better than fine.'

'Was it lurrrve?'

'Yes. On my part, anyway. And he said he loved me too. He was the perfect gentleman. He treated me as if I was some precious, fragile object he was afraid might break...'

Edwin makes a loud noise, an impression of a buzzer. 'Sorry, I'll have to stop you there. Do you mean in bed?'

'Everywhere. He opened doors for me, held my coat out for me – you know like waiters in restaurants do?' Edwin nods, frowning. 'He insisted on paying for everything...and he had a real thing about getting to places before me. So if we were meeting in a pub or a restaurant, he'd always make sure to be there half an hour early. I asked him about it once and he said he'd never leave a woman waiting on her own...'

'...in a rough den of iniquity like a pub!' Edwin rolls his eyes. 'The guy sounds like a twat.'

'What?' I'm puzzled. 'No, this is the good bit. This bit I'm talking about now, that was when everything was fine. Everything was brilliant.'

'No it wasn't. Why did he think you couldn't put your coat on, or sit in a pub on your own? You're not some ethereal waif. You're an opinionated, loud-mouthed ball-breaker.'

'Great. Thanks,' I say crossly. I do not want to be that, if I am. There is a love story in my head, albeit a desolate one. But its protagonists are not a loud-mouthed ball-breaker and a twat.

I doubt Edwin has been properly in love. I can tell, from his willingness to draw attention to himself. He is one of the breezy untouched. He is not like those of us who walk around with targets on our chests, desperately trying to cover them up, living in fear of the arrow. No, Edwin has no idea how it feels to meet someone and feel that instant tug, that flash of connection as you stare at what you suddenly realise is your idea of physical perfection.

Objectively there is no such thing as physical perfection, of course, but each of us has our own private definition. And when we meet it in human form we are unrescuable. A previously strong, secure person can be ruined by nothing but a face, or a body.

Not me, though. It was more than the right face that did for me (though the face *was* right – that square smile, those teeth one could easily imagine tearing into a hunk of flesh in the jungle, even when the attached body was wearing a suit, sitting in a Michelin-starred restaurant). It was the wooing, the well-organised chasing, the launching of what could only be called a campaign to win me over, one that spanned nearly a whole year and involved meals out that cost four hundred pounds and a necklace and earrings that cost even more than that. I wasn't used to it or prepared for it. It isn't the sort of thing that happens to women like me in the normal run of things. It might happen to ethereal waifs rather more often.

'Tell me about in bed, then,' says Edwin. 'Go on. Was he a missionary man?'

'Yeah. It was a bit odd, actually. I think he tried to be gentle with me, but…he was a bit *too* gentle. I mean, his kisses always started off light and sort of…stayed light. It was like having your mouth stroked by butterfly wings. There was never any sense of things accelerating or…becoming more urgent. He certainly never allowed himself to get carried away. It was like he was thinking, *Right, I'll do this now, I'll do that now.* And the way he touched me…his touch was so careful and almost weight-less, almost imperceptible. It didn't seem at all spontane-ous. You know those bits in films where Bruce Willis or someone is trying to defuse a bomb, and there are lots of different-coloured wires and he has to handle them *so* del-icately or the whole place will blow up? It was like that. But the funny thing was, he kept saying, "I feel as if I'm being too rough with you." I kept telling him he wasn't, but pri-vately I was thinking *What? How can you possibly feel as if you're being rough when you're barely allowing your fingers to brush against me?* I mean, did he think I was made of eggshells or something?' It is a relief to let all this pour out, finally. I haven't even told Susan and Susan, but I can tell Edwin and it won't matter, because he's only Edwin.

He groans, and covers his face with his hands. 'Don't tell me – you thought he was loving and sensitive.'

'Yeah, I did. I was quite…touched, I suppose, even though physically his moves were much too tentative to have any real impact. But noone had ever treated me like a delicate flower before.'

'Of course not, because you're a harridan! You're a shrew-bag.'

I feel it would be demeaning to point out to Edwin that ,even though I am opinionated, I still crave romance. I am still keen for men to be willing to sacrifice everything for me. I can't tell him this, though, or about the compliments: my clear eyes, my smooth skin, my hands. There is absolutely nothing beautiful or remarkable about my hands, yet even they attracted lavish praise.

'The guy sounds fucked in the head to me. He likes his women nice and helpless. He's a wife-beater waiting to happen.'

'Why do you say that?' There is, perhaps, more to Edwin Toseland than I realised. If only his mother's bedroom were not so hairy and didn't smell of a hamster's toilet.

'The fairer sex are a fucking nightmare – any sensible bloke knows that. Only the screw-ups who can't handle reality put women on pedestals as the embodiment of purity and innocence, or some such shite. Show a man like that a real woman and he turns into a frothing-at-the-mouth psycho. Oooh – is that what happened?' Edwin leans towards me, eager for the rest of the story.

'He is married,' I say, though I decided a few moments ago not to mention this.

'So you were a mistress. Goody! Well, go on, tell me. I've often wondered.'

'What?'

'Do wife-beaters beat their mistresses as well?'

'I don't know that he *is* a wife-beater. I hope he is.' To admit this is liberating. I would never say it to anybody else, but Edwin, being himself, is in no position to disapprove. I feel quite safe.

'Because then you'd be able to label him a grade A shitbird. Nothing that went wrong would be your fault,' says Edwin.

'Yes!' I am amazed that he understands.

'And never mind his poor missus, being beaten to a pulp every day of her life.'

'No. Never mind her.' We grin at one another.

'So what happened, for fuck's sake?'

'It was his birthday. I couldn't bear the thought of not getting him a present, even though I thought he might be annoyed if I sent one to his house, so in the end I decided to send it to his work.'

'What does Dickhead do?'

'He's a fireman.' But he is also writing a book about the history of the village where he grew up. And I've seen him in uniform, and with a pen in his hand, frowning, leaning over his notebook. And his voice is both hard and soft in a way that's impossible to describe. I hate the idea of trying to sum up why I was so drawn to him, but I try nonetheless, and suspect that the answer lies in the precise ratio of sensitivity to toughness.

'Fireman! The sort of job you choose if you're worried about the size of your dick. Or if you're gay and don't want to admit it.'

'Why are you so against him?' I ask. 'I mean, you keep saying he's a psycho and a dickhead and a wife-beater, but you don't even know what happened yet.'

'I know he's fucked you over. I'm just waiting to hear the details. Well?'

I sigh. 'We once had this conversation about baths. I said I'd never dream of having a bath in just water. I always put oil or bubbles or something in, something smelly...'

'Of course! Plain water! Pah!'

'He said he never put anything in the bath. He said he didn't know they did bubble bath and stuff like that for men. So for his birthday I sent him – I sent it to the fire station – what I thought was a nice bottle of bubble bath for men. I mean, it looked all masculine, the bottle was kind of dark and the letters on the label were in a sort of macho font. I made sure it wasn't at all girly.' Edwin is shaking his head despondently. 'It was from that range "The Tub". Do you know it?'

'Yeah. I might even have some. I have, in fact. At home.'

Rabbit cage flavour, I think to myself. I stop, to check that I feel reasonably all right. I do. I have succeeded in telling the story, so far, without feeling it, without reliving it. The crucial thing is not to picture the scene: me strolling along the aisle in Sainsbury's, picking up bottle after bottle, unscrewing cap after cap, comparing scent with scent. I was so determined to choose the perfect one. I considered smell, packaging, cream versus foam versus oil, suitability for his skin type (rough, dry). I consulted the shop assistants, and gossiped with them too, telling them the present was for someone special. I cannot stand to look back and see the old me, the innocent, hopeful Joanna, dawdling between the counters, not knowing what is about to happen to her.

I take a deep breath. 'A couple of days later, there's a ring at the doorbell. I go and answer it, and it's him. I smile, but he looks *awful*, his eyes are sort of dead. And he says nothing; he just slaps me across the face really hard and walks away.'

'Aha!'

There is a detail I cannot bring myself to tell Edwin. Before he turned and left, he stood still for a few seconds and watched me stagger backwards, clutching the side of my face. I steadied myself and was about to speak, and it was then that he turned and marched away, his hands in his pockets. He waited and watched deliberately, to check that he had hurt me enough, as much as he'd hoped to.

'I spent the next couple of days frantically trying to get in touch with him...'

'Why wouldn't you?' says Edwin. 'You bought him a thoughtful gift, he slapped you across the face – of course, you'd be keen to track him down.'

'I never got to speak to him,' I say sadly. 'He was determined to avoid me, and he succeeded.'

'But you couldn't stand to do nothing. That's your Achilles heel. You steam in and fuck things up even more. I'm the same.'

'I couldn't bear not understanding what had made him turn on me. I had to know. So I rang his best friend Dan, who'd introduced us in the first place. Dan's a colleague of mine at the lab. It was at his party...Anyway, he wouldn't talk to me at first, but I kept on at him and...well, I found out. And it was so ridiculous, I could hardly believe it.'

'What?'

'He thought I was taking the piss out of him for being fat.'

'Hey?'

'Because the bath oil said "The Tub" on it. You know, like, tubby. He thought I'd chosen it because I thought he was fat. But he wasn't, he isn't. He's got a bit of a beer belly, I suppose, but nothing serious. I never thought of him as fat; it just never crossed my mind. But when Dan told me, I remembered all the times he'd described himself as "lardy" and out of shape. Obviously he had more of a hang-up about it than I realised.'

Edwin scratches his testicles. 'The guy's a fucking freakshow.'

'I thought he was the love of my life. I still think he might be.'

'He isn't. Trust me, you're not that pathetic. He's made you pathetic, temporarily. You'll snap out of it.'

'I know it sounds wet and ridiculous, but I felt as if we were destined to be together, like Heathcliff and Cathy or something.' My one true love, my other half. A symbol, a bad idea. But nobody else has ever pursued me so determinedly. Noone will again. I took the highest opinion of me on record and dragged it down as low as it would go. I must be the worst kind of vandal. Edwin looks unconvinced. 'Heathcliff had a bad temper too,' I add defensively. 'He hanged kittens.'

Edwin, who I know believes *Wuthering Heights* to be overrated because of its reliance, for narrative purposes, on bad weather conditions, says, 'Jo, this guy isn't "the rocks beneath". He's just a twat.'

'You're probably right.' I take a deep breath. 'Anyway, once I knew the truth, I was a total wreck. I couldn't stand the thought that I'd hurt him when it was the last thing I wanted to do. I *loved* him.' The worst kind of pain is to know that you've hurt someone you love. It can never be undone, which makes you all the more desperate to try. You would give anything to have been hurt, rather than to have done the hurting. 'I wrote him a long letter explaining that I only wanted to buy him something really nice, and I honestly didn't mean any harm.'

'And did the fuckwit reply?'

This is hard. It's like sticking a needle into a scab and making it bleed. 'Well...this is, in a way, the most awful part. A few days later, he sent back the bubble bath, with a note that said, "If you kept the receipt, you might be able to get your money back".' I say this casually, as if it is just any old phrase. Edwin cannot know that these fourteen words dominate my waking life, that often I also dream about them. Fourteen utterly mundane yet impossibly mysterious words, stuck in my mind like stringy meat between teeth, impossible to dislodge.

'That's it? That's all it said?'

'Yup. And I've been in fucking torment ever since.'

'*Why*? I don't understand why you didn't just tell The Tub to stick it up his big, hairy arse. Anyone who reacts like that to being given some bath oil is too neurotic to live.'

One hears about epiphanies from time to time, but I have never had one before. I feel the clouds that have covered my heart for the past six months begin to disperse. Only slightly – I am still basically a soul in agony, condemned to suffer for ever, deprived for all eternity of the forgiveness of my one true love – but still, even a minor interval between bouts of anguish is welcome. And Edwin has created such an interval, by nicknaming my tormentor 'The Tub'. In doing so, he is making light of the situation, as well as, in some strange way, claiming it as his own, taking some of the burden off my back. He wants to turn the source of my misery into a shared joke.

I want to let him. I wonder if I can let the nickname stand, or if the ceiling will fall in or I'll be struck down by lightning if I do. I decide to risk it. 'I'm worried about myself,' I tell Edwin. 'You know I'm not usually a victim or a wimp, and I know, rationally, that The Tub's treated me appallingly. But I still love him, and that scares me. I don't think there's anything he could do to me that'd make me stop loving him. And that's worrying.'

'Beat you up, put you in hospital?'

'No, I'd still love him.'

'What if he raped you?'

'He couldn't. I would always sleep with him willingly.'

'Killed your mum and dad?'

'At least it'd prove he was bothered about me.' What am I saying? I don't mean it. I don't want him to kill my parents. I want the proof that he's bothered, minus the killing.

Edwin laughs. 'Forget him. He's a neurotic nincompoop. People should use the word "nincompoop" more often, don't you think? Look, clearly no sex is going to be had here tonight, so shall we go for a curry or something? I'm starving.'

'Okay. But...what about that note he sent me: "If you kept the receipt, you might be able to get your money back"?' Again I say the line that has flashed across the screen of my brain several hundred times a day ever since I read it. I am obsessed. I say the words to myself over and over again, unable to reach a conclusion, picking away at what I know in order to discover what I don't know, what I probably can never know. 'What do you think he meant by that? Was it an attempt to re-establish contact without losing too much face? Or was it an aggressive move, trying to hurt me by sending back my present? Sometimes I think he must have hoped I'd respond somehow, try to get in touch again. Maybe write back and apologise just once more, so that he could forgive me without feeling it was a climb-down. Because, let's face it, if he wanted nothing more to do with me, it would have been easier for him not to write at all.'

'Who cares?' says Edwin cheerfully. He is dressing. On with the maroon furry suit, no underpants. On with the pointy boots. I wish he would keep still and look at me, listen more carefully. He might miss something: a clue, a nuance.

A few minutes later we are strolling across cobbles towards a dingy Indian restaurant with a grubby purple sign outside it. I am no longer concentrating on our physical movements, so am unsure how we got to this dark road that is almost an alleyway.

I shout after Edwin as we go through the restaurant door, 'I've thought of writing to him and saying, "I need to speak to you." He'd have to say yes, wouldn't he? What if I had herpes and needed to tell him? That's bound to be the sort of thing he'd think of first. But there's always the chance he'd say no, and I'd never get to say what I need to say to him. So maybe I should write to him and say what I'd say if we met, and then at least I'd know he'd heard it.'

I have to pause as a waiter shows us to a table, takes our coats, hands us a menu each. It is torture, and I want to scream a torrent of hysterical abuse at him, for making me stop at such a pivotal point in my examination of the options. As soon as I can, I begin again. 'If I thought he wanted me to get in touch I would, of course I would, but I can't risk it. Because if him sending back the bubble bath was an act of aggression, a missile thrown into enemy territory, he'll be pissed off if I write to him. And then he might do something that'll hurt me even more and I can't risk that. As it is, he's nearly finished me off. I can't take any more.'

'Then don't. Shall we have popadoms or just a main course?'

'But what if my cowardice is the only thing standing in the way of some sort of resolution? If only I could know if he wanted a resolution or not. I can't even bring myself to ask Dan about it any more. I'm so afraid of hearing something that'd do even more damage to my psyche. Like that he's told Dan he hates me and was totally wrong about me. That's what I really don't want to hear.'

Edwin sighs. 'So what do you want, weirdy?'

'I just want to clear my name. I want an official pardon. I want him to know, and tell me, that I did nothing wrong.' And for him to love me again, and to die of pain whenever he thinks about the pain he's caused me, to burn for ever with regret. One of us has to, and I'd rather it were him. 'The thing is, if I wrote him a letter, what I wrote would inevitably be a defence. And in an odd sort of way, defending yourself only makes people keener to attack you. Whereas if you say nothing, they are more likely to come up with a defence of you all on their own. And if it comes from them, they won't resist it as much as they would if it came from you. Do you see what I mean?'

'Do you think they'll bring popadoms automatically?' says Edwin. 'I prefer it when they do, without you having to order them.'

I want to see Edwin again after tonight. I'd quite like to see him tomorrow night. I will have to come up with some sort of incentive. Perhaps I will need to masturbate in front of him after all. Talking to him is doing me good. I can feel some of the poison beginning to drain from my system as I talk. 'The awful thing is, you start to doubt your own behaviour. I've asked myself over and over again: what if he was right? What if, subconsciously, I did choose that bath oil because I saw the word 'tub' and associated it with him because he's…well, not thin. I mean, I didn't choose Radox, did I? I didn't choose Dove. Maybe I am guilty.'

'Oh, bollocks! Jo, put your menu down,' says Edwin. 'If the waiter sees you holding it, he'll think we aren't ready to order, and I'm fucking starving.'

'And the absolute worst thing is that, even though I know I'm not going to do anything, I can't allow myself to decide, officially, to do nothing, and then let it go. I keep having to go over and over the decision-making process, considering all the alternatives – I'm talking maybe twelve times a day, and it takes at least an hour each time – and I always arrive at the same conclusion. Which is that I'm trapped in this…inactivity.'

Our waiter brings us a basket full of popadoms and some small silver pots of various chutneys on a silver tray. This time I do not bother to wait until he's gone. I talk loudly over his attempts to take our order. 'I have to know, you see. I have to know if he'll *ever* forgive me, ever regret losing me enough to contact me. If he never does…well, then, I guess I'll know he isn't my one true love. That's the only thing that can prove it to me. And if I contact him, I'll never know what he would have done if I hadn't, will I? So I never can.'

'Forget The Tub,' says Edwin, through a mouthful of popadom and pickle. The waiter has gone. 'He's already forgotten you.'

'But what do you think was in his mind when he wrote that note?' I ask. It doesn't matter that I am obsessed, boring, trapped in a vice, screwed up beyond belief. I am with Edwin Toseland, who would have a cheek expecting better from me. 'What do you think he meant?' I demand. 'Was he being genuine or sarcastic? Was he paving the way for reconciliation, or was he having one last twist of the knife?' I ask the question over and over again, altering the wording slightly each time.

Herod's Valentines

'ADULTERERS FALL INTO two categories,' said Flora Gustavina. 'Those who have a talent for making more than one person happy, and those who have a talent for making more than one person miserable.'

'That's nonsense,' said Erica Crossland. 'There must be some who make their wives miserable and their mistresses happy. Or their wives happy and their mistresses miserable.' She spoke quickly. Through the window she could see TP, Flora's gardener, sitting cross-legged on the lawn, his large hands wrapped round a mug of Flora's milky hot chocolate. As soon as he'd finished, he would unfold his lanky body and lollop to the back door to ask for more. If he perched on the counter while Flora made it, he would be there for hours.

Erica dreaded the possibility of TP coming in and perching. It had happened before, several times. His knobbly knuckles repelled her; they stuck out, as if each of his fingers had swallowed a marble. She didn't like his dragging walk, or that he took Flora's money and never did anything to the grass apart from sit on it. Erica wanted to talk to Flora about money today, but she didn't want to cut short the conversation about adulterers. Like much of what Flora said, Erica thought it might turn out to be important, though she was not sure how. Nor was she convinced that she was the sort of person who would benefit from hearing important things.

Flora's house made Erica nervous. Other people were always appearing, interrupting. Frank, Flora's husband, was one culprit. TP was another. And sometimes there was Vesna the cleaner, Paul the financial adviser, Vicky the personal trainer, Craig the mechanic.

Flora didn't seem to mind them. She was the only interesting person Erica had ever known who was interested in boring people. She encouraged them all to speak. Erica listened with gritted teeth as they lumbered through their pedestrian anecdotes. And then she had to go. There was never enough time for Erica to listen to Flora, or for Flora to listen to Erica.

'Mistresses and wives?' Flora frowned. 'Spouses and lovers, please. No need to be sexist about it. Hmph. One would certainly expect there to be a third category – the postive-negative adulterer. But, actually, I'm not sure. I think they – we, rather – are all either double positives or double negatives.' She spoke as if she expected Erica to take notes.

Erica didn't need to; she had a good memory. The two women sat in the lounge part of Flora's kitchen. All the rooms in the Gustavinas' house had bits of other rooms in them, as if to convey the message that one might wish to do anything anywhere, and what would be wrong with that? So, the lounge had a bar and a large, curvacious, pistachio-coloured fridge at one end, the kitchen and bathrooms all had sofas in them that were more comfortable than the one in Erica's living room, her only one. The study contained two single beds, and there were desks, filing cabinets and bookshelves in many of the bedrooms.

When Erica stayed the night, as she often did, she slept in the easel room, so called because a large easel with a blank sheet of vellum attached to it stood in the centre of the carpet, with a box of watercolour paints and a brush on a table nearby. On her first overnight visit, Frank had noticed Erica's puzzled expression as he dropped her suitcase on the bed. 'Oh, didn't Flora tell you? This is Van Gogh's room. It's only avaible tonight because he's away.' Frank's demeanour was solemn. 'Gauguin's stag weekend.' He nodded, as if confirming the details to himself. 'They've gone to a rave in Milton Keynes.' There was a short, awkward pause. Then he bellowed 'No, not really!', making Erica jump, and hunched over, puffing out his chug-chug laugh.

Erica had stayed in Van Gogh's room many times since. She liked the easel and paints, at the same time as believing their presence to be almost daringly pretentious in a home where noone was an artist. If it was possible to be too fond of a house, then Erica was too fond of the Gustavinas'. She loved the stained-glass windows depicting rings within rings of multicoloured turtles (Flora had

had them specially made and installed by a friend of hers), the elongated, light, cluttered rooms (Flora had knocked down walls like dominoes on the ground and first floors), the spiral, see-through staircase that fell through the centre of the house ('I got rid of the boring stairs,' said Flora), the single, fat, cylindrical gatepost with its enormous round head that looked like a little man standing guard outside.

'You see, adultery isn't about the characters of one's wife and mistress, one's husband and lover,' Flora said now. 'The specifics of those people are almost completely irrelevant to the adulterer.'

'That sounds unlikely,' said Erica.

'I know. But think about it. Not everyone who's unhappy with their spouse has a fling, do they?'

Erica found herself unable to disagree with this.

'Exactly. And some people are perfectly content at home – like me – yet still have the odd…liaison. Because adultery isn't about dissatisfaction with one's partner. It's about appetites. Take you.' Flora was for ever taking Erica, in her speeches. 'You'd probably never be unfaithful.'

'How do you know?' asked Erica, who had nobody to be unfaithful to, or with. Nevertheless, she might be unfaithful. She liked to think she would. Erica couldn't rid herself of the conviction that, if she spent enough time with Flora, something would happen. She didn't know what; it was partly the suspense that kept her at Flora's side.

'The chocolates.' Flora nodded at the empty Guylian box on the table. 'All gone, and you only had one. I ate all the rest. And so far this morning I've had three lattes. You've had one cup of camomile tea. You're a person of small appetites.'

She made camomile tea sound like a puritan's soul-improving broth. For Erica it was a treat, one she only had when she came to the Gustavinas'. At home she drank instant coffee, the local supermarket's economy brand.

'I smoke,' Erica reminded her. Flora allowed her to smoke in the house when TP was in the garden. Flora found Erica's aversion to TP amusing.

'Yes. That's why we get on so well. You've got that little touch of transgression about you, just enough to make us compatible.'

'Smoking isn't transgressive,' said Erica. 'My parents both smoke and they're churchgoers.'

'It's different. They're old. For people of our age, smoking's a real no-no, and it's getting worse.' Erica was forty-nine. Flora was thirty-one, but assumed that Erica, as her friend, was the same age as her. They'd met at a yoga class, which was supposed to be the first of eight, but neither of them went back – Flora, because there turned out to be no men there, and Erica, because she couldn't afford it. 'Actually, even as a smoker you've not got much of an appetite. If I smoked I'd be on sixty a day. And that's the thing about adulterers – they inhabit the realm of excess. They're sensation-seekers, thrill-chasers on a grand scale. An ordinary amount of anything – but in this case, of romantic and sexual experience – isn't enough for them. For us, I mean. We have all this spare energy, all this extra capacity that we have to use or we feel empty and wasted. An adulterer without an affair on the go – like me now, for example – feels like a gorgeous extra-large Ivan Grundahl jumper with only a size eight anorexic inside it. Do you see what I mean?'

Erica did. It was easy to see what Flora meant. She always provided lots of illustrations of whatever point she happened to be making; a sensible practice if one is more imaginative than one's audience. Flora was not more imaginative than Erica, but she assumed she was. Coloured sunlight fell in beams around the two women – blue, pink, green, yellow – filtered through the plump bodies of the stained-glass turtles.

'So,' Flora went on, 'add to that the idea that each of us has, essentially, either an enhancing or a detracting force about us – and my point is proved. You're either the sort of person who brings joy, or you're the sort who brings misery. You don't vary your effect from person to person. An adulterer is someone who's attached but has joy-making energy or misery-making energy to spare, that's my point.'

'That can't be right,' said Erica. Flora giggled, wide-eyed. She often laughed when Erica disagreed with her, not sneerily, but with a sort of astonished admiration. Erica had noticed this, and tried to contradict Flora whenever she could. 'What about someone who has an enhancing force, or could have, but they're just in a bad relationship at the moment, so they're miserable, and they make their husband or wife miserable? And then they meet the right person, and suddenly they're happy and they make their new partner happy too. That must happen all the time.'

'Those people aren't who I mean when I say adulterers. I'm talking about habitual adulterers. Those for whom adultery is a hobby, like golf. Or an addiction. For them, it's not about a one-off transition from despair to fulfilment. No, they're quite content with their emotional landscape, whether it's a constructive or a destructive one. They just want a bigger portion, second helpings. And that initial heady rush, the massive novelty buzz of making someone happy or unhappy for the first time. Why do you think so many adulterers are fat?'

'I'm sure I could name some thin adulterers.'

'Fast metabolisms,' said Flora.

Erica saw TP spring up from the grass. He adjusted his pony-tail, fiddling with the blue elastic band that held it in place. He looked as if he might be about to come inside. Fearing her time would soon be up, Erica launched in. 'Flora, we still haven't talked about the work you want me to do.'

'Oh, yes! That.' She still sounded enthusiastic about it.

Erica was relieved. 'What exactly…?' But she got no further with her question. Frank Gustavina appeared in the doorway with a half-eaten pear in one hand and his briefcase in the other. 'Hi, Flor. Hi, Erica,' he said with a full mouth, his right cheek bulging.

Erica turned her grimace into a half-smile. Damn, damn, bugger, she thought. She could hardly bear to wait until next time to find out what Flora wanted her to do, to ask about the money. And Flora wouldn't say anything else about adultery now that Frank was home. Frank knew nothing of his wife's affairs.

'I might as well go,' said Erica.

'Darling, you're home early,' said Flora.

'I got run over at lunchtime,' said Frank. 'Big white lorry. Saw me in the road and just ploughed straight into me. I've felt a bit dizzy ever since, so I thought I'd better come home and see if I can get an appointment with the doctor.' He continued to munch on his pear as he wandered over to the fridge. 'No, not really! I just got bored, so I called it a day.'

Flora giggled. Frank opened a beer, raised it. 'Cheers!' he said. 'I'll leave you ladies to talk about Princess Diana's eyebrows, or whatever it is you talk about.'

'Oh, it's that,' said Flora, winking at Erica. 'See you later, darling.' The two women listened to his feet as they clattered up the transparent stairs. 'I'm worried about Frank, actually,' said Flora. 'I think he's feeling a bit insecure. He craves external validation. He was too successful too soon, and you know what it's like – the maintenance of success begins to feel like failure. Plus everyone assumes he knows how successful he is, so noone tells him.'

'Oh?' said Erica, wondering if it was worth raising the issue of the work again. TP was leaning against the shed, closer to the house, but, for the time being, not moving.

'He's started doing that awful mock-modesty thing.'

'What's that?' Erica wasn't interested in Frank's possible insecurity – he seemed fine to her – but she wanted to know what the awful mock-modesty thing was, to check it wasn't something she also did.

'Oh, you know. If Steven Spielberg did it, he'd say, "I made a film in the seventies, about a shark that ate people. It was called *Jaws*, and…." Etcetera, etcetera. And then the person he's talking to butts in and goes, "*Jaws*! Don't be ridiculous, I've heard of *Jaws*, it's a world famous movie!" And Spielberg gets to look all surprised. He says "Oh, really? Oh, how kind of you to say so." He gets the reassurance he was seeking that his film's as famous as he hopes it is, and at the same time he knows the other person's going to think Gosh, that Steven Speilberg's a really modest guy. *He didn't even assume I'd heard of Jaws.*'

'Right,' said Erica. She was fairly certain she didn't do the mock-modesty thing. She had no achievements that she could pretend she didn't assume people ought to have heard of.

'Until a few moths ago, when people asked Frank what he did, he used to say, "I'm Frank Gustavina." Now he says "I run a business, an estate agent's." And then, when people drag it out of him, and go, "Oh, wow! Frank Gustavina! I've seen your signs outside loads of houses!" he feigns pleasure and surprise – and it's boosted egos all round.'

TP knocked at the back door, making a plop-plop sound, as if his knuckles couldn't quite get it together to land on the wood at the same time. 'Give him a chance,' Flora whispered, getting up to let him in. She wore a square-necked jumper which, Erica noticed, appeared to be green from a distance, but when you looked closely you could see that it had bits of brown, yellow, orange, grey and mauve in it.

'Throat Pastille!' Flora exclaimed. 'Come in and talk to us.'

'All right.' It wasn't clear whether this was a greeting or an expression of agreement. TP slouched into the kitchen. He wore his usual outfit: skin-tight black jeans, a grey sweatshirt, grey fingerless gloves, a puffy blue waistcoat that reminded Erica of an inflatable bed, muddy white trainers. 'Well, I think the new version's finally finished,' he said.

'That's brilliant,' said Flora. 'Come on, then. Let's hear it.'

FLORA DID NO work. She had never done any, thanks to, first, rich parents and, second, a rich husband. 'It would cost Frank money if I worked,' she often told Erica. 'I'd need lots of suits, and then there would be the taxis there and back and the lunches. You can't get through a whole day on a home-made sandwich, can you? It would be too depressing. You'd really need to go to a nice restaurant at lunchtime, to make working in, say, an office bearable. A different restaurant every day, or you'd get into a rut. You know, sometimes when I go to London on the train, I see people getting out horrid little puckered brown rolls, tiny ones – they look like shrivelled conkers. And they've been sliced in half and some runny white gunk has been spread in the middle. They're always wrapped in clingfilm, that's what I can't fathom. Somebody prizes the withered brown lump highly enough to wrap it in clingfilm!'

'I never used to have lunch, when I was working at Muzorsgy's,' said Erica. 'I'd just work straight through.'

'That's you, though. You're sensible with money. But, for most people, working is a false economy.'

Frank Gustavina also had rich parents, who were friends of Flora's parents. That was how Frank and Flora met. Frank's parents gave him the money to start his business, but it was Frank who had made it profitable. 'I've worked for everything I've got, apart from what I've been given,' Frank once told Erica. Flora had guffawed, as if it were a hilarious joke. 'It's true!' said Frank indignantly.

Muzorsgy's, the health food shop where Erica had worked since she left university, had closed down six months ago. All the staff were made redundant. 'You're better off out of it,' Flora told Erica. 'Jobs in health food shops are the Jeffrey Archers of the employment world.'

'What do you mean?' Erica had asked eagerly. It sounded as if Flora might be able to make her feel better about having nothing to do with her days.

'They're dishonest. Though poor Jeffrey Archer, why shouldn't he lie about sleeping with a prostitute and dodgy bribes and stuff? Anyone would. Anyone who says they wouldn't is a hypocrite. Either that or lacking in self-knowledge.'

'Why are jobs in health food shops dishonest?' Erica persisted.

'Jobs are bad for you. Healthy food's good for you. The latter fact is intended to distract the employee from the former. You're supposed to think "Oh, wow, this must be so great for me. I'm surrounded by bottles of ginseng and evening primrose oil; I must be getting healthier every day."'

Erica laughed. She had thought exactly that. Flora was so right.

'You can work with me instead,' she'd said. With me, not for me. Flora did not think of Erica in the way that she thought of TP, Vesna the cleaner, Paul the financial adviser, Vicky the personal trainer or Craig the mechanic. Erica was a 'with', not a 'for'. Yet Flora did nothing, no work to speak of. Erica had been trying to get to the bottom of this for some time.

TP called working for the Gustavinas his 'day job'. His vocation was performance poetry. His stage name was 'The Throat Parrot', though Flora nicknamed him 'TP', and 'Throat Pastille'. 'He lets me,' said Flora. 'He wouldn't let anyone else.'

'What's his real name?' Erica had asked, when she first saw his stooping form in Flora's garden.

'I don't know,' said Flora. 'Everyone calls him 'The Throat Parrot'. I think he wants to make a complete break with his old identity.' Erica found it hard to imagine a previous incarnation that was worse than his present one. What could it have been?

TP had done several gigs, unpaid, in local youth clubs and libraries. For six months he was poet in residence at the head office of Frank Gustavina's estate agency. Flora laughed whenever Erica denigrated him, but she also frequently came out with some version of the following: 'Van Gogh led a miserable, poverty-stricken life, you know. He lived and died totally without recognition. People mocked him and thought he was a loser. Except his brother, Theo. He always had faith in... Van Gogh.'

Erica suspected Flora didn't know his first name. Both the Gustavinas appeared to have a Van Gogh fixation.

They mentioned him a lot, in all sorts of strange contexts, but had no reproductions of his pictures in their house. Erica had often thought this was odd, but Flora insisted that she would only display what she called 'originals', and so her walls were covered with black-and-white photos of rusting bed-frames and toothless, shoeless old women, and misshapen chunks of wood and board with netting, tissue and cardboard stuck to them.

'Not everyone who lives and dies without recognition is a genius,' Erica usually replied, though the precise wording varied. 'Some people who lead miserable, poverty-stricken, losers' lives are talentless nonentities. Come to think of it, that's probably the norm, isn't it? Van Gogh is the exception.'

'No,' Flora insisted. 'Loads of geniuses are unappreciated for absolutely yonkers, because the world can't handle their... vision.'

'Like who else?'

'John Kennedy Toole. Have you read *A Confederacy of Dunces*?'

'No.'

'You must. Loads of publishers rejected it, and he committed suicide. Then his mum persuaded someone to publish it – bit embarrassing, but he was dead, so I don't suppose it mattered – and now it's regarded as a great masterpiece. Which it is.'

'But TP's stuff is no good,' Erica pointed out. 'You know it's awful.'

'He is getting better. And I want to be like Theo... Gogh.' Flora's eyes shone when she said this. Erica realised that Flora thought the surname was 'Gogh', that Vincent's first name was 'Van', like Van Morrison's. Erica had noticed that Flora was extremely knowledgeable in some areas – literature, cinema, celebrity gossip and clothes – and utterly ignorant in others, such as geography, history and science. A conversation the two women had shortly after they met had revealed that Flora did not know the difference between the Isle of Man, the Isle of Wight and the Scilly Isles.

On the matter of TP's poetic abilities, neither Flora nor Erica was ever persuaded by the other's point of view. Once – only once – Erica was nearly convinced. Flora produced a new argument. She leaned her colour-flecked woollen elbows on the table and said, 'You know in books and films, where there's someone who noone has faith in? And everyone says, "You can't do it, you'll never do it, you haven't got what it takes"? Everyone says it, apart from the person themselves. Everyone underestimates them. You know the sort of book and movie I mean?'

Erica nodded.

'The maverick loser always succeeds in the end, and the people who didn't have faith end up looking like total dorks. That's their only role, in fact – to be the dorks who got it wrong. Well, not me! And TP is getting better.'

'Not at gardening,' said Erica, who hated to hear Flora defend him. 'Why does he never do any gardening? Why don't you mind?'

FLORA DIDN'T SEEM to mind anything. Erica minded lots of things: being unemployed, having no money, being single, sharing Flora with all her servants and with Frank – those were the big four, her main objections to her current situation. And there were subsidiary niggles: the black edges of the beige carpet in her flat, her inability to give up smoking, her parents' refusal to acknowledge that Erica was not a Christian, that she was different from them in this one significant respect.

'Okay,' said TP. He sat cross-legged on the granite-topped breakfast bar. 'It's called "Echelons".'

'Great title,' said Flora. Erica disagreed, but said nothing.

The first two words of TP's poem were the first name and surname of a well-known political leader. These were followed by '…you fucking lump of shit/Strangling children with your mitts'.

'Stop!' Flora held up her hand. 'Does he strangle children?'

'As good as,' said TP, a defensive edge to his voice.

'You mean, his policies are detrimental to children,' said Flora.

'Hey?'

'His policies harm children,' Erica clarified.

'Yeah.' TP didn't know what to make of Erica. She suspected he didn't know what she was doing in Flora's house all the time. She felt the same way about him.

'But to say "Strangling children with your mitts" – it's a very physical image,' said Flora. 'Mitts means hands – strangling children with your bare hands. I don't think you should say that if he doesn't. It's not a political objection. I just think you need to be precise.'

'Mitts makes me think of woolly gloves,' said Erica.

'Yes, which is another association you don't need. It's too cosy,' said Flora. 'Anyway, read the rest. I mean, perform the rest.' TP recited all his poems from memory. He was opposed to words on paper.

He started again from the beginning. After the 'mitts' line came a long, non-specific ramble about the uncaring and ruthless nature of the politician in question. Erica thought TP was making the same point, clumsily, over and over again, but Flora allowed him to finish the poem without further interruption. His voice deepened as he delivered the final couplet: 'No compassion for the kids/ No tin-openers for the lids.' He flicked his pony-tail over his shoulder and tried to look nonchalant, but Erica knew he was desperate to hear Flora's reaction.

'I loved it!' she said after a while. 'It's got real passion.'

'Do you think so?' TP was delighted. He hopped down off the breakfast bar. He looked as if he might run over to Flora and embrace her.

'I do. One query, though. Why "No tin-openers for the lids"? What lids? It seems an odd line to end with.'

'It's deliberately ambiguous,' said TP. 'I needed a rhyme for "kids".'

'But what tins and lids are you talking about?'

'No tins. No lids,' said TP impatiently. '"Lids" rhymes with "kids".'

'You can't put a line in a poem just because it rhymes,' Erica took great pleasure in telling him.

'Yes, you can! "Now and in times to be/Wherever green is worn/All changed, changed utterly/A terrible beauty is born." WB Yeats.'

'He wouldn't have chosen those words purely because they rhymed,' said Erica.

'What?' TP looked at Flora, appealing with his eyes. Flora was the judge. She had the final say. 'Oh, so I suppose it's just a coincidence that "born" rhymes with "worn", and "be" rhymes with "utterly"?'

Flora had missed the entire debate. 'Sorry, I'm still worried about these tins.'

'There are no tins, not in the way you mean. There are no literal, actual tins.' Erica thought she detected an edge of panic in TP's voice. She also felt edgy; how long would this nonsensical, irritating and entirely pointless discussion go on for?

Flora frowned, shaking her head. 'Yes, but if there are any tins at all, even poetic, metaphorical ones, they have to make sense. You need to clarify your symbolism. "No tin-openers for the lids" comes straight after "No compassion for the kids". It sounds as if you're suggesting that his lack of tin-openers is as damning as his lack of compassion. That's what doesn't work – because why should he have tin-openers? Are they his tins? If they're not his tins, why should he have openers for them?'

'There are no tins,' said Erica, in order to make sure she wasn't left out.

'He deprives needy children of food, that's the point,' said TP sullenly.

'Ah!' Flora threw both her hands up in the air. 'Why didn't you say so? I see! Oh, yes, that's good. Yes, I can see that it works, I can see it now.'

'I don't think it works,' said Erica, irritated. She glared at TP, who was smiling complacently. 'You said you only put it in for the rhyme. Now you're claiming it's an image of him starving the children. Which is it?'

'Both,' said TP.

'Perhaps there's something about the word "tin-openers", a certain clumsiness or…comic ordinariness…' Flora mused.

'You said it was good! You said it works!'

'Yes, well…maybe a clumsy image is a good way of unsettling people,' she concluded. 'Let's face it, you want your audience to feel uncomfortable, don't you, while they contemplate the deprivation of the have-nots?'

Erica was determined that TP should not get away with it. 'Even if you didn't only include that line for the sake of the rhyme, it sounds as if you did, and that's bad,' she said.

'What's your problem?' TP snapped. 'What do you know?'

'Who fancies a latte? Or a mocha?' said Flora.

Erica looked out of the window, at the uncut grass and unraked leaves. She was in danger of bursting into tears. She blinked hard. TP had broken the rules. The discussion was not supposed to turn personal.

What did Erica know? She had known a lot once, at university. She had got her degree, a good upper second, and then taken the first job that had come up. Muzorsgy's. The manager was the wife of one of her university tutors. It was only supposed to be temporary, but Erica had liked her boss and her colleagues; she would have felt disloyal if she'd left.

Flora made no attempt to discipline TP for his rudeness. She was busy putting drinks into the rotund, bumpy mugs she'd bought from a potter friend of hers. 'I don't want one,' said Erica, frostily enough to satisfy herself that she had struck back, but not so overtly that Flora would notice anything amiss. 'I have to go now.'

'Okay.' Flora stretched out a hand behind her and waved.

TWO DAYS LATER, Erica's mobile phone rang while she was in the supermarket. 'Erica!' It was Flora. 'Is everything okay? Is there something wrong with your phone at home?'

'It's been cut off.'

'Why?'

'I didn't pay the bill.'

'Oh, right.' Flora chuckled. 'I love your rebellious streak. I was expecting you hours ago. Why didn't you ring?'

Erica was thrilled. Flora had missed her. Her whole body was enlivened by the idea; her skin tingled. 'I can't make calls on my mobile any more,' she said. 'I've had it changed to incoming calls only.'

'I've got so much I want to talk to you about,' said Flora. 'And Frank's making a full day of it in the office, so come round as quickly as you can. Where are you? What are you doing?'

Before Flora phoned, Erica had been wondering if she ought to risk stealing some food that she couldn't afford.

If she did it at the same time as buying what food she could afford, surely noone would suspect her. 'Shopping,' she said, though she was already taking items out of her basket, depositing them on random shelves. She knew she wouldn't now have the patience to wait in the queue for the till. What could Flora want to talk to her about? It had to be the work.

'Shopping!' said Flora. 'Perfect. Can you do something for me? Let's call it your first assignment. I want you to buy three identical Valentine cards. Are you in a shop that sells cards?'

'Yes, I'm at the supermarket.' Erica began to retrace her steps, picking up the shopping she had just discarded and putting it back in her basket. If she was going to have to queue anyway, she might as well get the things she needed, save herself another trip tomorrow.

'Good,' said Flora. 'Choose a card that's tasteful and suggestive – nothing too…deterministic.'

Erica felt ridiculous and afraid at same time. She wished Flora hadn't called it an assignment. She'd have liked her to sound more serious, more professional, if this was the beginning of the work she wanted Erica to do. But if it was, what might the rest of it be? What would come next? It didn't sound like something that would last very long – certainly not as long as Erica needed it to. And she wasn't sure she understood exactly what Flora wanted her to do.

She tried not to sound anxious as she said, 'You mean the same card, three times? Not three similar cards?'

'No, the exact same card.'

'And…when you say not too deterministic…What do you mean, exactly?'

'Nothing that mentions either love or lust explicitly. Nothing that's clearly meant for either a long-term relationship or a purely physical, light-hearted thing. Something more all-encompassing that doesn't…limit the possibilities. Flattering to the recipient, without pinning anything down. Does that make it easier?'

'Yes,' said Erica, flustered, wishing she had a pen and paper with her. She tried to memorise Flora's adjectives: 'all-encompassing', 'flattering', 'suggestive'. She hurried over to the cards, worried in case another shopper, closer to the relevant aisle than Erica was, snapped up the last three identical non-deterministic Valentines.

An hour and forty minutes later, Flora and Erica sat at the table in Flora's conservatory with the three cards in front of them. The conservatory was also the music room. Enya's *Shepherd Moons* played in the background. It was Flora's favourite album. 'God would listen to this sort of music if he existed,' she often said.

'It's advert music,' Erica had once dared to reply, delighting Flora with her contrariness. 'Prudential, or Scottish Widows. God would only listen to it if he was thinking about getting his personal finances in order.' She'd made Flora laugh uproariously.

Today was not a TP day. And Frank would be in the office until at least four thirty. Bliss, thought Erica. Or, rather, it would be, it could have been, if she hadn't totally failed in the task Flora had set her. 'There was so little choice,' she explained for the fourth time. 'Most of them were so vulgar, or embarrassingly soppy. With messages that would only apply in very particular situations.' As soon as she'd started looking, Erica had understood what Flora meant by 'deterministic'.

'They always are,' said Flora. 'You know why, don't you? It's because noone has any initiative or creativity these days.'

'What do you mean?'

'Well…you know. The government tells us not to smoke or eat salt, motorway signs tell us not to drive while we're tired. Cups of coffee we buy from train buffet cars have "careful – hot" printed on them. Teachers go on courses to learn how to teach exactly like other teachers. Flair and independence are discouraged in every sphere of life, and as for risk-taking – huh!' She raised her eyes. 'And card manufacturers know this. They know noone has any gumption any more, so they make their cards really specific. Most people aren't up to the task of deciding what to write in Uncle Terry's bunion operation card, so Hallmark make cards saying "Get well soon after your bunion operation, Uncle Terry".'

Erica laughed. 'Yes, well, a lot of the Valentines in Asda were like that. One said, "If I show you mine, will you show me yours?" Another said, "Valentine, I've been searching for so long" on the front. And then inside it said, "There are so many pubs – you could be in any of them."'

'This one's perfect,' said Flora. 'Why are you so worried about it?'

In the end, despondent, Erica had chosen a plain red card with 'happy valentine's day' on the front in small white letters, all lower case. Inside it said 'be mine'. 'It doesn't really say anything,' said Erica. 'It's not suggestive or flattering.'

'It's fine,' said Flora. 'It's simple. Perfect. I like "be mine". One always wants full ownership, however briefly. And I can add my own message as well, can't I? Or, rather, you can.'

'Me?'

'Yes.' Flora giggled. 'That's your second assignment. To write the three cards for me, and the envelopes, and post them.'

This, it seemed to Erica, was a good moment to clarify the issue of the work. 'Flora, you know you said I could work with you? I'm still not sure what exactly you want me to do or how much you'd pay me. I mean, maybe you were joking...'

'Of course I wasn't.' Flora looked concerned.

'It's just...If I'm not going to be working with you, I really need to start looking for another job. I'm pretty desperate for money...'

Flora reached into the bag that was hanging from the back of her chair and pulled out a cheque book. 'Sorry,' she said. 'Yes, of course. I'll write you a cheque for five hundred quid now, is that okay?'

'But...'

'Or more? More. A thousand. And just tell me when it runs out.'

'Flora, don't be ridiculous. You can't give me a thousand pounds. I haven't done anything!'

'You've bought the cards. And you're going to write and send them for me.'

'But that's not work.' Erica felt like howling. 'I don't understand. You said I could work with you, but you don't work. Sending three Valentine cards will take me about five minutes. What else do you want me to do, to earn the rest of the thousand pounds?'

Flora sighed. 'I'm not sure yet,' she said. 'Things arise, don't they? I'm bound to need your help all the time. I like the idea that you're on standby.'

Erica shook her head tearfully. 'I need a proper job,' she said. This was a disaster.

'Would you prefer it if we said you were my secretary?'

'I can't even type.'

'Have I asked you to type? Okay, then, my personal assistant – how about that?'

'No. I don't know...'

'Come on, Erica, don't be so conventional. Just because I'm not giving you letters to type doesn't mean it's not a proper job.' Flora looked forlorn. 'If I pay you, that makes it proper enough, doesn't it? I mean, I don't know yet what I'll want you to do. It could be anything – maybe one week I'll want us to impersonate people. I might need you to help me shelter a wanted criminal. Who can predict the future?'

Erica nodded. It seemed that Flora was not teasing her; she was serious. And Erica hated the thought that she was in any way conventional.

Flora wrote a cheque for a thousand pounds, tore it out and handed it to her. 'Now, back to work,' she said, grinning. 'I've decided what I want the cards to say: "Interested? Or just curious?" What do you think?'

'Brilliant,' said Erica. She clutched the cheque in her hand, under the table. A warm glow of security spread through her body. No more loitering in the aisles of Asda, wondering whether to steal pork chops.

'Go on, then. Get writing.'

'You want the same message in all three cards?'

'Yes. Exactly the same.'

'Who are they for?'

'Paul.' Flora beamed. 'My financial adviser. You've met him a couple of times, remember?'

Erica did. He had the face of a footballer, or a soldier. A man with very short hair and hard features who did man's things. 'You've never said you fancy him.'

'I didn't. But last night changed all that.' Flora winked.

'What? You mean you've...'

'No, of course not. I had a dream about him. It was the most explicit dream I've ever had, and when I woke up I was passionately in lust with him. Have you ever had a sex dream?'

'Who are the other two cards for?' asked Erica.

'Ah. Well, the trouble is, I don't know Paul's address. I only know he lives in Silsford. I don't want to send it to his work address because his secretary might open it and tease him. She'd certainly see it. And if I asked him for his address, or asked anyone he knows, that'd look too suspicious. So I looked in the phone book. There are three P Sheafs in Silsford. I decided I'd just send the card to all three and one of them will be him.'

'What if he's ex-directory?' asked Erica.

'He isn't. I know, because when I told him I was, he looked puzzled and asked me why.'

'Why don't you ring all three numbers? He'll answer one of them and then you'll know.'

'No. Too risky. When the card arrived, he'd immediately remember the strange phone call, wouldn't he? He might hire a detective and trace the number.'

'Of course he wouldn't,' said Erica.

'I would,' said Flora. Erica believed her. Flora would do a lot of things that most people wouldn't. 'Or he might hear some background noise, something that would enable him to identify the house.'

'You could ring from a phone box. Or I could.'

'No! Look, to be honest...' Flora's eyes darted to the right, then back again. 'This is going to sound odd, but I like the grandness of the gesture. You know, sending it to all the P Sheafs in the phone book. I feel a bit like King Herod.' She laughed. 'Don't know which one you want? Right, target them all – that way you know you'll get your man. Do you see what I mean? If King Herod wanted to send a Valentine to his financial adviser, and didn't know his exact address, this is what he'd do. I like my plan – I think it's funny. It makes the whole thing more exciting. What's wrong with it?'

'I don't know,' said Erica doubtfully. 'Isn't it a bit unfair to the other two?'

'Unfair? The opposite, I'd have thought.' This time Flora looked as if she did not want Erica to disagree with her. 'Two people will get Valentine cards this year who might otherwise have got none. Think how pleased they'll be. I know Valentine's Day is silly in many ways, but you'd be surprised how many people would be bolstered for weeks, maybe even months, by the idea that they've got a secret admirer. It's an adventure, apart from anything else.'

ERICA WOULD NOT have been surprised. Her reservation about Flora's plan stemmed from her being able to imagine only too vividly the effect an anonymous Valentine might have upon a person. Especially one that said, 'Interested? Or just curious?' It was a clever, subtle message. Was it fair to make a person believe that they had an inspired and discriminating admirer when they did not, when they merely shared a name with the real object of desire?

Grateful as she was for the thousand pounds and for her unconventional job, Erica couldn't help wishing that she could avoid direct involvement in this mad Valentine-sending scheme. If she had not been working for Flora, she could have observed the goings-on from a distance; it would not have occurred to her to take an ethical position on the matter. It was different now that she was Flora's paid accomplice.

That evening she sat in her flat with the three cards on her lap and an empty tin of pork sausages and beans on the sofa beside her, wondering how Flora would react if she told her she felt uncomfortable about the whole business. She'd probably just laugh, and find someone else to write and post her cards for her. But then Erica would have to return the money; how could she not, in all conscience? What sort of employee refused her employer's very first request?

And since the cards would be sent anyway...Erica opened each one in turn and wrote the agreed message inside, in a style of handwriting that she had invented and practised: long, angular letters that tilted to the right. Nothing like Erica's small, neat script or Flora's round, unruly scrawl. Flora hadn't instructed her to do this, but neither had she explicitly told her not to, and Erica would have felt even more strongly implicated if she'd written the cards as herself.

She put them in their envelopes, sealed them, and fished in her bag for the piece of paper Flora had given her with the three addresses on it. She stared at them. 3 Bankside Close. 31c Brownsville Road. 19 Woodland Rise. Each one the home of a different P Sheaf, two out of three of whom were unloved by Flora. Perhaps nobody loved them. Erica felt sorry for these two strangers, and for herself. Tomorrow, before going to Flora's house – before going to work – she was supposed to drive to Silsford and post the cards. She wasn't entirely sure that she could or would do it. She looked again at the addresses, and decided to postpone writing them on the envelopes, as if to do so would be to commit herself. 'You must make sure to post them first thing,' Flora had said. 'I know Valentine's Day is three days away, but we don't want to cut it fine. It's nicer if they arrive early. I've always loved early Valentines. They allow you to feel a sort of advanced smugness. Not only have you got a card, but you know you've got one long before the actual day, so you can bypass the agony of waiting and hoping. I want Paul to know that his secret admirer is a considerate person, you see.'

When Erica was in her flat alone, she spent most of her time replaying recent conversations she and Flora had had. Home had become the place where – mentally, while sitting motionless on the sofa, staring trance-like in the direction of a fuzzy old black-and-white television – she archived and catalogued the footage of her life as Flora Gustavina's best friend.

'Shouldn't you post it more locally?' Erica had quibbled. She preferred to drive as little as possible. Her car, a boxy old Skoda that she'd bought from one of her mother's church friends for three hundred and fifty pounds, often stopped without warning and would not start again. 'Surely you want him to know the card's from you.'

'Of course I don't.' Flora had inspected Erica closely at that point, as if searching for an indication of her planetary origin. 'If I wanted him to know, I'd write it myself and sign it, wouldn't I? And then hand it to him. I wouldn't need three cards.'

'Yes, but you at least want him to suspect...'

'Exactly. I'd like him to suspect, but not be at all certain. That way, if he wants it to be me, he'll start to drop hints, perhaps invite me out for dinner...'

'But he'll only do that if he thinks it's likely to be you.' Erica had been surprised at her own vociferousness. Now that she was being paid, she felt obliged to give top-notch advice in the clearest possible manner. 'If the postmark says Silsford, he might not suspect you at all. Or your name might come way down the list.' Flora looked as if she did not like the sound of that. Erica continued, 'In which case he's not going to make a pass at you, is he? He's your financial adviser. He won't risk behaving unprofessionally unless he's convinced you're his mystery admirer.'

Flora had nodded. 'Everything you say would be true if it weren't for one crucial fact.'

'Which is?'

'I'm me.' Flora shrugged. 'Any man who knows me and gets a Valentine card is going to make me his prime suspect straight away. Sending an anonymous card is such a me-ish thing to do. Not many people are as keen as I am on mischievous and intriguing modes of behaviour.'

'But he knows you're married.'

'I'm still me,' Flora insisted. 'I'm telling you, when he gets the card, he'll think "Flora", immediately. Then he'll look at the Silsford postmark, and he'll remember that I'm married, and he'll be less utterly positive. Other women might spring to mind. But you see my point? I need the combination of Frank and the Silsford post mark to mitigate against the total obviousness of the card being from me.'

'What if he doesn't drop hints or invite you out for dinner?'

'I don't know.' Flora had frowned. 'If he doesn't do that, he'll do something else. Something will happen. Things will change between us.' She nodded suddenly, as if making up her mind. 'He'll know it's me, but he won't be able to prove it. It'll drive him crazy.' She grinned, her eyes twinkling with glee. 'And of course I don't have to admit it until it suits me...' She laughed. 'I've never been very good at making men wait for sex, but I love making them wait for information.'

'So you want to have sex with him? Just once, or...a proper affair?'

'That's a good point,' said Flora, wagging her index finger in the air. 'I must give it some thought.'

Flora had nodded. 'Everything you say would be true

WHEN ERICA ARRIVED at the Gustavinas' house the following day, she bumped into Paul the financial adviser on the doorstep. She made a startled, incoherent noise. The skin on her face tingled hotly. She clutched her bag against her chest, protecting it with both arms, as if she feared he might try to mug her. The smell of Paul's aftershave coated the air around them. It was sharp and citrusy, like a mixture of lime and acid.

Fortunately, Paul didn't notice that the sight of him had disturbed Erica. He waved vaguely without looking at her. She'd observed when she'd met him before that he (and Vesna the cleaner, coincidentally) preferred to look at things than at people. Paul gazed at printed columns of figures; Vesna stared at the piles of colourful pottery in the sink, into buckets of soapy water.

Today Paul stood still, legs planted apart, mobile phone to his ear. He wore a navy suit and a sky-blue shirt without a tie. His voice was deep and oddly lacking in inflection. *A dalek might sound like him*, thought Erica. The subject of his conversation, from what she could gather, was a forthcoming rugby match. He and whoever he was talking to would meet a group of surnames – Watkins, Carter, Clay – in the Red Lion before kick-off.

Erica lowered her eyes and waited. Paul didn't move aside, seemed unaware that he was blocking her route to the front door. He was a chunky, slab-like man. The skin on his face looked as if it had been heaped on top of the bones, then patted into place with a spade. Eventually, he ended his phone call with the word 'curry!' – a decisive announcement – and lumbered meatily towards his car.

Thank goodness, thought Erica. She'd been terrified that he would go back inside. But, no, he was on his way to the office, or to see another client. Or home, perhaps, to 3 Bankside Close, or 31c Brownsville Road, or 19 Woodland Rise.

Flora flung open the front door. 'Did you see him?' she whispered.

Erica nodded.

'Oh God! He's so gorgeous.' She took hold of Erica's elbow and steered her inside. 'I find just thinking about him more erotic than actually having sex with most people.'

'I don't think he's sexy at all,' said Erica, though she hadn't planned to mention it. But now that she'd started, it seemed important to carry on. Trying to save Flora from her own foolishness was certain to be in her job description, even if this had never been formally stated. 'There's something aggressive-seeming about him. Like a sort of anger, almost, just beneath the surface. I don't think he's very friendly.'

'Not sexy?' Flora was aghast. 'What are you talking about? What about his low, scary voice, like Hal the computer from 2001? Imagine that voice saying…certain things!' Her eyes gleamed.

'What did he say in your dream?' asked Erica.

'I'll never tell you that.' Flora grinned. 'Though I'll happily tell you what he did. Missionary position. The squashing and crushing variety, no arm support. Lots of silence, lots of rhythmic pounding. Camomile tea?'

'Yes, please.'

'I bet I'm right. I can't see him being a clamberer, or a there-there-er. Did you post the cards?'

It was the question Erica had been dreading. She hadn't. The three Valentines were still in her bag. She'd been terrified of Paul somehow detecting their presence when she'd run into him outside. She'd felt as if he were bound to intuit their existence and meaning through the thin fabric of her bag, even though she had not written his name inside the cards, nor, yet, on the envelopes. Now she was certain Flora would guess the truth straight away: that Erica had not successfully completed her assignment as instructed, that she had deliberately disobeyed.

'Yes,' she lied. Panic swept through her; soon she would be fired, friendless. Why hadn't she done what she'd been told to do? Why had she been unable to bear the idea of the other two P Sheafs, who were not financial advisers and did not smell of lime and acid, opening their cards and feeling their hearts swell with false pleasure, happiness that was based on a horrible lie, a ruse, Flora's stupid Herod plan? And they would never know, that was the worst thing about it. They might spend the rest of their lives believing in their secret admirer. But so what? Erica reminded herself that she didn't know these people. And worse things happened all the time. She was being idiotic. She cursed her own squeamishness. Flora was probably right to say that there was nothing wrong with lies that made everybody happy. Now Erica had lied to please Flora and, in doing so, had made herself considerably more miserable. I *must* post the cards on my way home, she thought. It wasn't too late. They would still arrive by Valentine's Day.

'You know you're a genius?' said Flora.

'I am?' Erica would have been delighted if she hadn't felt so guilty. She curled into a corner of the blue velvet sofa in Flora's kitchen and tried to forget about her own dishonesty, about the other two P Sheafs whom she would have, later, to defraud, and about the kernel of strained darkness she believed she had detected in Paul the financial adviser. Enya's 'After Ventus' drifted in from the conservatory. Flora had turned the volume up louder than usual.

'You are! You asked me if I wanted to have sex with Paul just once, or if I wanted a proper affair. I thought about it a lot, after you'd gone, and came to a startling conclusion.'

'What?' Erica's blood raced.

Flora came and sat down beside her, carrying their drinks. 'At first I thought definitely an affair. But there would be disadvantages. I've never strayed so close to home before. And Paul is Frank's financial adviser, too – it would be a bit much to have an ongoing thing right under Frank's nose.'

Erica's thorough and conscientious nature compelled her to ask a question that had been in her mind since she and Flora first met. 'What are your guidelines, if any, about what you will and won't do? From a Frank point of view, I mean. Do you make distinctions between one sort of infidelity and another?'

'Of course.' Flora smiled. 'That's so funny.'

'What is?'

'Watching you trying to find a polite way of asking me if I have any morals whatsoever. I have a very strict code. One: nobody threatens my marriage. Whatever happens, even if I fall madly in love and have to have a broken heart for a week, or a month, or a year, I don't consider leaving Frank. I never have and I never will. That's basic loyalty.' She nodded instructively at Erica. 'On that score, you won't find many people who are as moral as I am. Two: no flings with Frank's friends, colleagues or relatives – anyone who's more his than mine, in other words. Paul belongs jointly to both of us, but still – rule number three: one bonk only with shared acquaintances. And none with shared friends. Our coupley friends, for example – those men are totally out of bounds. Because of rule number four: no sex, or even mild flirtation, with the boyfriends or husbands of my female friends. So, for example, if you had a man, I would steer well clear of him.' Flora smiled reassuringly. 'Finally, rule number five: I'm allowed to have an affair with any man who hasn't been eliminated by any of the other rules, as long as the meetings aren't too frequent. I wouldn't want to be sneaking off every second night, lying to Frank.'

'So what would be a reasonable frequency?' asked Erica.

'One evening a fortnight,' Flora replied without hesitation. 'To coincide with Frank's squash nights. Or, if my lover lived too far away to make evening sessions feasible, one whole night per month.' She nodded gravely. 'Everything in moderation,' she said. 'But, then, once these things start, one tends to want more and more. Why do you think that is?'

'Emotions start to run riot,' Erica guessed.

'Yes, but why? Your question made me mull it over, and I think I've worked it out.' Flora raised herself to a kneeling position. She could never sit still when she'd had an idea. Erica craned her neck to look up at her. 'A one-night stand should be enough,' said Flora. 'Why does a relationship, if it's not your main relationship, need to drag on endlessly? You're not looking for a life partner – you've already got one. So wouldn't it be nicer to have just a small taster, a distilled…nugget of romance, sex, whatever, with a third party? Nicer, and also much more clearly delineated from one's marriage. Imagine the highlights of a six-month affair – all the best bits and none of the humdrum stuff – packed into one night. Wouldn't that be great?'

Erica sipped her camomile tea and said nothing. She thought about how she would have felt if she'd only been able to spend one afternoon with Flora. And they were just friends.

'One night would be enough, if people could only get it right,' said Flora. 'All one needs to do is apply the Emmylou Harris principle.' Emmylou Harris was Flora's second favourite singer, after Enya. Erica had noticed that none of the songs Flora loved were sung by men.

'Hi there!' The blonde bobbed head of Vicky the personal trainer appeared in the doorway, followed by her petite, muscular body in a pink tracksuit. 'Sorry to interrupt.'

Erica was enraged. Why was there always somebody hanging around? How could anyone concentrate on anything in the middle of this circus? Didn't Flora ever crave solitude? Erica resisted the urge to growl and wriggle.

'I've set it to "manual",' Vicky told Flora. 'But you can change it to "fat-burn" or "cardio" if you want.'

'Brilliant. You're a star.' Not a genius, Erica noted.

'I've bought a cross-trainer,' Flora told her. 'Shall we have a go on it later?'

Erica's anger intensified. They were supposed to be working. She smiled unenthusiastically. As soon as Vicky had retreated, she said, quickly, 'What's the Emmylou Harris principle?'

'When Frank and I went to see Emmylou Harris at the Maltings, she said we were a wonderful audience. She said we were special. She used those words: "wonderful" and "special". There was a real rapport between her and us. It was tangible, like a sort of force-field of emotion. And she kept saying what a great time she was having.'

Erica was about to ask how this was relevant to the previous topic of conversation when Flora raised a hand to silence her. She had more to say. 'Emmylou didn't arm herself with cautious indifference. She didn't say, "Look, you lot are just another audience to me. You do realise that, don't you? This time tomorrow I'll be singing these same songs to an equally appreciative crowd at the Birmingham NEC. Just so as you know." She wasn't scared that if she said nice things to us, we'd follow her home and demand that she entertain us every night for the rest of our lives. This is my point: when you know something's finite, you can relax and give it your all. Everyone involved knew that the gig was going to be a one-off – that was what made it so perfect.'

'That's totally different,' said Erica, thinking that Flora must know it was. She had a dreadful sense of anticlimax. She felt suddenly empty, hollowed out; she needed Flora to say something that was incontrovertibly true. Flora's fanciful analogies sometimes felt to Erica like a form of starvation.

'If I could guarantee that the Emmylou Harris principle would govern any one-night stand I had with Paul, I'd be totally content to sleep with him only once,' Flora summed up. 'It's when I imagine the unfortunate things he'll probaby do and say almost straight away that I think I'll need more time. You have to put in a lot of hours, often, to turn the awful things that might make you shudder for years to come into pleasant memories. That's why some affairs last longer than bloody degree courses,' Flora concluded on a note of bitter triumph. 'See? I'm a genius.'

'What nonsense,' Erica snapped. She had never snapped at Flora before. Why was Flora suddenly the genius? 'Your theory's got more holes than a golf course.'

Flora chortled contentedly. She did not enquire about the holes. 'Anyway, you asked yesterday what work you'd be doing, after the Valentines. This is it.'

'What?' Erica cowered. She wished Flora would forget all about the cards, never mention them again. King Herod! Why emulate him, of all men? While most people shuddered at the thought of his ruthlessness, Flora Gustavina admired his methodology. She must, Erica concluded, have missed the point of that particular bible story in quite a big way.

'I'm going to become a relationships expert,' said Flora. 'I am one already, but I mean, I'm going to become known as one. You see them on television all the time, on shows like *This Morning*. I'm always struck by how superficial their insights are: stuff like "if he tries to bash your head in with a hammer, leave him". So that's what I'm going to do, and I'm going to start by focusing on the one-night stand. The rules that should govern a one-night stand. That sounds good.' Flora appeared to be talking to herself.

'How... What...?'

'Have you got some paper and a pen? I'll give you my initial thoughts, and later you can take your notes home and condense them into something snappy and irresistible that we can send to newspapers and television companies.'

Erica began to chew the inside of her lip. Working for Flora, she was beginning to realise, was akin to being ambushed by a different alien creature every day. At Muzorsgy's, life had been predictable. Erica had ordered stock, put it out on the shelves, attended to the book-keeping, helped customers to find the products they needed. There had been a routine. It must be very conventional, Erica thought guiltily, to yearn for routine. She pulled a red gas bill and a black Biro out of her handbag, making sure Flora didn't catch a glimpse of the three unaddressed, unsent cards, and wrote 'One-night stand' on the back of the bill, on top of the pale blue italic print which explained that Erica could pay at a bank, by post, by direct debit, by cheque or postal order.

'How to have the perfect one-night stand,' said Flora, in a titular voice. 'Call it that.' Call what that? Erica wanted to ask. What would be the culmination, the eventual product, of this enterprise? And was it materialistic – philistine, even – to expect everything to have a result?

She heard a scraping sound and turned to face the window. TP loomed. He nodded at her through the glass and smiled furtively, as if suggesting a truce. Erica smiled back. This time she was grateful for the interruption. Perhaps Flora would forget about her plan to become the first television evangelist for the church of the one-night stand.

The scraping noise grew louder. Could it be the sound of TP grating his excessive knuckles against the wall, Erica wondered queasily. She couldn't see his hands. Then his eyes ignited with pleasure and he raised a large spade in the air as Flora turned to wave at him. 'TP!' she called out. He'd been scraping the spade back and forth along the ground, Erica realised; how very irritating.

Flora turned away from the window and muttered, 'What if Paul rejects me?' Erica was astonished. Flora had always seemed to her to be a person who never even considered failure. 'He won't, he can't. It isn't as if I'm propositioning him directly, is it?'

'You must have…' Erica began delicately. 'I mean, with all your experience…'

'I must have been turned down before? Of course. I'd say I have a sixty per cent success rate, which isn't too bad. And I always bounce back – I mean, I'm quite good at handling rejection. I used to be brilliant at it, but I'm getting worse with practice.' Flora giggled.

The back door opened and TP came in, holding a key in his bone-stuffed hand. He had his own key to the Gustavinas' back door. Erica's eyes filled with tears; she turned her face away to hide them. When did that happen? Why did he need a key? I ought to get up and march out of this house right now, thought Erica.

'How's my Throat Pastille this morning?' asked Flora.

'Pissed off. The Arts Council turned down my funding application for the Twenty-Two Parrot Gold tour.'

'Oh dear!' Flora turned to Erica. 'Throat Pastille was going to...'

'It doesn't matter now,' TP cut her off. 'It's not going to happen, is it?'

'How much money do you need?' asked Flora. Inwardly, Erica screamed.

'I asked the Arts Council for twenty grand,' said TP.

Flora nodded solemnly. Erica couldn't bear it. She had a feeling that Flora was going to try to compensate TP for the Arts Council's frugality, and she didn't want to be present to hear the mooting of such a ludicrous waste, not only of Flora's, but also of global, resources. For as long as there was only a finite amount of money in the world, Erica was of the view that TP should, to enable him to promote his poetry, be given none of it. '...nip to the loo,' she mumbled, grabbing her bag and leaving the room as quickly as possible.

The air inside the Gustavinas' downstairs lavatory had been stormed, at some stage, by Paul the financial adviser's aftershave. Erica narrowed her nostrils. Why was the smell so strong? Had he crept back inside to use the toilet a few minutes ago? Perhaps he too had a key.

Then she noticed a brown leather briefcase on the floor by the foot of the basin. It was open. A paper folder poked out of the top, and Erica read the words, 'Paul Sheaf Financial Services'. Her throat tightened. She tried very hard to remove from her mind the picture of Paul sitting on the toilet casting a leisurely eye over his company's latest brochure. The layers of aftershave that hung in the air were starting to make her feel sick.

She leaned over the large, square, white basin and washed her face. The green towel on the radiator smelled even more strongly of Paul the financial adviser than the general atmosphere did, so she used her sleeve instead. She opened the door and was about to leave the room when she thought of the cards. They were in her bag, which she'd – thank God, thank God! – brought with her. But she'd need to be quick; Paul could return at any moment. He was bound to come straight back as soon as he realised he'd left his briefcase at Flora's. There was no time to close and lock the door again, or to write Paul's name on one of the envelopes; in any case, Erica wouldn't have known whether to write 'Paul' or 'Paul Sheaf'. It wasn't an easy decision to make, when the name was not going to be followed by an address. Flora would no doubt have had firm views, but Erica couldn't work out what her friend and boss would want, so she just pulled one of the three envelopes out of her bag and stuffed it in between the pages of a pamphlet entitled 'Index-linked ISAs: your questions answered'.

She stood still for a few seconds, in a sort of reverie. She stared at the briefcase, letting relief and a sense of accomplishment wash over her. Now the two undesired P Sheafs would not have to be made fools of, and Paul the financial adviser would receive the card that was meant for him. It was the perfect outcome: Flora's romantic message had been delivered, yet King Herod had been foiled. This sort of rare happy ending almost made Erica question her atheism.

She carried the brown briefcase out into the hall and leaned it against the wall under the large stained-glass window, so that somebody would be sure to notice it. Briefly, she worried that, if Paul found the card too soon after having his case returned to him by Flora, he would know it was from her, but then she decided that was unlikely. Why would he check his briefcase on the way from one client's house to another? He would be much more likely to find the card tonight, when he unpacked his things.

Jubilant, Erica returned to Flora and TP. TP seemed to look her up and down, inspecting her in a more thorough manner than usual, and Erica wondered if her face was red, or her sleeve obviously wet. She did her best to look casual and innocent.

'I wrote a poem this morning!' Flora announced, beaming. 'I've been meaning to tell you, Erica.'

'You wrote a poem?' TP sounded worried.

Flora ignored him. 'It's because of you-know-what.' She winked at Erica. 'I feel as if I've got this massive…surge of energy and creativity.'

'What's you-know-what?' TP whined.

'Nothing,' said Flora and Erica together. Ha, thought Erica.

Flora pulled a small piece of paper out of her cardigan pocket. Erica could see the back of it, on which was written 'bacon, smoked salmon, quince jelly, cheese, bics for cheese, avocados'. A heavy exhaustion took possession of her brain, dulling her senses. The trauma of the last few minutes had taken it out of her. Thank goodness the assignment was now complete and the deception was over. Well, sort of over. Erica would never be able to tell Flora that she had jettisoned the Herod part of the plan.

Flora began to recite, in a slow, theatrical voice:

'Peter and Christopher Hitchens
Are my favourite famous brothers.
Although there is stiff competition –
The Marxes, the Coens, and others –
Who are no doubt preferred by their wives
And must surely appeal to their mothers,
Peter and Christopher Hitchens
Are my favourite famous brothers.'

There was silence. TP slid off the breakfast bar. 'I'd better get on with some work,' he said, and stomped out into the garden.

'It's better than anything he's ever written,' said Erica. 'That's why he's in a huff.'

'He isn't in a huff; he's just upset about his tour,' said Flora. 'Twenty grand, though – it's a bit much, isn't it? I didn't want to tell you while he was in earshot, but the reason I wrote the poem is because I had an extremely horny dream last night, involving both Hitchenses. At the same time. Which is completely impractical, because I've heard they don't get on, don't even speak. It's a shame, isn't it?'

'Another dream?' said Erica, alarmed. 'We don't have to send Valentine cards to them, too, do we?'

Flora giggled. 'Don't worry. They'd both think I was an airhead, I'm sure. I wouldn't even waste my time trying. Anyway, I have to be faithful to Paul,' she added coyly.

'I don't see why, when you're not faithful to Frank,' said Erica, regretting the comment straight afterwards.

Flora didn't seem to mind, thankfully. 'That's different,' she said. 'You can't be unfaithful to the person you're being unfaithful with – that's very bad form. Maybe after we've sorted out the rules for one-night stands we can move on to some more general guidelines for adultery.'

'So what happened in your dream?' Erica asked quickly. Anything but the one-night stand project. She stiffened. Herod's Valentines were behind her, but the future would be full of new and imaginative ordeals of Flora's devising. Erica wasn't sure she liked her new job as much as she'd hoped she would.

Flora looked wary, as if she were considering something. Then she said, 'No, I'd probably better not say. I don't think Peter Hitchens would approve of me talking about him in a carnal context, even if Christopher wouldn't mind. Erica, look!' Flora leaped up off the sofa, pointing outside.

TP was mowing the lawn.

HOW TO HAVE A PERFECT ONE-NIGHT STAND
  1. Apply the Emmylou Harris principle. Limit your-self to one night only. That way, you will need no other limitations on the character, mood, quality and intensity of the occasion.

2. *If in doubt, don't do it. Don't go ahead but allow misgivings to ruin the occasion. Don't reveal indecision and guilt by saying, 'Is this a good idea?' or 'I need to decide whether I'm going to get my last train home', thereby shifting responsibility on to the other person. Any lack of wholeheartedness during the preliminaries is appalling etiquette.*

3. *Don't make the mistake of thinking that, just because your time together is limited, there is no point in saying anything romantic or signifi-cant. Obviously it would be futile to say, 'I want to spend the rest of my life with you', since that isn't an option, but there is no harm in saying, for example, 'I'll never forget you', or 'This has been one of the most amazing nights of my life.' A one-night stand has to be short but it does not have to be sordid, throwaway or worthless. It can (should?) have as much resonance as a decades-long relationship.*

4. *You shouldn't make grand claims (see above) that aren't true. That doesn't mean, however, that you must say everything that is true. If the sex has been unsatisfactory, there is no need to mention it. You won't sleep with the person again, so there is no opportunity for improvement. Therefore, women: behave as you do when you are given an unfortunate coat for Christmas by a well-meaning relative. Do not say, 'Bloody hell, what a disappointment. Couldn't you do any better than that?' Be politely appreciative and spare the man's feelings. Men: your part of the deal is pretending to be unaware of the hopelessness of your*

performance. Women hate nothing more than to have to comfort a man after bad sex; it adds insult to injury.

5. *If you're married and your one-night stand partner knows you are, do not remove your wedding ring, especially if you're likely to meet him or her again in a non-sexual context when you will, once more, be wearing the ring. There is no need to bring the hackneyed symbolism of deception and betrayal into the proceedings. Remember: you are not two different people, nor should you try to be. You are one person doing something worthwhile and life-enhancing. So, while you should be tactful and ensure that your husband or wife doesn't find out for the sake of their happiness (see unfortunate coat point above), you should in no way behave as if you are ashamed or guilty.*

6. *Ideally, you should spend the whole night together. This should include breakfast (continental, definitely not full English, irrespective of whether you are at one of your houses or in a hotel). It is perfectly acceptable to leave as soon as breakfast is over, whatever time this may be. If you absolutely cannot stay all night, say so before the sex begins. Give the other person plenty of notice that you will need to dash off at four in the morning. Otherwise, they will feel desolate and abandoned and wonder what they did wrong.*

7. *If your one-night stand partner is someone you know and will see again non-sexually, you will need to work very hard on a new manner. You absolutely must not treat them as if nothing has changed, and*

revert to an everyday chumminess or professionalism. That would suggest that you want to pretend nothing happened. The new manner must somehow reflect an underlying connection, and could involve such elements as: fewer words more carefully chosen; an increased solemnity in your bearing; significant private looks; an increase in the amount of respect and awe accorded to the other person; emitting a faint aura of regret and missed chances – a sort of if-only-ishness.

8. Women: your underwear must match. It is not sufficient for the bra to be merely the same colour as the knickers, or even the same colour and material. They must be a set. It is irrelevant that many men will never notice a detail like this; it should be a matter of personal pride. Men: your underwear should be clean and, if not brand-new, then at least new-looking. It is totally unacceptable to present a pair of boxer shorts that, for example, is fraying at the top, around the elastic.

9. While it would be absurd to insist on no mention of spouses, assuming you are both married, it is very bad form either to praise or denigrate your life partner. So, stick to factual references only. 'I had to come by train because Philippa has got the car tonight' is fine. But 'You're so gorgeous. Philippa's body fell to pieces after she had our third child' is not, nor is 'Philippa's a brilliant gardener. She's so capable round the house. She can make anything, grow anything...' etc. Avoid, in particular, a combination of praise and criticism, which conveys the

impression that your spouse is everything to you, fills up every possible corner of your mind and life.

10. *The biggest faux-pas of all, and one men are often guilty of, is to ask your one-night-stand partner if she still has sex with her husband, or – worse still – how often. If you ask questions of this sort, you will appear to be an oaf who knows nothing of social norms. If you do ask, you deserve, and should expect, a lie by way of response.*

11. *The sexual positions you choose should reflect – or at least not directly contradict, in terms of their symbolism – the mood you hope to create. If you're highlighting pure physical pleasure and cheerful experimentation, almost any position is acceptable. If, however, you're aiming for a deep bond and a lasting emotional imprint, avoid anything too innovative and technically demanding. Choose, instead, a position that allows a lot of eye contact. Men: avoid, at all costs, torso-kneeling (kneeling, upright, at the end of a woman's torso and looking down at her from on high). While intercourse is possible in this position, it will make her feel like something unsavoury on display at a car-boot sale – a single floppy shoe with a brown-stained inner sole, for instance. Torso-kneeling is also incredibly risky for any man who isn't absolutely confident of his sexual prowess. If you're no good in bed and you torso-kneel, your lover will suspect that you're trying to be towering and manly in the only way you know how.*

12. *Always fake an orgasm if it becomes clear that you aren't going to have a real one. Never ask*

your lover if he or she has had one. Also, do not assume that if you have occasioned an orgasm (real or feigned) in the other person, that your work for the night is done, unless both of you are only in your teens or early twenties. If your partner is in his or her thirties or forties, you should aim to provide three orgasms. Anything less appears niggardly, like arriving at a dinner party with only one bottle of wine.

13. You need to give careful consideration to the balance between sexual activity, comic tension-diffusing banter, intimate whispered conversation and sleep. Certainly no more than four hours should be spent sleeping (you can always catch up the following night). The sexual activity should be broken up into at least two chunks. Two two-hour sessions are preferable to one four-hour stint.

14. Remember that ill-judged one-liners such as 'Aren't you going to take off your pants?' can ruin everything. A good example of this in a non-sexual context is the 1985 Band Aid single 'Do They Know it's Christmas?', in which the line 'Tonight thank God it's them instead of you' destroys the whole effect.

'YOUR PHONE'S BACK on!' Flora cheered.

'I paid the bill,' said Erica. 'I've just finished writing up your one-night stand...'

'Don't bother. I've changed my mind about that. I thought about it after you left and I realised, if my guidelines became famous, you know, really caught on, then everyone'd know what to do to tick all the right boxes, and people's behaviour wouldn't tell you anything about their real selves. It'd give oafs the tools to masquerade as civilised, and that's the last thing I want to do. Oafs. Oaves. It should be "oaves", shouldn't it?'

Erica felt as as if a small stone, thrown from a great distance, had landed in the pit of her stomach. 'But I've spent hours on it!'

'Oh, God! Sorry!' Flora's voice was a loud combination of anguish and the need to make haste. 'I'll give you a bonus or something. Now, listen. There's been a development on the Paul front.'

'What? Already? Has he said something?'

'No, no, I haven't seen him or spoken to him. But…I've met someone. Someone else.'

Another small stone. 'Who? When?'

'Last night. I can't go into detail now. I'm not sure whether Frank is in or out. Sometimes he lurks, or drifts around silently while he makes up his mind whether to go in to the office or not. So I'll tell you later. But, anyway, Paul – nothing I said about him applies any more.'

'You don't fancy him?'

'Yuck, no. He's a monosyllabic neanderthal who thinks an expensive suit and a talent for adding up is enough to conceal his essential brutishness. It isn't too big a leap of the imagination to picture him clubbing someone to death, his face smeared with blood and wolf saliva. Don't you agree?'

'Yes,' said Erica in a tight voice. She was angrier with Flora than she had ever been. She had put such effort into producing a definitive document that accurately and eloquently summarised all Flora's thoughts on the one-night stand, only for Flora to dismiss the whole thing in a casual aside. Now the hours the two women had spent discussing Paul were to be flushed away as well. But it wasn't the waste of her time and energy that infuriated Erica – it was Flora's knack for making her feel ridiculous. Flora was the one who had dreamed up the absurd idea of marketing herself as a relationships expert; Flora it was who had decided to send a Valentine card to a stocky and uninspiring financial adviser. Yet somehow Erica had ended up, in both cases, as the one to whom it had to be explained, as if she were a child, how preposterous an idea it had been from the start.

Flora sighed. 'I wish I hadn't sent Paul a Valentine. Too late now, though, isn't it?'

'Maybe not,' Erica said, without thinking. Then she blinked a couple of times, as if she had just woken from a deep sleep. Damn! She saw instantly that she had committed herself to a full confession. She bit down hard on her lower lip.

'Maybe not?' Flora perked up; she was ready to be convinced.

'Has Paul been back to collect his briefcase?'

'Hey?'

'He left his briefcase at your house. It was there two days ago. I found it and put it in the hall. I…'

'What's this got to do with anything?' said Flora impatiently.

'Flora, I didn't send the three cards. I couldn't do it. I felt too…mean, that it just wasn't fair to the other two, the ones who would imagine someone was interested in them who wasn't, so I…'

'But you told me you posted them.' Flora sounded confused. Not angry. Yet, thought Erica.

She took a deep breath. 'I lied. I'm sorry. I'll completely understand if you want to sack me.'

'Don't be daft, you're my best friend,' said Flora.

'I was going to post them, honestly!' said Erica. A small tear of relief escaped from the edge of her eye and trickled thinly down her cheek. 'On my way home the other day. They'd still have got there in time, I'm sure. I would have overcome my silly scruples and sent the cards, but then when I went to the loo I saw Paul had left his briefcase, and I just thought it'd be so much better to stick one of the cards in there and...'

'He hasn't been back for his briefcase, and I haven't seen it,' Flora interrupted. 'This is most odd. He can't not have noticed that he hasn't got it. He's so attached to that briefcase, it almost qualifies as an essential organ. Where did you say you saw it?'

'I found it in the downstairs toilet, and I moved it into the hall.'

'Hang on.'

Erica heard a loud clunk. She chewed the skin around her fingernails. Please let it still be there, she prayed. Flora could retrieve and destroy the card, and no damage would have been done.

'Erica? It's not there. What did it look like?'

'Dark brown leather, with two pockets at the front. It's an Armani one, I think.'

Flora screamed with glee, a circus spectator's scream. 'That's not Paul's briefcase, it's Frank's!' she giggled.

A sour taste filled Erica's mouth. But it wasn't true; she knew that perfectly well. 'No, it's not. I've seen Frank's – it's black.' She didn't appreciate the joke; what could its aim be, other than to terrify and embarrass her? And that wasn't like Flora.

'His old one was. He's got a new one. I should know; I bought it for him.'

'But...' Erica's mind began to spin. 'It was Paul's, it had to be. It was full of loads of boring stuff about financial thingies. I put the card inside a pamphlet about ISAs.'

Flora was still laughing, but sounded as if she were trying to stop, out of respect for Erica's anxiety. 'Well, Paul must have given Frank the boring stuff during one of their meetings. Frank's briefcase is a mobile dustbin – he crams it full of all sorts of crap he's never going to need again. Oh, this is brilliant!' She hooted. 'I wonder if Frank's found the card yet. Shit!'

'What?' Alone in her living room, Erica ducked when she heard Flora's sudden change of tone, as if she'd just spotted a sniper in the window of the house across the street, with a gun pointed in her direction.

'Frank might find the card and pass it on to Paul. Then Paul's even more likely to suspect it's from me than he would otherwise have been.'

'Surely not.' Erica felt feverish; her skin was suddenly clammy. 'Who'd put a Valentine card for a...prospective lover in her husband's briefcase in the hope that he'll pass it on? Anyway, why would Frank think the card was for Paul?'

'It was inside an ISA leaflet Paul gave him, it had Paul's name on it...'

'No, it didn't,' Erica blurted out. 'I didn't write his name on it; there wasn't time. I just stuffed it in the briefcase. Paul's name's nowhere on the card or the envelope. If Frank's found it, he might think it's intended for him.' Thank God Erica had altered her handwriting. She thought of all the thank-you cards she had sent to Flora and Frank, after staying the night at their house. Then panic took hold of her. What if she hadn't disguised her writing sufficiently? What if Frank thought she was in love with him? Two strangers had escaped, but Frank was now the innocent victim of King Herod. Oh, God; this was the worst disaster imaginable.

Flora was laughing again. 'If Frank found it, he'd think someone had given *Paul* a Valentine card, which Paul stuffed into his ISA leaflet and forgot about, and passed on by mistake. Anyway, there's no need to worry because Frank *never* reads those glossy financial brochures Paul gives him. Neither do I. We're always saying, in fact, how pointless it is for us to have a financial adviser when we're too lazy to read any of the information he gives us. All our money sits in the building society, year after year, doing nothing.'

'You mean Frank might not have found the card yet?' said Erica, trying not be upset by the idea of all the Gustavinas' money.

'He definitely won't have,' said Flora. 'Relax. When he gets in later, I'll whip it out and shred it. I'll destroy the evidence. God, how funny! Who'd have thought this would happen, hey? It's like in *What's up, Doc?*, when all the briefcases get mixed up...'

'What time will Frank get back?' Erica interrupted.

'I don't know. Look, don't worry. I'll attend to it. You can rely on me. The last thing I want is Frank finding the card and passing it on to Paul. Especially now that I've met Hugh.'

Erica ignored Flora's fluttery sigh. She didn't have the mental strength even to consider Hugh at the moment. She admired Flora's stamina; most people, she guessed, after vigorously desiring and then mercilessly spurning one man, all in the space of a week, would want to wait at least a few days before hurtling towards the next.

Still, who was Erica to criticise Flora? Flora was a loyal best friend – and, it seemed, a compassionate boss. Most people would have fired Erica for her failure to complete her first task as instructed. Flora wasn't even cross about it. 'I'm sorry I didn't post the Valentines,' Erica said again. 'I would have done, if I hadn't…'

'…decided to target Frank instead!' Flora chuckled. 'Don't worry. I'm glad you didn't send them. If you had, it'd be too late. Maybe you're psychic. As it is, I'll be able to fish the card out of Frank's briefcase and noone'll be any the wiser. And, since there's no name on the card, I could even send it on to Hugh! I've got until tomorrow, haven't I?'

Please, please, shut up about Hugh, thought Erica. 'Thanks for being so understanding,' she said.

THE NEXT MORNING, Erica was in the middle of trying to lower a split white bin liner full of rubbish into a black refuse sack when her doorbell rang. She swung round, and red oil from a takeaway curry carton spilled out of the slit in the bin bag, pooling on the already stained linoleum. She sighed, dropped the lot and ran to the door. Please let it be Flora, she prayed. She didn't even mind if Flora wanted the two of them to proceed straight to the home of Hugh, whoever he was, to deliver the Valentine card by hand.

Flora hadn't phoned her yesterday evening, and every time Erica had tried to call the Gustavinas' house she'd got an engaged tone. The same had happened this morning. Flora's mobile wasn't even taking messages. A cold male voice said, 'The Vodafone you are calling may be switched off. Please try later.' Erica had been trying every five minutes since seven o'clock this morning. She was desperate to hear that Flora had successfully retrieved the card.

She ran to the door and swung it open, gasping with relief when she saw Flora wrapped in a long brown woollen thing that was either a very soft coat or a very long cardigan. 'Thank goodness! I've been worried sick,' said Erica. 'Come in. Did you get it? Is everything okay?'

'I'm afraid not.' Flora didn't move. She looked burdened; miserable, even. Erica's hands flew to her mouth. She couldn't believe that the situation was not resolved. Flora had assured her it would be. 'I can't come in. We've got to go,' she said, nodding in the direction of her red Mercedes.

'Where to?' Erica smoothed down her hair with one hand. She was wearing a shapeless old sweatshirt and tracksuit bottoms. She couldn't go out without changing.

'My house.'

'But what...?'

'Come on, I'll explain on the way. Don't worry, I've already thought of a way round the problem,' said Flora. But Erica noticed that she didn't smile.

She abandoned her wish to attend to her appearance and followed Flora to the car. She was desperate to ask more questions, but felt, somehow, that it was not her place to do so. Flora would talk when she was ready. This is all my fault, thought Erica. I've caused everybody so much trouble. She climbed into the Mercedes. It smelled of oranges. Erica rested her feet on the two small piles of battered paperbacks that filled the footwell.

'Right. Let me update you on the catastrophe.' Flora laughed grimly. The car accelerated steadily, smoothly, as she spoke. 'I looked in Frank's briefcase and there was no card anywhere in sight. I was a bit puzzled, because Frank hadn't said anything to me and I was sure he would have done if he'd found the Valentine. I was just wondering what to do, whether to bring it up, pretend *you'd* wanted to send Paul a Valentine and mistaken Frank's briefcase for his…'

'*What*?' Erica thought she might have a seizure.

'I said I was wondering,' Flora snapped. 'I didn't actually do it, all right? Anyway, as I was mulling things over, deciding what my next step ought to be, Throat Pastille turned up.' She stopped, sighed.

'And?' Erica demanded.

'There's no easy way to say this, Erica, so I'll just say it, okay? Throat Pastille had the card.'

'He…Oh, no.'

'He saw you put it in Frank's briefcase. He was in the hall. How could you not have seen him?'

Erica felt too sick to answer. She'd been so nervous, she'd just stuffed the card in, leaving the door to the hall wide open. But TP had been with Flora, hadn't he? Perhaps he'd been on his way to the upstairs bathroom, but had stopped when he saw Erica shaking and sweating over Frank Gustavina's briefcase. She pressed her eyes shut. She considered throwing open the passenger door of Flora's car and launching herself out.

'TP was curious, understandably,' Flora went on. 'He decided to investigate, while we were busy chatting in the kitchen. He found the bloody card, and turned up last night to announce to me and Frank that you're a scheming traitor and we ought to have nothing more to do with you.' Flora's voice shook. Erica couldn't tell if she was angry, frightened or upset. 'I was so surprised, I didn't know what to say.'

'What did Frank say?' asked Erica. Oh, God. Frank Gustavina thought she fancied him. She would have to make it clear, as soon as possible, that she didn't. Without offending him, of course. Was such a thing possible? Oh, God!

'What do you think he said? "What sort of friend makes a play for her best mate's husband?" – something along those lines. He and TP were pissed off, on my behalf. They're both saying I should get rid of you. But I don't want to get rid of you, because you're my best friend and, as we both know, you *aren't* trying to steal Frank behind my back.'

'I can't believe this,' Erica whispered. 'What can we do? I can't bear the thought of Frank thinking that about me. We'll have to tell him…'

'What? Tell him what? I've considered all the options. One: the truth – obviously we can't tell him that. Two: we tell him you thought it was Paul's briefcase, and that you meant to send the card to Paul.'

'No!' Erica protested, horrified. This plan had been mentioned once already, and it sounded no more appealing the second time round.

'I decided against option number two, because – if I can be blunt – TP really doesn't like you, and he'd be absolutely sure to tell Paul you've got the hots for him, just to embarrass you and make life difficult. And you really don't want to get on the wrong side of a hulk like Paul. I could order TP to keep it to himself, but I couldn't be a hundred per cent sure that he would. I think the temptation'd be too great. He'd tell Paul, but make Paul promise not to tell me. Anyway, even if he wouldn't, I just…I still think of Paul as mine, somehow, rather than yours. Do you understand? Even though I don't fancy him any more.'

'I don't want Paul!' said Erica. 'I don't want even a tiny bit of him, and there's no way I'm going to pretend I sent him a Valentine.'

'Okay. So, then, option number three: we say that you intended the card for Frank, and I'll just be very tolerant and understanding about it. I can say, "She's single, she got carried away, she's sorry, there's no harm done", etc. etc.'

'No!'

'Well, it wouldn't be convincing, anyway,' said Flora. 'There's no way I'd ever overlook such a huge betrayal, and Frank knows that. He'd be very suspicious.'

'So what can we do?' Erica asked, shaking in her seat. 'We have to come up with something, don't we?'

'There's only one thing we can say: that you thought the briefcase was TP's, and that you meant the card to be for him.' Erica opened her mouth, aghast, but Flora silenced her with a raised palm. 'TP was the only man in the house at the time. His zip-up case, the one he keeps his poetry cassettes and CDs in, is brown. You'll say you thought the case was his, and he'll believe you. You just shoved the card in, and you didn't notice the financial brochures...'

'No. No!'

'It's the only way, Erica.' Flora turned to face her with a solemn expression. 'What's the alternative? How else do you propose to explain why you put a Valentine card in Frank's case? If you meant it to go to Throat Pastille, I won't have to banish you from my life for ever. Erica, I don't want to lose you! As a friend or as an employee. There's Project Hugh to think of, remember?'

'You can't do this!' said Erica quietly. She didn't want to know a single detail about Hugh – not where Flora met him, nor his surname, nor his job. She was determined not to ask. How dared Flora refer to TP by an affectionate nickname when she'd admitted only minutes ago that TP couldn't stand Erica? It was so disloyal. 'You can't play with people and...fancy one person one minute and another the next and...' She was unable to expand, though she was certain that she had many excellent points to make. If only she weren't so distraught and confused. 'I won't do it,' she said. 'I don't have to say anything to Frank. He can think what he likes, and so can TP. Let me out. Stop the car.'

'Oh, they can think what they like, can they?' said Flora angrily, speeding along the dual carriageway. 'You mean, I can deal with it? That's what you mean. You might be able to walk away from this, but I can't.'

Erica began to cry. 'Go on, you might as well say it. I can walk away, even though this whole disaster is my fault. If I'd posted those cards...' 'I don't want to lose you', Flora had said. 'As a friend'.

Flora sighed. 'Erica, the last thing I want is for us to fall out over this. Yes, it's a mess, but let's just deal with it and move on. I'm sorry that this TP thing is the best idea I can come up with, but I'm afraid it is. Can you think of a better one?'

'What about telling Frank the truth?' Erica sobbed.

'Don't be ridiculous. Do you want to ruin my life?'

Yes, yes, yes: the word stormed Erica's head.

Neither woman spoke for a while. The only sounds were the hum of the car's engine and Erica's occasional sniffs.

'Do you know when I first cheated on Frank?' said Flora eventually. 'It was after a huge row we had. He'd said some awful things to me. He apologised, of course, but I knew I could never forgive him, not unless I armed myself with something, a secret. I simply refused to be the more injured party. So I contacted an agency for married people. I found their address in the back of *Private Eye*. I met a man and we had a four-month fling. And ever since then, whenever I've been cross with Frank, I've thought "Ha! Little do you know."'

'What's that got to do with this?' said Erica. She wished she had some cigarettes with her.

'You said I play with people, before. I don't mean to. But I have needs just like everybody else. I do what I need to do. It might seem frivolous to you, but believe me, I'm deadly serious about all my...enterprises. Whether they last a long time or only for a moment.'

'I'm not doing it,' said Erica.

'Why do you think I sleep with other men? It's not because they're any better at sex than Frank is. Most of them are worse, actually, technique-wise. But...Look, men enjoy sex whatever the circumstances. All they need is some repetitive rubbing and they're away. Whereas we women need mental excitement to generate physical excitement, don't we? Novelty is essential. The first time you have sex with someone is always the best.'

Erica looked up. 'That can't be true,' she said. Once again, one of Flora's hooks was in her and she couldn't ignore it. She had to follow it up.

'It's true,' said Flora. 'The newer a man is, the less knowledge and experience we have of him, the less real he is to us. He's a blank slate, on to which we can project all the necessary fantasies. And let's face it, if we're honest, it's only by concentrating hard on our own fantasies that women can achieve satisfaction. It never comes about because of anything a man does. Not in my experience, anyway.'

'That's not true,' Erica protested tearfully. What Flora was saying did not reflect what Erica had read in books and women's magazines over the years. 'Your partner can learn how to please you, but it takes time for you to... get used to each other's ways. The first time isn't the best, hardly ever.'

Flora raised her eyebrows. 'Erica, that's crap. Everyone lies about sex. Except me, now. Most women have far more orgasms on their own than they do with men. It's the concentration thing again, the necessary psychological build-up, the focus on creating precisely the right conditions to achieve one's own pleasure. Any distraction ruins it, and what woman can concentrate single-mindedly on her own pleasure with a man around? Even when he's doing his best to be selfless, one always feels the lurking presence of his ego, its wish to be attended to in one way or another. Even if all it wants is to be recognised for not wanting anything at that precise moment.'

Erica's mind buzzed. She didn't want all this information. Or rather, she did, but she knew she ought not to. It was possible to know too much, more than one could handle.

'That's why, the less well you know a man, the better,' Flora went on. 'Because you'll be less aware of what he's thinking, what he wants and needs. You can ignore him more. In a good way.'

'This has got nothing to do with me pretending to have sent the Valentine to TP,' Erica protested. 'That's what we were discussing, and I'm not doing it. Okay?' Flora smiled politely. 'Anyway, it's not true, what you're saying. What about intimacy? Women need intimacy, not novelty, in order to feel...stimulated.'

'I agree intimacy's important. But again, all my best intimate moments have involved virtual strangers. When I'm with a man I hardly know, secrets and confidences pour out of me. But all that staring into eyes, sharing deep truths and insights about one's most private selves – you want to do that with someone who doesn't already know you too well, don't you? Otherwise, it's just embarrassing. I mean, you don't want to be having orgasms in front of the person you go to Waitrose with, the person you bicker with about whether to buy a block of Parmesan or the ready-grated stuff. I couldn't bear to…roll up every bit of myself – the everyday me and the ideal, private, fantasy me – into one giant ball and give it to just one person. I'd feel owned, like a slave. I'd feel as if I had no leeway.'

Flora had captured precisely how Erica felt, in her present bind. 'I won't pretend to fancy TP,' she insisted tearfully.

'Then say the card was a joke!' Flora's eyes sparkled with sudden inspiration. 'He annoys you, and you wanted to wind him up.'

Erica felt as if the oxygen in the car were running out. She wished Flora would open a window, didn't dare to do so herself. 'It's not fair. You can't expect me to…'

'Erica, we can't tell the truth. My whole world'd be wrecked. Look, please! I'll buy you a new car,' said Flora urgently, glancing at her watch as she drove. 'Your Skoda's a disgrace. Your parents can't drive. You're always ferrying them around; you need reliable transport. If you do this, I'll buy you whatever car you want – a BMW, a Jag, whatever.'

Erica wondered why a Rolls-Royce wasn't on the list. Wasn't that supposed to be the best sort of car? Dully, she considered her options. She decided that she had none. 'I can't lose you,' Flora had said. Erica had to do what Flora wanted. She wasn't sure why. It was partly the offer of a car, partly that she had already spent most of the thousand pounds Flora had given her on getting herself out of debt. And they were only in this predicament because Erica had totally disregarded Flora's original instructions, something Flora was decent enough not to point out. Fear, also, was involved. Erica had a strong suspicion that the world would immediately become a barren and hostile environment if she disappointed Flora Gustavina.

'Maybe I'll say it was a joke,' she said. She imagined setting fire to Flora's hair.

'Yes! That's the way to do it,' Flora gushed, relieved. 'I can completely understand why you don't want to fake lust for TP. Who knows what that might lead to?' She stopped the car. Erica, who had been utterly unaware, for the duration of the whole hideous conversation, of a world outside the Mercedes, finally looked out of the window. They were here, at the Gustavinas'.

'Let's get this over with,' said Flora. Erica forced her stiff legs to move in the direction of the house. She couldn't bear to think about what was going to happen. Why wasn't she running away? What could Flora do to stop her, if she chose to escape? 'I'm back,' Flora shouted as she unlocked the door. There was something fake, something staged, about the way she said it. 'I've got

Erica with me. Go through to the lounge,' she whispered to Erica. 'What?'

'You go first.'

Flora looked impatient. Then her expression softened and she smiled. 'It'll be okay, don't worry,' she mouthed. She turned her back on Erica and marched confidently into the lounge.

Erica trailed after her, dragged by a force that both controlled and despised her, one she didn't understand. Frank Gustavina lay stretched out on the sofa, with a bumpy pottery mug in one hand and the *Daily Telegraph* in the other. He was wearing a grey suit and only black socks on his feet, which brushed against Erica as she entered the room. He leaped into an upright position; it was as if he feared that even the smallest physical contact might commit him to a relationship with her. TP sat cross-legged on the floor, tracing a pattern on the carpet with his bony fingers. He stared at Erica in sullen defiance.

What was TP doing here? Erica couldn't believe Flora – or perhaps it was Frank? – had invited him to witness the showdown, the show trial. She had an unpleasant thought. What if Flora had only discussed the options with Erica to make her feel she had some say in what happened next? What if she had told Frank and TP last night that Erica had intended the Valentine card for TP? That would explain why he was here this morning.

For a few seconds, nobody said anything. Then Flora nudged Erica. 'Go on,' she said officiously, like a primary school teacher. 'Erica has something to say, about the Valentine card. Go on, Erica.' They can do and say what they like, thought Erica, but surely it's up to me whether I choose to feel degraded. She stared at the window ahead of her and imagined that she was playing the lead role in a very demanding drama; it was hard work, it was torture, but it would be worth it.

'It was supposed to be for TP,' she said. 'I thought the briefcase was his. I mistook it for that brown case, with the zip.'

'My poetry portfolio?' said TP. 'It's nothing like it.'

'I just assumed…' Erica blushed. 'You were the only person in the house at the time, and…I thought Frank's briefcase was black. I didn't know he had a new one.'

'Understandable.' Frank nodded. 'Right, well…there's no problem then, is there?' He looked at Flora, as if seeking permission to leave the meeting. She shook her head. Frank stayed put.

Erica tried to work out what she ought to say next. She needed to make it clear, tactfully, that the Valentine had been a prank. 'Interested? Or just curious?': it was hardly the sort of thing one would write if one were joking. It didn't sound at all light-hearted. Why hadn't this occurred to her before? Had Flora thought of it? Erica felt dizzy. She didn't want to humiliate TP. He annoyed her, but she had no wish to turn him into an object of public ridicule, not in a romantic context. That would be too hurtful; he didn't deserve that. Flora was staring at her with sharp, shiny eyes that urged her to speak up.

'How could you think I'd be interested in a middle-aged frump like you?' TP looked Erica up and down. 'I wouldn't touch you if you were the last woman in the world.'

'There's no need for that, TP,' said Frank. 'Shouldn't we all just…try to get back to normal?'

'What's normal?' Flora snapped. 'Erica, tell him. The card was supposed to be a joke.' Stick to the script, for God's sake, said her eyes.

'I…I…' Erica stammered.

'She's a joke,' said TP. 'She's only interested in me because I'm a poet. If I was just a gardener, she wouldn't look twice at me. But, I mean, how desperate would I have to be?'

'TP, shut up, for fuck's sake!' said Frank.

'She's got a moustache!'

Erica turned and left the room as quickly as she could. A loud humming filled her head, like the sound of a large insect becoming agitated. That had not just happened. It had not happened. It couldn't have. She was opening the front door when Flora caught up with her and began to breathe desperate jollity into her ear. 'Good old Frank! He put TP in his place, didn't he?' She tittered nervously. 'God, that was excruciating! Are you okay? You haven't taken it to heart, have you? TP's a fool. He doesn't know what he's talking about.'

'I'm fine,' said Erica.

'Phew! What an afternoon! Look, let's go and do something nice to cheer ourselves up. Cocktails! I know just the place.'

'No. I have to go.'

'Come on, Erica, don't sulk.' Flora lowered her voice. 'We need to talk about Project Hugh.'

'No. I've got...things I have to do,' said Erica, edging past Flora and out on to the street.

'Tomorrow, then? Let's go out for lunch. And then shall we go and buy you a car?' Flora shouted after her.

Erica stopped walking. If she said no, if she left and never came back, Flora and Frank and TP would all think she was too ashamed, that TP's cruel words had destroyed her. She couldn't let them think that. She had to come back tomorrow and perform, credibly, the role of someone who didn't give a damn what some grubby scrounger thought of her.

'Tomorrow?' Flora called out again.

Erica turned and gave a small nod.

'Excellent!'

Erica never wanted to see Flora Gustavina again in her life. She would see her tomorrow, and the day after, and the day after that.

You are a Gongedip

THERE OUGHT TO be a word to describe the person we most wish we had never met. I won't invent one – I shudder at the thought – but somebody should, so that we know to expect that person in our lives, even if they haven't arrived yet. Such a word, such a concept, might help us to recognise them while there is still time to escape, before they have shattered our calm and orderly existence.

A Devittoris. Wasn't the first Mercedes called after a woman of the same name? I believe it was.

My own orderly existence was shattered on the seventh of May last year, when Maria Devittoris ambushed me outside my house. I had done a satisfying morning's work, eaten my usual lunch of a baked potato with tuna mayonnaise and a rocket and watercress salad, and was setting off on my customary bike ride. I have found cycling to be an excellent way of banishing from my mind the dizzying effects of sustained mental concentration, and I rarely miss a day. In order to be happy and productive, I need exactly the right balance of the indoors and the outdoors, the cerebral and the physical. This was what I was thinking about – how essential this mixture was if I were to flourish, how impressive my determination, daily, to achieve it – as I opened my garage door and emerged into the sunlight with my bike.

I noticed immediately that there was a person standing next to my front garden, on the other side of the hedge. I glanced at the figure out of the corner of my eye. The head and shoulders were all I could see above the neat rectangular wall of privet, and these were covered by a bizarre item of clothing that was a cross between a shawl and a hood. Is such a garment called a snood? I believe it is; I wouldn't have dreamed that word up out of nowhere.

I took in that the figure was wearing a snood, then – a woolly, emerald green thing that was quite extraordinarily ugly. I wondered what sort of idiot would choose to wear knitted headgear in early May and, even more worryingly, to waste his or her afternoon dawdling on a pavement. Merloncing: now there's a word I did make up, as a schoolboy. My friends and I use it to this day. To merlonce: to loiter idly, deliberately, or be unoccupied in a subtly obtrusive way, while somebody else is busy right next to you, making it impossible for that person to concentrate on what they're doing. Did the green-topped merloncer have no work or hobbies to pursue? I've always loathed time-wasters, and, when I saw the figure begin to turn to face me, I averted my eyes, keen to avoid any contact that would cut into my cycling time.

Head down, I pushed my bike out on to the road and steered it away from the snood-wearer. I had one foot on a pedal when I heard a woman's voice call out, 'William!' I was considering pretending I hadn't heard when I felt a sharp tapping on my back and heard laboured breathing that sounded as if its source were adjacent to my left ear. Whoever she was, she had hurried over in order to draw herself to my attention. That was sufficient to make me dislike her.

I had no choice but to turn. Inside the green snood's oval-shaped aperture I saw a slender nose with a moist red tip, waterlogged eyes, two blotchy expanses of cheek, a small flexing mouth. I noticed these features individually before I saw them as a whole and realised, with immense frustration, that the hooded dawdler was Maria Devittoris. I had forgotten her almost entirely, but there was no denying that we knew one another. Therefore, I deduced, she was not standing here by chance. She intended to speak to me, perhaps at length.

'Maria. I was just on my way out. I can't talk now, I'm afraid.'

'When can you?' Her tone was knowing and bitter, her question confusing and unanswerable. I was trying to work out what to say next when she said, 'Why do you think I'm standing outside your house in disguise?' With her right hand, she yanked off her hood. The action was savagely abrupt. I had the impression that she was trying to blame me for subjecting her to the indignity of wearing the green snood, when in fact neither her presence nor her attire had anything to do with me.

Nor did her two questions, both of which were designed to suggest that she and I were jointly involved in an ongoing situation. She had the look of a woman who thought she knew all about me – a look I have seen on several female faces over the years. I was particularly alarmed by Maria's second question – 'Why do you think I'm standing outside your house in disguise?' – which was surely based upon a conviction that her motivation ought to be of interest to me. I cared not one jot.

I will not go into detail about my history with Maria. I would find that too tedious – as dull, in fact, as the party at which we met. Maria works for Collegiate Press, who have published all my work. They are excellent publishers of scholarly books, but hopeless party hosts. All this is irrelevant, however. The only salient point is that I had spent some time with Maria a year or so previously and then lost touch with her.

'I have no idea why you're standing outside my house in disguise,' I said honestly. If I'd put my mind to it, I'm sure I could have come up with a workable theory, but as I had nothing to gain by doing so, I didn't bother. I pushed my bike back and forth, listening to the tempting click and whir of its wheels, wishing Maria would disappear. Then it occurred to me that appearing to cooperate might be a more efficient way to get rid of her. So I applied myself, and tried to think about why she might, a year after we'd last spoken, be lurking outside my house with her head and shoulders encased in a knitted green tube.

The effort took all my willpower. My brain vigorously resisted any sort of imaginative speculation about Maria's actions. My focus slid away from her into abstraction. I issued an order to myself: 'Think about Maria Devittoris.' Obediently, my thoughts struggled to latch on to her, but they were dragged away each time they got close, like feeble swimmers in the strong current of my attention and enthusiasm, which pulled in the opposite direction, towards the hills, solitude.

'I've no idea,' I said again, and shrugged.

'I've been watching you for a while,' said Maria. 'I didn't want you to see me until I was ready.'

'Oh. Well, I didn't see you,' I said, swallowing a yawn.

A tear rolled from the outer corner of her right eye. 'Aren't you going to ask me, ready for what?'

I felt exhausted by the unfeasibly high level of involvement she expected from me. If she wanted to tell me what she was ready for, she was free to do so, though God knows I was keen to preserve my ignorance on this score. By now it was clear to me that my plans for the afternoon were an endangered species. I wanted to lie down in the middle of the road and hug my knees to my chest. I pictured myself in bed, cocooned in my duck-down duvet. Maria's demands were making me feel nooberly. This word is another one I invented while at school. My friends and I couldn't have managed without it over the years, so perfectly does it describe a particular state. Nooberly: tired, sensitive, vulnerable, shivery, or otherwise in need of curling up under a quilt.

If only Maria had known how difficult it was for me to stand there and converse with her, I was sure she'd have granted me a sympathetic release. I was so bored by the whole idea of her that I found I was having to remind myself every three seconds that she was still in front of me, that convention and politeness required me to respond to her nonsense. The concept of Maria Devittoris drained from my mind even as I looked at her; I kept having to gather it up and drop it back in, pat it into a more solid shape.

She sighed. Did that mean she had given up on me? I was cautiously optimistic.

'How's the phonetics business?' she said.

'Don't call it a business.'

Her mouth twitched. 'Still the same old William. How's work, then?' She moved closer. Her lips were brown, glossy, ribbed with vertical lines, like two worms.

'Fine.'

'What are you working on at the moment? This morning? You still work in the mornings, don't you? From eight until twelve.'

'Why do you want to know?'

She let out an abrasive snigger. 'Only you could ask that. How are James and George? Do you all still go to the Lord Nelson every night?'

'Not every night, no.'

'Do you still speak in that silly code the three of you made up at your public school, with its many helipads?' I found her inaccuracies tiresome. Our school had possessed only one helipad. The silly code, as Maria called it, was something I'd devised alone. James and George merely used it.

I vaguely remembered that Maria had always resented the private language I shared with my two oldest friends. Hadn't she once insisted that she 'deserved' to know what all the words meant? Yes, that's right: there was some tearful nonsense about her feeling excluded. She'd assumed she had the right to know everything about me. Now, over a year later, it seemed that assumption remained in place.

I refused to discuss James and George with Maria, so decided to deflect her attention by answering the question about my work. 'If you must know, this morning I was proofreading my introduction to Collegiate's new *Dictionary of Rhymes*.' I announced the title proudly; it was my suggestion. When I'd first seen the proposal, the book had provisionally been called *The Rhymer's Dictionary*. I had successfully persuaded Rachel, the language reference editor, that this sounded twee and amateurish.

'We need a new one?' Maria sneered. It had always infuriated me that she referred to Collegiate Press as 'we'. Her job there was a menial, manual one – she fiddled with commas and semicolons once all the serious editorial work had been done – yet she spoke as if she were to Collegiate Press what TS Eliot was to Faber and Faber. 'What's wrong with the old one? I assume cat still rhymes with hat.'

And with fat, I nearly said. There was a bulge around Maria's middle that had not been there the last time I saw her. 'Among other things, the introduction is what's wrong with the old one,' I said impatiently. 'Naunton Ralph wrote it.'

'Who?'

'He's a professor of English Literature at Oxford, an intellectual casualty of the sixties and seventies. He knows nothing about linguistics. His introduction's all about the politics of rhyme, its cultural significance.' This was one of my favourite rants, but even so I soon ran out of steam. It is impossible to find anything interesting, or to be interesting oneself, in the presence of somebody one finds wholly boring. Just as I would have been unable to eat a baked potato if there were a cowpat on the plate beside it, I had no desire to disparage Naunton Ralph with Maria as my audience.

'Words mean things to people,' said Maria. 'Some people, anyway.'

My fingers were starting to hurt. I loosened my grip on the handles of my bike. 'Maria, I have to go. Is there something specific that you want from me?'

'What do *you* want, William?' she said in a flirtatious voice. 'Apart from to be immortal. Poor William! Let's face it, noone's ever going to pay much attention to your work.'

'This is…Get out of my way!' I pushed her and she staggered backwards. In the history of my paltry acquaintance with Maria, I had said not one word to her about wanting to be immortal. How dared she invent random wishes and attribute them to me without my permission?

She bobbed back up, like a rubber duck in the bath. 'Perhaps your introduction to the rhymer's dictionary will be the one, the piece of work that propels you towards stardom.' She sniggered. 'If it doesn't, you can always become a rapper. Or a gigolo, I *don't* think!'

'Maria, I've listened to enough of your inanity. Now, I've got the rest of my life to get on with, and I'm rather hoping you won't be in it, so if you'll excuse me...'

'Ah!' she said, clapping her hands together, as if she had coaxed from me a crucial revelation. 'So you did lie about call waiting.'

'*What*?' I was beginning to despair. Would I ever get rid of the woman? Not this afternoon – I had kissed goodbye to this afternoon a long while ago; indeed, my grieving process for the hours between two and five was already well under way. But now I was beginning to fear for the evening, for tomorrow, next month, next year. In order to persuade Maria to leave me alone, I would have to work out what she meant and respond to it in a way that would satisfy her. Call waiting? I had no idea what she was referring to.

'Our last phone conversation. There was that bleeping noise on the line, your call waiting signal. You said, "I'd better go and see who it is. Ring me again." Those were your exact words.' I wished that I could confidently have accused her of lying, but I had no memory of any of it. And even if it were true, so what? I'd taken another call; it was hardly a momentous event. 'But I didn't call you again, did I? And you didn't call me. And that was that.' Maria's voice vibrated with menace and misery. Her oral portrayal of that being that was a bleak, apocalyptic one.

'And that was that,' I enthused, in a far jollier tone. 'So why are you here?'

'*I* phoned *you*. I always did. If you had a call waiting and had to go, you should have said *you'd* phone *me* back, not "ring me again" in that presumptuous, offhand way!'

I felt a creeping sense of alarm.

Maria straightened her back. 'I think most reasonable people would agree that the onus is on the callee, not the caller, to phone back if the original call is interrupted by the callee's call waiting noise. And you could easily have ignored those bleeps and carried on talking to me! The other person would have been diverted to your voicemail. They'd have left a message. Why couldn't they be the one to wait for *ever* for you to ring them back?'

My brain was reeling from her outburst. Should I rip out her entire belief structure at the roots, I wondered, or content myself with trying to trim around the edges of her insanity? I couldn't decide, so settled on a mixture of the two approaches. 'There are no onuses between us, Maria. I barely know you. I'm not going to bicker about the minute detail of something that happened a year ago. I don't remember any of it. Perhaps the other call was urgent.'

'You barely know me? You knew me pretty well at the Marriott County Hall. And then you lost interest in me immediately afterwards. I know why. You and George and James! You're mentally straight, but physically gay. You're so enamoured with the idea of yourself as heterosexual, and it's enough to get you through the odd encounter with a woman, but you can't sustain it. The people you want to see again and again are your male friends.'

I was stunned. I began to have a sense of how much time Maria had devoted, since we'd last met, to formulating theories about my character. She was quite wrong. If I find men, on the whole, more appealing than women, it's because they talk about interesting things; women talk mainly about themselves. I had lost interest in Maria immediately after the night we spent together for two reasons: first, the chase was over, and second, she had flat nipples. I prefer nipples which jut out even when their owner is not aroused.

I considered telling Maria this in the hope that it might clear things up once and for all. In the face of the stark truth, surely she would have to submit, abandon her far-fetched hypotheses. I opened my mouth, but she interrupted my first inhalation. 'You never really wanted to have sex with me, did you? You wanted to invite James and George that night! You didn't want us to be alone. You didn't have any condoms! You must have hoped I'd refuse to have unprotected sex.'

'Maria, we're in the middle of the street.'

'I bet you never make the first move, do you? You're attractive, so women chase you. Like I did, idiot that I am! Why did you never ring me back?'

'You could have rung me. How was I to know you'd gone off in high dudgeon?'

Maria screwed up her face. '*High dudgeon?*' she repeated scornfully. 'Is that another of your infantile code words?'

'I didn't invent the term "high dudgeon", Maria. Ask any educated person.' She had no business working for a publisher; she didn't even know the rudiments of the English language.

'Those made-up words were all about me, weren't they? Insults that you could say in front of me so I wouldn't know what they meant.'

I laughed. 'Nothing I have ever said or done has been about you, Maria.' My bike wobbled beneath my hand, as if boredom and hopelessness had weakened its vehicular spirit. Enough was enough. I leaped into the saddle and pedalled away with the urgency of a getaway car driver.

'I'll get you back!' Maria yelled after me. It was unclear whether she was talking about revenge or retrieval. I didn't care. I turned the corner of my cul-de-sac and the notion of her began to disperse. She was rather like a cloud of midges: irritating, but easily left behind.

I returned from my bike ride two hours later. The road outside my house was empty. I closed the front door, savouring the knowledge that Maria Devittoris was on the other side of it, and that was the last thought I had about her until, five months later, my editor at Collegiate sent me an advance copy of the *Dictionary of Rhymes*, the new edition, with my introduction.

I turned immediately to the contents page and was proud to find the words I knew I would see: 'Introduction by William Handysides'. I cannot deny that I love – loved, rather, before Maria ruined everything for me – to see my own words, my name, in print. I don't see anything wrong with taking pride in one's achievements. I sat down and re-read my introduction. I was biased, of course, but leaving that aside, I could see that, objectively, my essay was incredibly impressive. I remembered Maria's sarcastic comment about this piece of work propelling me to stardom. How ironic it would be, I thought, if that were to happen. Maria's limited imagination would never have been able to conceive of such a thing. It occurred to me that I did not at all like the idea that Maria worked for my publishers. I wondered how successful the *Dictionary of Rhymes* would need to be in order for me to be able to demand that they get rid of her.

After I'd spent a couple of hours admiring my introduction, I leafed randomly through the pages, savouring the feel of them. Collegiate use good-quality paper, which is something most publishers don't seem to bother with any more. Idly, I began to read lists of rhymes, lulling myself almost into a trance. 'Bill, dill, drill, fill, gill, hill. Fetch, gretch, sketch, wretch.' Something bristled at the back of my mind. 'Fetch, gretch...' I gasped. My brain juddered back into focus. 'Gretch' was one of my creations. To gretch: to whine or complain loudly in an attention-seeking, self-indulgent and unwarranted manner. I swallowed a mouthful of bile. How could this be happening? It wasn't possible. It couldn't be. Nobody knew that word apart from James, George and me.

I think I might have blacked out for a while, but if I did I came to almost immediately. I pushed the pages frantically, not caring if I creased them. I searched for the word 'merlonce'. There it was, alongside 'ponce', 'bonce' and 'ensconce'. With panic simmering inside me, I looked for and found all my own words: 'mawmby', 'stidge', 'grolph', 'nooberly', 'swoggle', 'ponk'. What sick joke was this?

After a few seconds, panic gave way to rational thought. My stomach churned and my gullet quivered. I could hear my digestive juices squelching inside me. One other person knew all those words, aside from me and my friends: Maria. She'd heard them all, every single one. James, George and I had made a point of including them in every conversation after Maria had blubbed that it made her feel left out.

I marched round my study in small circles, muttering, clenching my fists and threatening inanimate objects with all manner of violence. Working was out of the question, as were cycling, sitting down, eating and sleeping. I paced the floor for most of that night, and by the time morning came I was a red-eyed desperado.

Maria had done this. Commas and semicolons hadn't been enough for her this time. She'd sabotaged the dictionary; it was her pathetic, cowardly revenge, and for what? I owed her nothing. We'd had sex once. End of story. At five in the morning, I crawled round the house on my hands and knees, hunting in old notebooks and diaries for Maria's number. I thought I would never need or want it again, so I had not taken care of it. I yelped with savage satisfaction when I found it scribbled on the back of an old Collegiate Press catalogue. The handwriting was Maria's. I made a mental note to burn the catalogue later, as soon as I'd dialled that repugnant number for the last time.

Maria answered after only three rings. Despite the hour, she did not sound as if I had woken her up. 'Maria!' I breathed into the receiver. 'It's William. You're going to fucking regret this!'

'I thought you hated split infinitives,' she said merrily.

'As soon as I tell my editor, you'll be looking for a new job.'

'Rachel? Tell her what, precisely?'

'That you fucking went and put all the words I invented into the dictionary.'

'What words?'

I fell silent. I couldn't list them; it would have been too humiliating.

'William, what have you done?' Maria's voice was slow and emphatic as she feigned shock. 'You haven't... you *haven't* gone and put your silly made-up code words in the new dictionary, have you? Oh, my God. Rachel'll go mad when she finds out. You'll be lucky if she publishes you again after this. William, how could you be so *immature*?'

'But...' I bent my body into painful shapes, tangling the telephone wire in a mess of limbs. She was right. How could I say anything to Rachel? How could I prove that Maria had done it, not me? They were my words. I'd invented them. Maria could prove it; she could tell Rachel to ask James and George. I pictured myself explaining to Rachel how this act of vandalism had come about. I didn't think I could bear to tell her such a ridiculous tale, even if there were a chance she might believe me. It was so undignified, so unprofessional. I would have to direct her attention towards the relevant words. No, it was unthinkable.

'You and your public school pranks,' said Maria fondly. 'Don't worry, William. I won't breathe a word!'

'I'll fucking kill you, you fat nonentity!'

There was a silence, after which she said nasally, 'I don't know why you're so angry, anyway. I thought you loved to see your own words in print. And these ones are yours in every sense. You should be delighted. Immortality, William, remember?' There was a loud click. She had slammed down the phone.

I stood in the middle of my living room, arms by my sides, feeling as if I were about to choke or suffocate. What ought I to do now? I forced myself to walk towards the dictionary, but couldn't even contemplate opening it. If I'd been able to bring myself to touch it, I would have taken it outside and put it in the dustbin. Instead, I closed my study door, trapping the dictionary inside. That door has remained closed ever since.

I limped through to my lounge. There were books there too, books which were not the *Collegiate Dictionary of Rhymes* and which had not been vandalised by Maria, but my fingers scrunched into a tight ball every time I tried to open one. Over a period of weeks, I tried every day, with a range of volumes – novels, atlases, recipe books – but it was no use. Every time I even thought about lifting a cover or turning a page, my mind zoomed back to that awful moment when I had first seen the word 'gretch' in the dictionary and my brain had been crushed by an avalanche of fast-falling horror.

I was, it seemed, allergic to books, the thing I had always loved most in the world. I became somewhat of a hermit, and for months I did little but lie in bed and drink bottles of absinthe, which I ordered on the internet

(I used the local library's computer; I would have done without rather than venture into my study). Pretty soon my income dried up, and I had no choice but to plunder my trust fund.

I was forced to avoid James and George, since the prospect of confiding in them was abhorrent to me. Maria had been a joke to us, insofar as she was anything at all; I couldn't bear to confess to them that I had been felled by a joke. I refused to be thought of as the man whose made-up childhood words found their way into an important book he was working on, via his deranged ex-lover. Also, I began to suspect that my book phobia was too extreme a reaction to what Maria had done, and was filled with an even greater dread than my dread of books when I considered what this might indicate about my mental health. Surely a sane, well-adjusted man would have shrugged it off, perhaps even laughed about it in time. I became convinced that I was some kind of pathetic wimp, which drove me to hide myself from the outside world even more comprehensively.

A few weeks after the day of the dictionary's arrival and my abusive phone call to Maria, I received a post-card from her. I was going through a particularly bad patch, spending whole days and nights lying on the floor sobbing and chewing my hands, when it arrived. It said, 'Moofmips are red, nooglips are blue, you are a gongedip, and I grax you.' I read it once, then tore it up immediately, but it was too late: I knew the words by heart. Her aim was clear: to make me feel left out in the way she had, because I didn't understand the stupid words she'd made up. No doubt she wanted me to wonder what they meant, but I wasn't going to fall for that trick. It was obvious to me that they meant nothing whatsoever. They were pure gibberish. Maria wasn't interested in inventing new words; all she cared about was upsetting me. And her words sounded so stupid: what on earth could a 'moofmip' be? Anyway, I absolutely refused to speculate. There was no such thing as a 'gongedip', not in the world and not even in Maria's mind.

I am slightly better now, though it has taken nearly a year. I go out occasionally. James and George have been very understanding; they took me at my word when I told them that it was stomach problems that had laid me low. I still get palpitations when I think about opening a book, although I am now – finally, thank God – able to open newspapers, journals and magazines without suffering any adverse effects. And I will never give up on books; I am absolutely determined to beat whatever psychological syndrome I have acquired. Last night, for example, I was able to sit for two hours with Halldor Laxness's *Independent People* on my knee. Closed, of course.

If only the dreams would leave me alone, I think I would recover more speedily. After many months of sleeping for about eighteen hours a day, I now hardly sleep at all. Oddly, it is not the corrupted dictionary that haunts me in the night; it is Maria's postcard. My recurring nightmare is that I receive another card from her, exactly the same as the last one: 'Moofmips are red, nooglips are blue, you are a gondedip, and I grax you'. I see myself reading the card, hear the words inside my head, just as if the scene were real. I jolt awake, soaked in sweat. I don't know why I am so afraid of it happening, since it has already happened.

The Most Enlightened Person I've Ever Met

I AM NOT an enlightened person. I don't entirely understand what it means to be enlightened, but I understand enough to know that I'm not. Even my psychotherapist, who is more enlightened than I am, does not regard herself as fully enlightened. She once described someone she met on a spiritual retreat as 'the most enlightened person I've ever met', and said that, compared to him, she still had a long way to go.

I have even further to go, though I have made progress since last year. And although enlightenment is not the same as knowledge, I am also more knowledgeable than I was. I now know that there are six Betty's Tearooms: one in Ilkley, two in York, one in Northallerton, one in Harrogate and one just outside Harrogate, at Harlow Carr. When I phoned Nathan to confirm today's meeting, I made a point of saying 'Don't forget, it's the Betty's at Harlow Carr, not the one in Harrogate.'

He said, 'I haven't forgotten. Was that a dig?'

'No,' I said. 'I just want to make sure we'll both be in the same place: Betty's at RHS Harlow Carr.' I didn't know before I discovered Harlow Carr that RHS stands for Royal Horticultural Society.

It is likely that many people are aware of these facts that I'm boasting about having in my possession – I am not the only one. However, I like to think that I know them in a more fundamental way. The knowing of them is at the core of my being, because of the injuries I sustained in the process of acquiring the knowledge. Let's just say they've been burned into me.

I have been to all six Betty's Tearooms, several times each in the past year. It helps to be thorough. I have had a process to complete, and each stage is crucial. Today should be the last. Perhaps it's fate that the Betty's at Harlow Carr is my favourite. It's a lovely shape, spacious, and there are beautiful views from all the windows. After I gave up my job – after it gave me up, rather – I started to come here every day: a long walk round the gardens in the morning, then a Betty's Yorkshire rarebit for lunch, with a dollop of apple chutney and a dollop of tomato chutney on the side.

I am early for my meeting with Nathan. I sit by the window, as I have promised Greg I will. Five minutes before Nathan is due to arrive, I see Greg outside, near the trees. He is wearing his green overalls and gives me a thumbs-up. He is smoking a cigarette, holding it backwards, inside his palm, so that it's not obvious. If his boss caught him, he would lose his job.

Greg is one of nineteen full-time gardeners at Harlow Carr. I first met him when I started to come every day. He wants us to live together, but I've told him I can't think about that until my business with Nathan is concluded. I think he understands.

When Nathan arrives, he doesn't look older, fatter, sicker or in any way worse than he did last year. Because I am not enlightened, I resent this so deeply that my head starts to ache. Still, at least I know how I ought to feel, so I suppose that's progress. I ought to realise that even if Nathan is well and happy, that doesn't detract from my own wellbeing. It isn't as if miseries and deteriorations heaped upon him would make my good luck stocks rocket sky-high, as if he and I are on some kind of fortune see-saw.

I talk over his 'hello'. I can't help it. 'Look around you,' I say. 'Do you see the shops of Harrogate? No. Do you see the famous Victorian Turkish Baths? No.'

'What?' He looks baffled.

'Harlow Carr might have Harrogate in its address, but any sensible person would agree that we're outside Harrogate, not in it. Ask the waitress what she thinks, when she comes to take our order.'

He groans. 'Not this rigmarole again. Is this why you wanted to meet?'

'No. I wanted to get it out of the way, that's all.'

'It is out of the way,' he snaps. 'It's a year out of the bloody way, a year past its sell-by date!'

Greg is waiting outside for me to give him the signal. When I touch the bottom of my ear, he starts to move. 'Someone's got something to tell you,' I say to Nathan.

'What?' His face wrinkles in bewilderment. 'Who?'

'He's called Greg Massarano.'

'Who is he?'

'A gardener. He works here.'

'And this affects me how?'

'Wait and see,' I say. He might have said 'us': 'And this affects us how?' He never wanted there to be an 'us'.

Greg arrives at our table. 'Go on,' I say.

He clears his throat. 'On the twenty-fifth of August last year, Lindsay was sat at that table there from about three until closing.' He points. 'She was crying. I saw her, watched her the whole time.' Word-perfect. I nod at Greg, smile. He makes himself scarce.

'You see?' I say to Nathan. 'I wasn't lying. I wouldn't lie about something so important.'

He sighs. 'Lindsay, I always believed you. I just…I wanted out. I couldn't see a way to extricate myself – you were so clingy. So I…'

I am no longer listening to him. My proof, my precious evidence: Nathan has made it worthless with a few casual words. I feel as if he's shot me in the gut.

I couldn't believe my luck when Greg told me. He hadn't been planning to, he said, but then I was honest with him so he decided he ought to be honest back. When I finally decided, months after he started pursuing me, to tell him about Nathan, he admitted he'd first noticed me one afternoon long before we met. He hadn't mentioned it, in case I was embarrassed by his having witnessed my distress. He told me he'd thought I was beautiful and wished he could cheer me up, stop me crying. His sister had had her first baby that morning, he said, and he was so happy that he wanted everyone else to be happy too. Especially a woman as stunning as me.

That was when I started to realise that there was hope, that I could finish my unfinished business with Nathan. I had proof. I could exonerate myself. After that, I let Greg kiss me, though I wouldn't go all the way with him. I won't, not until my mind is free of Nathan.

'Did you do it deliberately?' I ask. 'Last August. You suggested the venue. "Betty's in Harrogate", you said. Did you know there were two in…the Harrogate area? Did you hope I'd go to the wrong one?'

'Course not. I was going to tell you, if you turned up, that it was over. Or rather, that it couldn't start. I'm married, Lindsay. I've got kids.'

'But I didn't turn up.' The truth settles over me slowly, like a fine mist that penetrates to my bones. 'And you were relieved. Of course you were. And when I rang you later, distraught because I'd missed you, you decided it'd be easier to blame me. I told you I'd waited for two hours, panicking and desperate, trying to get you on your switched-off mobile, before it occurred to me to ask a waitress if there was another Betty's in Harrogate. Do you know what she said?'

'Lindsay, what's the point of this?'

'She said, "Not in Harrogate, no. But there's the one at Harlow Carr, just outside town. And I raced back to my car, drove there at a hundred miles an hour…'

'I'm not proud of my behaviour,' Nathan interrupts me.

'...and you'd gone. And when I phoned you to explain, you savaged me. You said I'd stood you up, and when I told you my story, you called me a liar. You said you didn't want anything to do with someone who could lie so easily.'

'I'm sorry.' Nathan opens a menu to avoid having to look at me. While he offers me his apology, he is looking at the words 'Fat Rascal' and 'Apple and Cinnamon Pancake'. An enlightened person would choose to believe that that didn't necessarily invalidate his apology.

'Someone who could lie so easily,' I repeat. 'You were describing yourself. You don't want anything to do with yourself.'

'Must we drag this out?' Nathan asks irritably.

I say, 'I came to tell you that I'm healing.'

'Have you been ill?' he asks.

'I pitied you when I thought you didn't believe me. And, since it now turns out that you did, I pity you for the lack of self-esteem that allows you to harm yourself by lying to me and rejecting my love. You can treat me as if I'm worthless if you want, but that doesn't make me worthless. I don't have to internalise your attitude to me.'

Nathan mutters, 'You could do worse.'

'I'm lovable and valuable,' I tell him. I wait for a sense of inner peace to suffuse me. I'm sure it will happen soon.

'And I'm not normally a liar,' Nathan snaps. 'In fact, I can't think of any other significant lies I've told in my adult life. I was...so desperate to get rid of you, Lindsay.' He shrugs. 'Maybe it'd do you good to...internalise someone else's view of you once in a while, or whatever the mumbo-jumbo terminology is. You might end up behaving more normally.'

All he had to do was accept that he was a liar. That was all.

'I want to show you something,' I tell him.

'Where? What?'

'Come on.'

I am not at all enlightened. It isn't going to work. It only works for people like my psychotherapist – calm people.

Nathan follows me outside, around the back of the building. When we get to the right door, I pull a key out of my pocket and unlock it. 'Where are we going?' he asks.

'There's a flight of steps. Be careful. You go first.'

'Where are we...? Lindsay, it's dark. Is this really necessary? I can't see a thing. I don't care if you've got forty people waiting down here to tell me how lovable and valuable you are. I still...'

I cut him off by saying, 'Do you still smoke?'

'Yeah, why?'

'You've got your lighter on you?'

'Yeah,' he says.

'When we get to the bottom of the steps, spark up the flame. That way you'll be able to see what I want to show you.'

In the dim glow of the small flame, he surveys the room, the large pile of sacks in one corner. 'Greg and I come here,' I say. 'When the gardens are closed. Those sacks are comfortable to lie on.' Greg made a copy of the key for me. He calls this 'our place', says it'll do for now, until we move in together.

'Am I supposed to be jealous?' asks Nathan. 'I'm not. Good luck to you and Greg. I hope you'll be happy together. Can I go now?'

'Do you know what's in the sacks?' I say. 'Fertiliser. Tons of the stuff. For the gardens. And see there?' Against one wall are dozens of containers full of petrol. 'For the lawnmowers,' I explain, walking towards him. 'It's a bit odd, isn't it? We're directly under Betty's. You'd think they wouldn't be so stupid as to store fertiliser and petrol under a busy café. It's an explosion waiting to happen.'

Nathan opens his mouth, says nothing. I am quick: I grab the lighter from his hand. The cellar goes dark. I hear him running to the steps. 'Don't bother,' I tell him. 'I locked the door.'

He can't see where I am. While he screams, pleading with me, I pick up a canister of petrol, open it, and start to pour it over the sacks of fertiliser. When they're soaked, I flick the lighter with my thumb. A bright flare; heat. Terrible heat. And a glow rising from my body, blazing in the dark. I am the most enlightened person in the world.

Acknowledgements

I WOULD LIKE to thank the following people: Jenny Geras, Adele Geras, Dan Jones, Morgan White, Peter Straus, Nat Jansz, Mark Ellingham, Ray French, Tom Palmer, James Nash, Suzie Crookes, Susan Richardson, Chris Gribble, and Michael Schmidt.

About the Author

SOPHIE HANNAH is the *New York Times* bestselling author of numerous psychological thrillers, which have been published in 27 countries and adapted for television, as well as *The Monogram Murders*, the first Hercule Poirot novel authorized by the estate of Agatha Christie.

Discover great authors, exclusive offers, and more at hc.com.